Changeling Press, LLC

ChangelingPress.com

Red/Demon's Little Lamb Duet

Marteeka Karland

Red/Demon's Little Lamb Duet
Marteeka Karland

ISBN: 978-1-60521-826-7

Publisher:
Changeling Press LLC
315 N. Centre St.
Martinsburg, WV 25404
ChangelingPress.com

Printed in the U.S.A.

Editor: Katriena Knights
Cover Artist: Marteeka Karland

The individual stories in this anthology have been previously released in E-Book format.

Table of Contents

Red (Salvation's Bane MC 9)
Marteeka Karland

Rosanna: Salvation's Bane's been good to me -- more of a family than I've ever had before. And I want that. But I'm not a kid anymore, and I know what I want. Red. I need him to see me as more than just another mechanic. No matter how good I am, working beside the man is never going to be enough. I'm going to break him down. Get under his skin, until he realizes I'm a grown-ass woman, and I know my mind.

And if that bitch of an ex of his doesn't leave us alone, she's the next thing I'm gonna break.

Red: I'm headed for a special hell. Rosanna knows her way around cars, I'll give her that, and she looks sexy as hell with a wrench in her hands and a spot of grease on her nose, but she's just a kid. I know she's got a past she can't or won't talk about, and she may think she's all grown up, but she's younger than my son, Anthony. Pretty sure that makes me some kind of a pervert.

And now that Anthony's the assistant DA, he's got a bee up his ass to take me down. Be damned if I'll let him take Rosanna with me. I should send her far away from me and this life, but one kiss is all it takes to pull me under. I could no more give her up than I could give up the air that I breathe. I'd kill to protect her. And from the looks of things, I may have to.

Chapter One

"Get the lead out, boys," Red gruffed to the dozen or so men in the garage he owned. "We got less than forty-eight hours to deliver these two cars and I still need to go over them to make sure you fucks didn't miss anything."

"Go to hell, Red!"

"Like we ever miss anything, you motherfucker!"

"Fuck you."

One guy just flipped him the bird without looking up from under the hood of the car he was working on.

"Lazy as you fuckers are, if I let it slide once, you'll fuck me over the next time and it's my ass in trouble with Thorn." Red tried not to grin, but it was hard. He worked with good men and loved every one of them like a son. At least, he loved them like he wanted to love his own son. That ship had sailed, though.

"I can help if you need me."

The groan came before Red could repress it. "No," was all he said.

"But --"

"Said no, girl. Now get on with you."

Her name was Rosanna Creamer, and the image her name presented just... *stuck*. Because, seriously, he could envision her creaming on his cock for hours and hours. Every day. Forever. She was also so young any thoughts he had about her were probably illegal. If not, they should be. He was forty-eight years old. Rosanna said she was twenty-three, but he had his doubts.

The disappointed look on her face got to him every time. He wanted to call her back and give her a job to do, but if he did, the kid would walk all over him.

"Fine. But I'm ten times better than any of those fuckers," she muttered.

"No swearing." He said it automatically, like he might scold a naughty child. The second he did, he winced.

"Fucking fine, motherfucker," she shot back. There was venom in her voice, but Red didn't mind. His head whipped around almost of its own accord to watch her stomp away. Because, really, she had an ass to make angels weep. When she hit this level of angry, she always flounced off with that little ass jiggling like his hand might make it jiggle if he'd smacked it. Sure enough… yeah. There she went. And just like that, his cock was at full attention.

"Fuck," he muttered, rubbing his hand over his mouth.

"And don't think I don't know you're looking at my ass," she shot back over her shoulder. Then, just to torment him, she flashed him a cocky grin and bent over at the waist to pick up a wrench from the garage floor where some dumb fuck had left it.

He turned away from her. Had to. Otherwise, he'd have her bent over the hood of the GTO she was working on. Red's garage was a legitimate business. They fixed and maintained cars of all kinds, from luxury to ordinary, beat-up Fords. It also fronted a chop shop and sold stolen cars overseas. Rosanna was a huge asset to him in so many ways. The girl could fix anything. She even had an affinity with the newer, high-end cars with sophisticated security systems.

The sound of her giggle snagged Red's attention. She'd just been flirting with him, but now she was trying to ensnare Julio? What the fuck?

"Don't the two of you have something to be

doing beside playing hide the wiener?"

"Ain't nothin' more important than that," Julio muttered.

"Nope," Rosanna said at the same time. "Hide the wiener is the most important task I have. Though, poor Julio here isn't allowed. His woman took his man card."

Roars of laughter all over the garage.

"Then perhaps he should get away from you so he don't get fuckin' castrated. Can't afford to be a man down now."

She patted Julio on the shoulder. "Much as I adore Julio, he's not the man for me."

He wasn't rising to the bait. If he did, he'd be hard all fucking day and masturbate all fucking night. He wasn't going to ask…

"Well, just who is the fuckin' man for you, little girl?"

"Oh, I imagine he's someone a little older than Julio." She winked at Red.

Every Goddamned time she said something like that, Red just had to open his big mouth. And every Goddamned time, she was more outrageous.

And, yeah, the guys jumped all over that shit.

"Oh, yeah, Red. Girl wants you."

"Maybe you can tame the bitch," one guy muttered. "Last time I tried, she took a wrench to my head. Damned near knocked me out."

"That's 'cause Rosanna there don't fuck no pussies."

More laughter.

"All right, that's enough of that shit. Y'all got shit to do. I suggest you get to it or there's a replacement for every single motherfucker in here."

They still laughed but went back to work.

Rosanna, the little witch, gave him a cute little wave over her shoulder and blew him a fucking kiss. The shit of it was, Red couldn't help but grin.

"Brat," he muttered, trying like shit to keep the smile off his face.

"I totally am," she fired back. "Don't like it? Spank me." The laughter that had been dying down roared again. Then she went back to her work.

The GTO was a piece of shit, but Red knew she'd have it purring like a kitten before she was done with it. She was the most gifted mechanic he had. On some things, she was even better than him. Like the newer cars with the fobs and all that computer shit he hated. Cars should be about mechanics. Not technology. He was getting too fucking old for this shit.

Red was about to move to a '71 Torino when he heard another female voice. This one was not nearly as pleasant as the first.

"Ian! Are you too dimwitted to even check your phone? I've been calling all week!"

Red sighed. He was not in the mood for this. He tried to put on his best neutral expression, but he was sure some of his irritation bled through.

"Hello to you too, Joy. Been a shade busy. Besides, you know how I hate being tethered to a phone." The tall, voluptuous woman approaching him was a world away from the little pixie he fantasized about. Tall and elegant, Joy had been part of his life for close to thirty years. Though they never married, they'd had a child together. Both mother and son seemed to make it their mission in life to make Red miserable.

"I don't care what you hate, you have an obligation to me." She thrust several crumpled sheets of paper with their envelopes at him. Red was hard pressed not to drop any of them. The result was him looking like he was juggling while trying not to drop anything. "You see those? Those are past-due bills. Are you trying to ruin my credit?"

"Electric. Phone. Three credit cards? Joy, these are not my bills. I told you the last time you brought me your shit I wasn't paying them anymore. You want stuff? Get out and work for it."

"If you'd just pay the alimony and child support --"

"Stop it right there," he growled. "I paid every dime of child support the judge ordered me to, up until Anthony graduated from law school. I could have stopped when he turned twenty-three, but I kept it up so he could get his law degree without having to worry you with money. You and I were never married so there was no alimony to be paid. I consider the extra I've given you both over the years more than enough."

"You're just trying to make yourself feel better! They're going to cut off my electricity, Ian! And I have to have the credit cards to live. Not having a phone is dangerous for a woman living alone. You have to pay these!"

That was Joy. She always knew how to pull at his sense of responsibility and protectiveness. He hated her, but she'd been in his life for a very long time. It was hard to just ignore her. So, here he was. Leave her to fend for herself or help her out. *Again.* Sure, it reinforced bad behavior, but what choice did he really have?

Stomping to the register, Red took out six hundred dollars. It wasn't the whole amount she needed, but it would pay the phone and electric bills and give her some to pay on her credit cards. She could choose which one she wanted to pay.

"There. Don't come back for more."

She counted it with a frown, then turned her angry gaze to his. "This isn't enough."

"It's all I can spare. You can pick which bills to pay."

"I don't know what I ever saw in you," she snapped. "You're as worthless as the day I met you."

"Then why do you keep coming back?" Red was done with this. "Excuse me, I have fucking work to do. Someone has to make money to keep your ass in designer clothes. You sure as hell don't."

Red turned his back on her sputtering form. God, he hated that woman! What he ever saw in her was a mystery to him now. She was still stunningly beautiful, but the appeal of all her glamour had faded to nothing over those years of trial he'd put up with her.

"Aren't you going to see me out?" she demanded.

"Found your way in. I suppose you can find the way out." If he took her outside where no one could see, he'd kill the bitch. His self-restraint only went so far.

"I've always known you were worthless. You could at least be considerate to a woman."

Before he could respond, one of the guys called out. "I'll walk you out. Just let me get something to wipe my hands on."

"Keep your filthy paws to yourself! The last thing I need is for some filthy grease monkey to ruin my outfit."

"You sure?" another man answered. It sounded like Julio. "We were just talking about a new game I came up with. I could teach you how to play."

"I can assure you I have no interest in any game the likes of you would play." Her snooty tone grated on Red's nerves. He just wanted her out of his garage. Out of his fucking life. Unfortunately, Julio just had to continue. Red knew he'd catch hell for not defending her, but, really. She came into this garage knowing exactly what she was walking into. Not his fault when the boys offended her.

"It's called hide the wiener. Teaching an uptight rich bitch like yourself would be the highlight of my fuckin' day!"

The place erupted in laughter. He tried to hide his grin, but had to duck his head before she saw it. Cause, yeah, his face was split wide with it.

"Ian?"

"Not my circus, honey. You don't like the language, stay outta the fuckin' monkey house. Only my problem if you're actually payin' for a service."

"You'll be the one paying!"

"Just did. Six hundred dollars' worth." More laughter.

"Is there no way you could have taken me to your office? Do you have to insist all our conversations be in public, or do you just want to humiliate me?"

"Last time we had a conversation about money in private, you lied and convinced a judge I'd agreed to buy you a car as part of our custody battle. How I'm not sure, but I had a feeling there was sex involved. So, no. None of our conversations get to be in private, and all my security cameras have audio as well as video. As to the humiliation? It's not my intention to humiliate anyone. But if you are humiliated? It's just a fucking bonus for me."

Finally, *finally,* the fucking bitch stormed out. To the catcalls and laughter of the entire garage.

* * *

Rosanna witnessed the byplay between Red and

his ex. It was never pleasant. The thing she hated most was the way the woman put Red down. He was so far from worthless and irresponsible it wasn't even funny. Rosanna wanted to scratch the woman's eyes out on sheer principle. It made Rosanna insanely jealous that Red had a kid with another woman, even if neither seemed to be in his life. He deserved so much more than what he'd been given.

After such confrontations with his ex, it always took Red several hours to get over the train wreck. She knew today would be worse. The irresponsible and worthless comments had gotten to him. She could tell by the way he'd completely closed down to everyone after Joy had left. Leaving him alone to lick his wounds was always hard, but she had to give him a little time. Then she'd do something outrageous to take his mind off the incident.

She was done with this GTO piece of shit. The owner ought to be shot for letting it fall into such disrepair. It would run like a beast now, but, though the car would appreciate everything she'd done, the owner would just wear it down again. She kept tinkering with it because she had nothing else to do and didn't want to leave the garage with Red in this state.

Helping the others was out of the question. Not only would they not accept help from anyone, but it would grate on their masculinity to have a girl offer to help. Besides, each man -- or woman -- had his own projects. You did your own work and got paid accordingly.

With another hour to kill, Rosanna just cleaned engine parts, shining up the cosmetics and making the outside look at least half as good as the inside would be.

"You headin' out soon?" That was Julio again. The man really didn't like that she'd turned him down.

"Nope. I'm here for a while."

"I'm still good to get that drink if you want."

"Told you, Julio," she said, not looking up from her task. "I don't have drinks with taken men."

"Look, we're not even really together."

"She know that? Because she thinks you're gonna make her your ol' lady."

"I never told her that."

"Yeah, you did." Red stood behind Julio, his massive arms crossed. There was a significant amount of gray in his beard, particularly at his chin and temples, and his hair was liberally streaked with the stuff, but the bright orange/red was still a stark contrast with his pale skin.

Julio spun around, obviously not liking the bigger man at his back. "She might have assumed --"

"Heard you the other day. Said you had her property patch in the works for her cut."

Julio looked nervous. One thing everyone knew about Red was that you didn't disrespect women if there was a way around it. Probably why he hadn't told his ex off yet. "You know how women are, Red," he said in a conspiratorial voice. "You have to keep them happy if you want to keep them puttin' out. Besides, you got your own woman. You probably told her you'd make her your ol' lady back in the day."

"Nope. Ask her. Even she'll tell you I never indicated we were exclusive. She had other men. I had other women."

"You had a kid with her. Don't seem like something you'd do if you didn't intend to keep them both safe."

"You're right. But I never intended to have a kid

with her. Women are just as devious as men when it comes to getting what they want." Then he snagged Julio by the neck and walked him away from her. "Stay away from Rosanna unless she approaches you on her own. Get me?" He shoved Julio out the door to the garage. Red turned and met Rosanna's gaze before stalking into his office. The man was definitely intense.

"Hey, Red!" she called out to him even as she jogged to his door. "You knocked out that Torino?" He didn't look up from the stack of papers on his desk, grunting at her. Not an answer, but more than she usually got from him. "I could help you finish. Been hopin' you'd let me work on something with you so I could get a feel for how you work. We'd make a great team."

"Ain't got no use for a little bit like you. Just keep doin' your assigned work and we'll be fine."

"But I could learn from you. You could be my mentor." Despite his repeated and vehement rejections, Rosanna was dogged in her determination. Not only did she want to learn from him, but she just plain *wanted* him. His age should have put her off, but it just added that much more of an appealing aspect to him. He knew what he wanted, and he'd protect those he took under his wing. Red represented everything she was missing in her life.

"Ain't got time." He still didn't look up at her.

"Sure you do. Just imagine how much faster --"

"I said no, Rosanna." This was how most of their conversations ended.

She sighed. "Fine. It's not like you don't know where to find me when you need me."

Did she imagine he groaned when she left the room? A glance back proved she hadn't. He was thumping his head on his desk, his fingers laced where they rested on the back of his head. Did she frustrate him that much?

Then, as if he sensed her looking at him, he lifted his head. The fire burning there nearly made her knees crumble. It was such a mix of anger and carnal desire it was hard to reconcile one with the other.

"Get out, Rosanna. Now. Go home." Yeah. Might be a good idea.

She wasn't afraid of Red. Not even when he'd been at his most angry. But there was something in his voice, in his eyes, that gave her pause this time.

Her station already cleaned, the GTO ready to go, she decided it was probably a good idea to exit stage right, make like a sheep herder and get the flock outta there.

She'd never invested in a ride of her own. The garage was only a couple of miles from the clubhouse where she lived. So she rode a bike wherever she needed to go. Not a motorcycle. A bike. Like, a bicycle. Got her from point A to B, and the maintenance was little to none. It did not, however, make for a speedy getaway. Thank goodness Red didn't follow her out.

The ride to the clubhouse took less time than usual. The adrenaline charge she'd gotten when Red had looked up at her still hadn't worn off when she rolled inside the gates to the converted fire station. Then it was all she could do to get her legs to stay under her.

She made it to the common room before her legs finally refused to support her any longer. With a groan, Rosanna collapsed into the first chair she saw.

"Rough day?" Poison, one of the patched members of Salvation's Bane, brought her a Captain and Coke. *Bliss*!

"Na. Just Red being his usual grumpy self." She

waved him off as she snagged the Captain and Coke. "He can be a cranky bastard."

"He givin' you shit?"

"Na. He had a rough afternoon." Which was code for…

"Ex came by, huh?"

"Yup. And it was everything you'd imagine." She turned to look more fully at Poison. "Why does he put up with that shit? Does he still love her?"

Poison shrugged. "Before my time, but I'm not sure he ever loved her. From what I understand, she was a manipulative bitch from day one."

"I can certainly see that. But, hey. None of my business."

Poison gave a snort. "Yeah. I hear ya. Let me know how that works out for ya."

"What?"

"Joy and Red's past not being your business. Pretty sure you're making it your business."

Rosanna froze with her glass at her lips. "I am not. I was just making an observation."

"Girl, everyone sees through you. You're hot for Red."

"Fuck you, Poison," she snapped. "You don't know shit."

He chuckled, which just infuriated Rosanna all the more. "I know plenty. I know you watch every move he makes."

"'Cause he won't teach me what he does with cars! A girl's gotta learn, and he's the best!"

"Every time Joy comes around, everyone's afraid you're gonna attack her with a wrench or something."

"If I wanted to, A, I'd have already done it. And B, she'd deserve it. She's a cunt to the first degree! Doesn't mean it's got anything to do with Red."

"You keep to fixin' and soupin' up cars. 'Cause you're a horrible liar."

"Fucker," she muttered. That wasn't embarrassing or anything. Poison gave her a mock toast with his beer bottle and wandered off. Jesus, she had to get herself under control or she was going to be the laughingstock of the fucking club!

She'd just flipped off Poison when the object of her torment walked through the door of the club. He went straight to the bar. Once Wrangler handed him a twenty-ounce bottle of Bud Light, Red unscrewed it, turned it up and guzzled it. He slammed the bottle on the wood counter and snagged a second one from Wrangler's hand. He gave the man a hard look as he glanced at the second bottle he'd been given.

"Seal's broke."

Wrangler shrugged. "Just tryin' to help a brother out."

"Not by breakin' the fuckin' seal on my fuckin' beer, prospect." He shoved the bottle back at Wrangler. "Get me a new one, you little fucker." Harsh even by Red's standards. Wrangler took the bottle and started to place it in the fridge. "No! You pour that swill down the fuckin' sink. Broken seal means flat beer."

"Lighten up, man! It's just a beer."

Red lunged forward and snagged the smaller man by the throat. Instinctively, Wrangler's hands went to Red's wrist. It didn't budge the hold Red had on him. "You do what the fuck I tell you to or you're out," he snarled. "Thorn has the final say, but all prospects have to be approved unanimously. Right now, I'm your fuckin' holdout."

The room had gone quiet, and Wrangler glanced around before putting his hands up, the beer still in one of them. "I hear ya, Red. Down the sink."

Red shoved him backward and motioned for a fresh beer. Wrangler complied, then emptied the opened bottle down the sink.

"Man, someone's in a pissy mood," Rosanna said before she could stop herself. "Maybe you need to get laid."

Red growled at her when every man in the club chuckled at his expense. "Don't push me, Rosanna. You're about two seconds away from takin' your ass back to wherever you fuckin' came from."

That got her full attention. And pissed her off. "Why don't you go fuck yourself? I ain't done nothin' to you. What the fuck?"

"There a problem?" Thorn approached, a frown on his face. Rosanna ducked her head and looked away, wrapping her arms around herself protectively.

Red sighed. "No. Sorry, Rosie. Been a pisser of a day. Didn't mean to take it out on you."

She shrugged, not looking at either man. Red and Thorn both knew her story. It was Red she'd come to first six months earlier. She'd been broke and homeless, and, she thought, on the run from the cops. Red had listened to her story, then taken her back to the Salvation's Bane clubhouse and made her tell Thorn. Thorn and his ol' lady, Mariana, had found a place for her in the clubhouse to live, while Red had given her a job in his garage.

"That was a dick move, Red," Thorn said softly. "Don't do it again. You need to hurt someone, take a prospect to the ring and pound on 'em."

"I hear ya, boss."

Thorn squeezed her shoulder before leaving. Red stood there a long while before sitting next to her. "He's right. I won't do that again."

"Whatever," Rosanna said, then stood and left to

go to her room. She'd deal with it all tomorrow. This wasn't the first time Red had hurt her feelings. It probably wouldn't be the last. But, damn it, he was the first person to give a damn about her since she was thirteen years old. It was hard to stay mad at him, no matter how rough he got. This was the first time he'd ever said anything like that, though. Kicking her out of the only home she'd ever known? Yeah. It was beyond cruel. But she'd forgive him. She always did.

Chapter Two

Red knew he was a jerk. Worse than a jerk. He'd hurt Rosanna worse than anyone in her life other than maybe her mother. She didn't talk about her mother, though Rosanna admitted she'd hurt the other woman when she'd split. She didn't talk about it, and Red had never asked. All he knew was that her mother had been abusive and moved them from one little hick town to another. Wherever the drugs were. Rosanna hadn't said much else other than she'd had all she could take and had split. Bottom line, if she left Bane, Rosanna had nowhere to go. Red had known that. An apology wasn't nearly enough.

He scrubbed a hand over his face. "I'm too fuckin' old for this."

"Hi, Red." Retta was a beautiful woman, if a bit hard. She'd been with the club for years and seemed to have no intention of moving on like some of them did. After a while, being a woman in a club full of horny bikers probably got old. "Heard you had a rough day." She slid onto his lap and wrapped her arms around his neck. "How about I take care of you tonight and make you forget all your troubles."

Her purr was as erotic as hell. Normally, Red'd take her up on it. Hell, more than once, he'd taken her and a couple more club girls. Not now, though. "Sorry, honey. Not tonight."

She pouted prettily. "You sure? I can get Trixie and make you forget all about your bad day."

"I'm sure. Run along now." He swatted her ass when she stood up, and she giggled like a girl. Retta was as far from a girl as Red was from a boy. She just wasn't as old as he was.

Red gave Retta time to find someone to play with

before he stood to find Rosanna. Last thing he wanted was for a club girl to follow him to Rosanna. She'd be pissed all over again. And, yeah, he knew his little Rosie had thoughts of seducing him.

As he climbed the stairs to her room, Red thought about that. The girl was younger than his son. *Younger than his fucking son!* Even if he wanted to fuck her, he'd feel like a pervert the entire time.

No. Scratch that. He'd enjoy the fuck out of it. *Then* he'd feel like a pervert. He could make Rosanna enjoy it, too. Fuck. Even covered in grease after a hard day in the shop, Rosanna had a way about her that just screamed sex. The guys in the garage noticed it. Fucking Julio wasn't the only one hitting on her. Red was always careful to shut that shit down if Rosanna didn't. So far, he'd only had to intervene once. If Julio came on to her one more time, he'd be number two. As far as Red knew, the first piss-ant was on his way to Washington state. Julio might not make it out of Florida if Red had to warn him again.

Once at Rosanna's door, Red knocked lightly. "Rosanna? You in there?"

There was a scratch, then he heard her stomping to the door. "Go away, Red! I don't want to talk to you!" she yelled at him through the door. "Fucker!"

"Yeah, baby, I know. Open up so we can talk."

"How 'bout you go to hell! I'll meet up with you when it freezes over!"

"Guess I deserved that." He waited a few seconds. She didn't retreat but didn't open the door. He placed a palm on the wooden door. "You gonna open up?"

"I said no."

"Yeah, but you're still there so you must want to. Come on. We can talk about you joining the team on the next batch of cars."

That got her to open the door. Fast. "Really?" Her smile was wide and her eyes bright.

Red looked at her a long time. "Tell me something. And you gotta be truthful."

Her smile faded to a wary look. "Depends on what it is."

"Is it the jackin' cars or the soupin' 'em up that turns you on?"

She let out a giggle, her body relaxing to lean against the door frame. That smile was back and dazzling as ever. "You want to know the answer to that question, you're going to have to figure it out yourself."

"Let me in. We can discuss it."

"Nothing to discuss."

"How about seeing which group you need to be in on the next job?" He raised his eyebrows, determined he was getting into her room. "Can't do everything, and I need to see which you're best at."

"I'm good at all of it," she said confidently. "So just put me wherever you need someone. Bye!"

She tried to shut the door but Red stuck his foot just inside. "Rosanna," he said warningly.

"Look, I'm tired. I worked on that fucking junk-ass GTO all day. It runs like a dream now. No one but you could have done a better job. Now, please. I need some time to wind down and thicken up my skin for another round of verbally-beat-the-shit-outta-Rosie."

"Stop, Rosie. Just stop."

"I am stopped." She shrugged easily, like it really was no big deal. "I'm stopped and going to bed. We can pick up where we left off in the morning."

Somehow, she managed to kick his foot out of the doorway and shut the door before he could do anything about it. He pounded on it a couple of times, but she didn't answer.

"Fuck." He scrubbed his hand over his face. This was not the way he'd wanted to end this day. Not by hurting Rosanna. Sure, he was surly to her most days, but it was the only way he could keep from throwing her against a wall and fucking the shit out of her. And it wasn't just her looks. The girl was smart as they came. Given enough time, there wasn't anything she couldn't figure out. She kept telling him she wanted to learn from him, but the fact was, he needed to be learning from her. And fuck if her intelligence didn't turn him on.

Finally, knowing he'd gotten all he was likely to get from her tonight, Red headed back to the garage. He was more at home there than he was in the clubhouse. Mostly because the club whores ganged up on him. Apparently, he'd gotten a reputation of being a hard ride in the sack, and the women who'd yet to experience sex with him were determined to crawl into his bed. It could happen in the clubhouse, but at the garage… Well, that was his place. Had been before he was ever a part of Salvation's Bane.

The ride back was the only solace he had. It wasn't long, but he made a couple swings around the block, policing the area. He didn't really care much other than, by keeping the riffraff off the streets, it kept the police away from him.

He pulled into his parking bay and shut down his bike. Shutting the door, he stretched before locking everything up and setting the alarm. Damn, he was getting old. Too old to even be looking at a woman like Rosanna. So old that, every time he saw her look over her shoulder and catch his gaze through his office window, that stupid Toto song ran through his head --

I can see your face still shining through the window on the other side. His last thought before he lay down and dozed off on the tiny cot in his office was that he was so fucked.

* * *

The peal of the alarm jolted Red out of fitful sleep. He was so startled, he stumbled out of bed, got tangled in the unzipped sleeping bag he used as a cover, and face-planted on the concrete floor.

"Mother fuck!" He was sure his bellowed rage could be heard over even this deafening noise. "Some motherfucker is gettin' ready to fuckin' die!"

"Sorry! Sorry!"

Was that Rosanna? "Goddamn it, woman! Turn that fuckin' thing off!"

"I can't! Did you change the code?" She sounded desperate. Red stumbled out into the big bay where Rosanna was bouncing with anxiety at the keypad. He reached over her, trapping her body between him and the wall, and keyed in the code. Instantly the noise stopped.

Rosanna had her hands over her ears when she turned to look up at him and immediately dropped them to her sides. There were faint smudges under her eyes and her long, auburn hair was up in a thick ponytail, but she still looked beautiful. And so, so, fucking good. She was so close he could pull her into his fucking arms and just hold her to him. Would she let him, or would she pull away in disgust?

"I tried to turn it off," she said, pleading with him to understand. "But the code wouldn't work!"

"It's Wednesday, girl. Code changes automatically at midnight on Tuesday. You know that."

"It's Wednesday?" She blinked up at him. Most

people he'd call bullshit on for that. But Rosanna probably had forgotten what day it was. She measured time in jobs. She was scheduled for a certain job on a certain day, so whatever job she was working on, well, that was what day it was. She was still scheduled to be working on that GTO, but she'd gotten done early... Shit.

"I forgot to update your schedule," he said with a sigh. He still didn't step out of her space, because she hadn't moved to go around him. How long would she let him stand over her like this? And why was he pushing her?

"I'm sorry," she said, still looking up at him like she was afraid he might fire her ass. Fuck. He'd like to set fire to her ass all right. With his hand. Her lying over his lap. Naked. Her ass sticking up for him to smack...

"Um, Red?" She laid a tentative hand on his chest and pushed ever so slightly. Which was when he realized he'd run out of his office that doubled as his bedroom in nothing but a pair of boxer briefs.

"Fuck," he muttered as he turned and walked back toward his office.

"If it helps, you've got a really nice ass," she called out. Was that a giggle?

"Mind what day it is next time, little girl. You can't remember what day it is, how'm I supposed to trust you to remember what we're doing in the pit?" The pit was the chop shop and illegal garage. It was where they put freshly stolen cars until they were safe enough to pass any police inspection if they got raided.

"'Cause that's just how I work. You know that! It's why I gave you that fucking app in the first Goddamned place!"

"You're old enough to keep up with your shit on

your own. I suggest you start doing it."

"Can you please get a little more grumpy? I don't think I've had my fill of you this week. Please make me want to scratch your eyes out before the weekend so I don't feel bad about leaving you with all the shit Julio and Reys are behind on."

He popped his head back out of the office as he tugged on his jeans. "What the fuck? They're behind again?"

"They're always behind, Red. I keep them caught up, but Julio was trying to get handsy, and Reys is just a dick."

"'Bout had enough of those little fuckers."

"You and me both," she muttered. "Anyway. GTO is good to go. See what I did there?"

He pointed a finger at her, but couldn't say anything for fear he'd laugh if he did. Ducking back inside his office, he threw on a T-shirt and his boots. Lots of work today, and he was behind. If he wasn't careful, Julio and Reys wouldn't be the only ones she had to help out with work.

"Oh!" she called, following him when he really just wanted to be away from her before he did something stupid. Like bend her over his desk. Fuck! He needed to get a fucking grip! "By the way. I think I've solved the little computer problem we have with the newer car models." She gave him a cheeky grin.

"Yeah? What?"

"Nuh-uh. You have to see it in action." She motioned him to follow her. "Let me get a car, you come with me, and I'll show you all the bells and whistles."

He snorted. "Right. Is that code for you try to jack a car, we can't bypass the OnStar security, and you get me arrested outta spite?"

Little brat had the audacity to look offended. "I would never! And, frankly, I'm insulted you'd imply I'd try to get revenge that way!"

"Just remembering having to bail out Dusty a couple of months ago."

Rosanna shrugged. "Well, he deserved it. *And* it was his fault. I told him what to do, but he just had to do it his way. So, when I heard sirens, I split. I'm not taking the fall for his stupidity."

"Fine. We'll talk about it. You'll show me what you've got, and we'll try it out on my ride. Just like I make everyone else do before pulling some hare-brained stunt to try to get on the A team."

She flashed Red a brilliant smile. "You got it, boss!" Then, with a flourish of all that long, red hair as she spun around, she was gone. Red knew he was definitely going to hell, because all he could think about was wrapping a length of that hair around his cock and jacking off with it.

"Fuck. Me."

* * *

The morning passed uneventfully. Rosanna finished Rey's project while Red worked on Julio's. Neither man had shown up for work. Which put Red in a worse-than-foul mood. It was all Rosanna could do to keep the mood light. Fuck, the man was high maintenance!

She'd worked through lunch, only grabbing a sandwich, which she laid on the edge of the car she was working on. So what if she ingested the tiniest bit of grease? She was fucking hungry! She had a bottle of water on her workstation at all times but, with the working lunch and all, she was out. Time to refill.

The heat sometimes got sweltering, but, honestly, with the bays going up and down and people coming in and out, it was easier to just use fans to circulate the hot, humid air. Most days she didn't mind it, but there was a storm coming in off the coast and that had made the humidity go through the roof.

Going inside the break area where there was air conditioning was almost a misery because it was so comfortable. She'd have to go back outside, and she didn't really want to. With a sigh, she filled her water bottle and took a healthy swig before topping it off again.

The sweat beading on her skin chilled in the cool air, and goose bumps erupted over her arms and legs. Hell, her nipples were probably straining the sports bra she had on. She wore overall shorts, steel-toed boots, and a tank top. Her cap was on backwards and served to keep most of the sweat out of her eyes. She was pretty good at keeping herself clean -- years of practice because her mother didn't think it was lady-like to look like a grease monkey -- but she had a few smudges on her overalls. As if that bitch knew what a lady even was.

As she came out of the break room, she heard a decidedly female voice, screeching at several decibels above human tolerance. Fuck if it wasn't Joy. Again! What the fuck? Did the woman never stop?

"I told you I had to pay those credit card bills, Ian." Joy practically sobbed with hurt. "Now, if I miss a payment, it could cost Anthony his job! Do you want him fired because you wouldn't help his mother with a simple credit card bill?"

Oh, the bitch was good. She even sounded distraught. In reality, Rosanna would just bet they'd cut off her credit use until she caught up her payments. She'd used the money Red had given her to pay the phone and electric, then probably pocketed the rest.

"What does your debt have to do with Anthony's job?" Red sounded pissed. Well, more pissed than usual. Pissed was his default setting. At least, it had been for the six months Rosanna had known him.

"Because…" This was a male voice. Anthony? Rosanna snuck around the corner to stand with Grease where he worked on some kinda fucked-up Pinto. "I'm working in the District Attorney's office. My family must be above reproach, or it looks like I'm compromised. Anyone could use her debt as pressure for me to help them, and I can't have that."

"Then pay her fuckin' bills yourself," Red snapped. "I'm done being used by the two of you."

"You'll give her the money," Anthony said. "Or I'll make your life a living hell, old man. Just like you've made mine and my mother's." What the fuck? Had Rosanna misjudged Red? He was grumpy, yes, but he was never needlessly cruel. Hell, he was good as gold to Joy and all her demands. Had something gone on before Rosanna arrived that Red deserved this?

"Exactly how have I made your life miserable, Anthony? I paid for your education. I made it so your mother never had to worry about money while you were in law school. You don't owe a fucking *dime* from school loans. All because of me. Anytime Joy breaks a nail, she comes to me to pay for the fuckin' manicure, and *I've* made *your* lives a living fuckin' hell?"

Anthony gave Red an evil grin. "How is it, do you suppose, that a grease monkey who owns a garage barely hovering over the red managed to pay for all that law school? Huh? I'll tell you how. You're dirty. You're using this garage as a front to launder money or something." Anthony looked like he knew he had the upper hand and was enjoying shoving it in Red's face. "I'm launching an investigation into this place. You're going to have police swarming you night and day until I find out what you're doing, then I'm going to personally put you away for the rest of your life!"

Red looked positively livid. Even Rosanna was a little put off by what she could see in his eyes. Beside her Grease whistled low. The whole garage was so quiet Rosanna winced, because she knew everyone had heard Grease. The last thing any of them needed was to attract the trio's attention.

"Gonna use your old man to make a name for yourself, eh?" Red's voice was a low, deadly whisper.

"That's right," Anthony continued, either not realizing or not caring about the beast he was about to release. Red was quick to anger and quick to calm down. But this was a whole other ballgame. Red looked like he was ready to kill. "By taking down my own father, I'll prove I'm willing to do whatever it takes to shut down crime in this city. I'll happily bury you if it means I make lead Assistant DA before I'm thirty."

"Yeah," Red said, crossing those arms over that massive chest. "Real fuckin' hero there, boy."

Anthony took the three steps separating him and Red, jabbing a finger right in Red's face. "I'm a man, fucker! You never treated me like one, but I am!"

"No," Red said calmly. "You'll never be a man until you learn gratitude and self-sacrifice. You're just like your mother. Out for yourself in all things. She found what she needed in me. First it was about fuckin'. Then money. Both of you have bled me dry for the better part of thirty years." Red uncrossed his arms and took his own step forward. Anthony had to back off or be trampled by his older but much larger and stronger father. "So, go on, you little weasel. Take your best fuckin' shot. You only get one."

"That a threat, old man?"

"It's a promise. I never treated you as anything but my son. At least, until Joy decided you might give me more attention than you did her. It gutted me when she refused to give me any kind of visitation, but I resolved myself to abide by her wishes. Believe what you want, but I never treated you as anything less than my son."

Anthony sneered at Red, looking to his mother. "What did you ever see in this Neanderthal, Mom? He's so far beneath us. Why didn't you just drop him a long time ago?"

"I did, sweetheart. But he wouldn't leave me alone. Stalked me." Red growled but said nothing. "Probably because he couldn't get another woman after he left me to fend for myself. It was hard enough on him before I took him on. If I hadn't, I have no doubt he'd have been all alone these years."

Rosanna had heard enough. "That's so much fucking bullshit," she muttered and took a step forward.

Grease slid in front of her, careful not to touch her because, yeah. His name said it all. He was not as careful about getting muck all over him as she was. "Whatever you're thinking, Rosie. Don't. This is between the three of them."

"I'm not letting them berate Red like this."

"You have no idea what went on before you got here. You sure he doesn't deserve it?"

"You saying he does? If so, tell me and I'll gladly let the fucker take whatever they dish out."

Grease sighed. "You're gonna be in so much trouble, Rosie…"

She nodded. "That's what I thought."

Rosanna moved away from Grease and near the

break-room entrance once again. She tossed her cap to the floor. Her hair was parted in the middle and woven into two tight French braids, leaving the ends to swing freely nearly to her waist. She didn't have time to fix that, but she figured it was sexy in an innocent kind of way. Hell, her whole outfit was sexy in that context. Time for some fun.

She let out an ear-splitting squeal and bounded in the trio's direction. "Red! Red!" she shouted excitedly. "I've missed you so much!"

Red turned to her, his eyes wide. He shook his head slightly, either to warn her off or to convince himself he was really seeing what he thought he was seeing. Rosanna grinned from ear to ear as she jumped into his arms, wrapping her arms and legs around him and hugging him tight. Red's arms came around her instinctively, but he didn't try to push her away. In fact, did she imagine he squeezed her to him just as tightly as she squeezed him? This whole thing might have been a huge mistake on her part. Not because Red might be pissed at her. Because now she knew what it was like to be held tightly in his arms. And it felt fucking good.

When she pulled back it was to grab his face with both hands and pepper it with kisses all over. "I tried to call but knew you wouldn't have that stupid phone with you," she said between kisses. "I'm sorry it took me so long to get back!" Then she made her second mistake. One of her kisses landed full on his mouth. Electricity seemed to zing through her body, and she stiffened. She might have pulled back then, but Red's deep growl warned her to stay right where she was.

Then he deepened the kiss.

Red shuddered around her, like he, too, was trying to absorb the shock of what was happening.

Darting his tongue inside her mouth when she gasped her surprise, Red took effortless control of the situation, his arms squeezing her tight. Rosanna tried to fight to regain her footing. This wasn't supposed to be their first real kiss. Not like this. In front of not only the entire garage, but Red's ex and his son. When she tried to pull away, however, Red shifted one hand to the back of her neck and squeezed, keeping her in place for precious seconds. Then he was the one to pull back. It was like he wanted Rosanna to know it was him stopping the madness. Not her.

Red pulled her to him to rest his forehead against hers, but his eyes were open and staring right into hers. Gradually, Rosanna became aware of her surroundings. Joy's outraged sputtering, Anthony's angry threats. The jeers and raucous laughter of the guys in the garage. When she would have climbed off him, though, Red squeezed her tighter until she relaxed. Then he pulled her head down to his shoulder and rested his chin there for several long seconds.

"Missed you, too, little brat," he said softly. Rosanna got the feeling it wasn't all for show, but that might have been wishful thinking. Finally, he let her down. She didn't miss the fact that, like the kiss, he let her go on his terms. Not hers.

"I take it we're staying in tonight," she said with a nervous giggle, trying to play the part when that ship had long sailed. This was no game she was playing. She wanted the real thing.

"Oh, you have no idea," he said. Now, his voice was no longer husky. He was back to his surly self. "We'll definitely be stayin' in tonight." That wasn't ominous or anything. But he didn't let her go. Instead, he pulled her closer and kissed the top of her head. "Go on, lil' bit. Pretty sure you got work to do." When she turned to leave, he swatted her ass. Hard. She yelped and turned to glare at him, but the heat in his gaze made her knees weak. To cover up her reaction, she bared her teeth at him, trying to make it look like she wasn't as affected by him as she was. Which was more for him so he didn't see her as weak. If he did, if he smelled blood in the water, he'd cull her like he had so many men in the garage in the six months she'd been there.

With an exaggerated twist of her hips, Rosanna sauntered back to the Pinto she was working on for Marge from Tito's Diner. Much as Rosanna loved Marge, the car was still a piece of shit. But Rosanna was determined to keep it running for the older lady. And for Red's reputation as the best mechanic in town. In fact, she was pretty sure Marge brought it in just to see how long they'd keep fixing it.

Glancing over her shoulder, she met Red's gaze. Joy and Anthony were still laying into him, but his focus was on her. Not them. Finally, he put a hand up in the air, a gesture for them to stop. Amazingly, they did.

"There's only two things the two of you need to understand," he said. He wasn't loud, but the whole of the garage was watching and listening. A few of them tried to pretend to work but a few, like Styx, had pulled up chairs, grabbed beers, and were watching the show avidly. Which pissed Rosanna off, that they'd get enjoyment out of Red's problems. She knew Styx at least had Red's back if it came to anything physical so that was something. "This is my fuckin' garage. Mine. Anything goes on here is my business. Not yours. Second --" He looked straight at Anthony this time. "This is private fuckin' property. Unless you got somethin' you need fixed, or a fuckin' search warrant, stay the hell away. I'll call the fuckin' cops and see just exactly how much pull you have in the fuckin' DA's office. *Boy*." Red had thrown in the "boy" just to piss off Anthony. Rosanna had no idea what had gone on between Red and Anthony, but it was obvious Anthony hated his dad and Red had hit his limit with Anthony. Surprisingly, Joy just looked shocked. Sure, she'd gotten her two cents' worth in, but she kept glancing over at Rosanna as if pondering how the two of them were together.

"Christ, Red," she hissed, using his road name for the first time in the six months Rosanna had seen her coming around to berate her ex. "She's younger than Anthony. Are you really replacing me with a child?"

"Joy, you were never mine to replace. I was never yours. The only tie we have between us is Anthony, and you've made damned sure I was never going to be part of his life. Now, you both have to live with that. You more than him. We had a good relationship until he was about six. Then you got jealous or some shit. Don't know. Don't care. It's done."

"If you think your little whore changes anything, you can think again," she spat. "There's too much history between us to ever let go."

"Honey, I let go a long fuckin' time ago," Red said in a weary voice. "And you know what? It really wasn't that hard. Only part I had a rough time with was lettin' you have Anthony."

The younger man snorted, as if he doubted how true that was. "Don't beat yourself up over it, old man," he said. "I made something of myself, no thanks to you."

"Uh-huh. Your mama paid for all your

schoolin'." Red said. "I suppose she paid for every little thing you wanted. Only problem with that is we all know I paid for it. I paid for everything. The fancy boarding schools so Joy didn't have to be bothered with actually raising you. The Ivy League schools I had to use everything I made to pay for. I pulled every string I knew how to pull to get you grants and scholarships so you could go to those stupid, fancy schools, then you come after your old man for being a biker. Yeah. Your mama's the real saint, boy. I'm the fuckin' devil. Now get your fuckin' ass outta my fuckin' garage."

Red spat in front of Anthony, clearly disgusted with the whole mess. "Styx!" he called, never looking away from Anthony. "They ain't gone in thirty seconds, call the fuckin' cops!"

"Got your six, boss." Styx raised a beer in salute to Red before downing it and crushing the can.

Rosanna watched as Red stomped into his office and slammed the door. She breathed a sigh of relief. At least he hadn't taken her to task over her little stunt.

"Rosanna! Get the fuck in here!"

She cringed. "Fuck."

Chapter Three

There was a rage building inside Red. One he hadn't seen coming and wasn't sure he could contain. Joy and Anthony were both going to be on him like stink on shit now. He'd seen the astonishment and hurt in Joy's eyes when he'd sent Rosanna on her way with a swat to her ass. Fuck, how he wanted to do that again! That firm, luscious globe had jiggled just the briefest of heartbeats before settling. He wanted to watch that again. And again. Hell, he could get off on just spanking her ass!

But Joy wasn't the problem. She'd long ago killed anything between them. Anthony was another story altogether. With his ties to the DA's office, he had every intention of making Red's life a living hell. It wasn't that Red minded the harassment. He was a fuckin' biker. He was used to it from "civilized" people. It was the fact that Anthony would go after Rosanna as hard as or harder than he went after Red. And Rosanna had as many ghosts in her past as any of them.

While he was letting Joy and Anthony vent their anger at him, he'd been plotting through all the scenarios in his head. His first reaction was to send Rosanna away. As far as he could get her. But, considering her reaction the night before, he discarded it almost immediately. Even as one scenario after another rolled through his mind, there was one he tried not to acknowledge. Anything he did to send her away to safety took her away from him. The thought blinded him to anything else, because all he could think about was ways to make her have to stay. Given the explosive nature of what had just happened between them, he decided he had to get her pregnant.

Then there would be no way she could leave him, because she wasn't Joy. Unlike his ex, Rosanna would want him in their son's life. Red knew firsthand having a child together created a permanent link. As much as he'd never be rid of Joy, he wanted that same situation with Rosanna. Which just pissed him off further, because having a kid with a woman who didn't love him was what got him into this scenario in the first Goddamned place.

He opened the door. "Rosanna! Get the fuck in here!" His bellow rang out across the whole garage. Though he had to talk to her about this, all he could do was feel the blind rage attacking him from all sides.

Joy. Anthony. Rosanna. They all wanted something from him. Of the three, he knew Rosanna was the only one willing to give anything in return. Hell, she'd give without expecting anything at all, but a woman didn't kiss a man like she just had unless she was willing to take him on. And Red couldn't do that. He was too fucking old. Too set in his ways. Joy had wanted to be with him because being with a biker was exciting. Red had no idea what Rosanna wanted beyond just having a home and family and maybe a happy life. After six months of her being under his feet constantly, he'd learned her better than he should have.

Rosanna entered the office quietly. He turned, then pointed at the door. A silent command for her to shut it. She did.

"Look," she said. "I'm sorry about that. I was just tired of hearing both of them spout their venom about how you weren't good enough and shit." She shrugged. "I was just trying to show them you meant something to someone."

She sounded at once contrite and combative.

Trying to justify her move when there was really no justification for it.

"What you did was make Anthony double down on his promise to take me down. Only now, he's gonna have his eyes on you too." He stalked toward her, making her back up against the door. "My God, girl! What the fuck was all that? I'm too Goddamned old for you, and you're a pain in my ass!" He scrubbed a hand over his face. "You made me look like the horny biker Joy's always accused me of being."

"So? You are a horny biker! Everyone here is! Why do people get so fucking hung up on other people having sex? What's wrong with sex? I happen to like sex!"

"So does everyone else. But when there are power dynamics involved, the first thing they go after is that primal instinct everyone has. Anthony is going to paint me as a pedophile at worst. What he's really going to do is use that as an excuse to raid the garage and see if he can figure out what it is we do here. He's got no imagination, so it will take someone smarter than him to figure it out, but he won't stop until he does. All thanks to that little fuckin' stunt you pulled."

Rosanna looked like he'd slapped her. Her face grew red and her jaw clenched. "I might have started it, but you finished it. I was content with little pecks all over your face. But you had to pull me in and stick your tongue down my throat. I certainly didn't start that shit."

"No. You didn't." He could concede that, but he wasn't ready to give up the fight. He had to push her away so she would cut him out of her life. "But once you started it, I had to follow through. Joy knows me and knows how I'd react to that shit. A woman throws herself at me like you did, practically offering herself to me, I take her. Right there. Wherever we are. The fact that I stopped short of fuckin' you right there in front of everyone was me being considerate to you. You try that little stunt again, you'll get more than you bargained for."

"I'm sorry, all right?"

He spun around and slammed a fist down on his desk, making her jump. "Sorry doesn't fuckin' cut it, Rosanna! You put yourself directly in their path. We both know you have a past. What do you think will happen when Anthony starts diggin' up shit on you? I may not know your story, but you do. Thorn does. You know exactly what he's liable to find." She paled and put the back of her hand to her mouth. "Uh-huh. That's what I thought. Now, either get back to work or go back to the clubhouse. But stay outta my way. You hear me?"

Rosanna nodded, then fled out the door. She left, but Red had no idea where she went. Hopefully back to the clubhouse. He texted Thorn to be on the lookout but didn't tell him why. Only to text him once she got to the compound.

Four hours later, she hadn't showed. Red wanted to pull his hair out. "Goddamn it!" He threw his phone across the room in a fit of temper. If she wasn't at the clubhouse, there was only one other place she could be. And he knew exactly what she was doing. He'd watched her there before. *Fuck!* Girl would be the death of him.

* * *

This was twice in twenty-four hours. Rosanna grumbled as she emerged from the ocean to sit on her beach chair. Toes in the warm sand, setting sun warming her body, crisp, salt air playing over her wet skin… Yeah. This was just what she needed after that fucking confrontation with Red. It had taken every ounce of willpower she'd had not to leave the garage immediately so she could have a good cry. She'd taken shit from the guys about it, especially Grease, but she'd finished the Pinto before leaving.

The little stretch of beach she currently enjoyed was technically private. But she happened to know the owners were out of town, and fuck 'em anyway. Beaches should be used by everyone as long as they kept it clean. Uncaring if anyone saw her naked -- being caught nude swimming and sunbathing was currently the least of her worries -- she chucked her bathing suit and just let the warm sun beat down on her.

God, it felt good! She sighed and stretched her arms over her head. Yeah. This made it all better. She thought about the conversation she and Red had had. Well, it wasn't much of a conversation. It was more him yelling at her. As usual. God, the man was a fucking asshole! Why did she even bother? It was obvious he didn't want her around. Or anyone for that matter. Man was as antisocial as they came.

But that kiss…

No doubt about it, he'd wanted to kiss her. He might try to play it off or pretend like he was only doing what was expected, but that man had wanted her. Rosanna might not be the most experienced in sex, but she'd been around men enough to know when one wanted a woman. Red wanted her. His biggest hang-up seemed to be the age gap between them, but she didn't see that as a problem. All she knew was that Red, even if he was the grumpiest man she'd ever met, was a good man at heart. He'd made sure she'd had a place to go after a really dark time for her, and he and Thorn had practically given her a family when she'd never had one.

She sighed. This was helping her relax, but it wasn't helping her situation. She needed to think this through. What to do next?

Absently, she snagged a bottle of Hawaiian Tropic suntan oil in one hand and her beer in the other. She took a healthy pull of the alcohol, then set it back in the sand before unscrewing the bottle of oil and squeezing a thin line down her torso.

At once, the smell hit her. There was nothing so wonderful as Hawaiian Tropic suntan oil. She could just inhale. Best aromatherapy ever! Instantly, her mood lightened even further, and she started rubbing the silky oil into her skin.

She took her time, applying oil to her legs and arms, then her inner thighs and her bare mound. That last made her shiver. Which led to decidedly naughty thoughts. Every single one of them involved Red applying the oil to her body. Like one of those erotic massage scenes on the free porn sites.

Moving her hands back up her body, Rosanna cupped her tits, letting the nipples poke through her fingers. She scissored her fingers tightly, tugging the pebbled buds over and over. The evening sun played over her like warm fingers, and she uttered a soft moan.

Yeah, this was happening. Out in the open, under the sun, while the ocean crashed against the shore. Rosanna let one hand slide down her body to her pussy. Her bare mound was slippery with the oil. When she dipped her fingers to her slit, they came back wet with her own moisture. What would it be like for Red's fingers to be playing her? His hands were big, the fingers thick and long. They'd be callused. Rough. She circled her clit with a finger, moaning when pleasure rolled through her.

"Oh, God," she whispered. What if that were Red's tongue? What if his dark auburn head were between her legs, tonguing her clit, sucking her lips and finger-fucking her pussy. Could she take that? She thought she could. "Red."

He was her fantasy. Her rough biker with a soft heart. When he let it show, which wasn't often. She was so stupid to be fantasizing about this, because it wasn't likely to ever happen. But, God, she wanted it to! She wanted it to be his fingers instead of hers plunging in and out of her cunt. Wanted his dick readying to plunge into her instead of three of her fingers. Out here, on the beach where anyone could see her, it made her thoughts even more kinky.

She'd been to the club during the parties. Most of the club girls didn't care where they fucked. The men didn't care either. In fact, most of them seemed to thrive on it. Could she have sex with Red at one of those parties? Everyone would watch them. He'd pull her onto his lap facing away so she could see everyone staring at them, and spread her wide for the club to see that big dick of his disappearing inside her. He'd cup her tits, squeeze them and tug the nipples all while he fucked her. Even with her on top of him, he'd be in control.

Then, when he was ready, he'd stand with her, her thighs draped over his arms as he moved to the pool table or the bar. He'd turn her over and fill her again, this time with her facing him. So she knew exactly who was fucking her. He'd lean over her, his hands braced beside her head and fuck her hard. Fast. Rough.

"Who do you belong to, Rosie?"

"You, Red."

"Only me!"

"Only you! Only you!"

He'd roar his release, coming deep inside her, his hand wrapped around her throat to hold her down. He'd bellow his pleasure as his cum filled her. Then his other hand would go to her belly, stroking and massaging just above her bare mound.

"That's it, baby. Now fuckin' come on my cock. Milk the rest of my cum from my dick."

With a scream, Rosanna orgasmed. Her body seemed to fragment into a thousand pieces, and warm liquid leaked around her fingers where they were plunged deep inside her pussy. She gasped as the waves continued to crash around her both literally and figuratively.

Finally, she was spent, her body limp. The water lapped around her ankles with the rising tide.

"Rosanna! What the fuck?"

Ok, that wasn't in her mind. That sounded like the real Red and, by the sound of things, he was fucking pissed. Right. She sighed. When was he not? Hopefully, he hadn't heard her cry his name when she came.

"I could ask you the same thing. This is a private beach."

"Yeah, but not your private beach. After our talk, you're risking getting caught on private property." He loomed over her, scowling. "You're naked."

"Well, yeah. What's the good of having a private beach if you can't be out naked?"

He scrubbed a hand over his mouth, his gaze eating her up. "Is that suntan oil?"

She grinned. "Well, yeah. You wouldn't want me to burn, would you?"

He pulled his gaze away from her body and bent

to pick up the bottle of oil sitting in the sand. Glancing at, he found his scowl again. "Ain't got no sunscreen in it."

"Are you sure?" She took the bottle from him and gave a fake surprised look up at him. "Well, shit. What do you know?" She reached into her bag and pulled out another bottle. This time it was aloe vera gel. "I bet my skin is already damaged. This should do the trick. You might want to help me with this. You know. Make sure I don't miss any spots." Without waiting for him to refuse, she tossed the bottle in his general direction and turned over on her stomach.

"You don't look burned." His voice sounded dazed. A quick glance at him under her lashes told her that, yeah, he was zeroed in on her ass.

"Light's fading. Besides, you probably can't tell until the next day. You wouldn't want my ass to be sore, would you?"

"Oh, I'd like it to be sore, all right," he muttered. But she heard him flip the top of the bottle and squirt a dollop into his hand. "Just not from a sunburn." She watched as he absently rubbed the green gel between his palms. Then, eyes still glued to her ass, he laid his hands on her back and gently rubbed.

It felt heavenly. Rosanna knew better than to make a sound. He had to be completely focused on his task, otherwise he'd start thinking again and stop. Those big hands of his easily took in the skin across her back, rubbing up and down from her shoulders to just above her buttocks. His fingers slightly grazed the sides of her breasts, and it was all she could do not to moan.

"How long you been out here like this?" His voice was husky and soft. He cleared his throat right after. "'Cause your skin's hot."

"Is my ass red?" she asked, trying not to sound too eager for him to squeeze and knead her cheeks.

"Don't

know. Why I asked." Again, he cleared his throat.

"What about my legs?" She didn't really want to take his focus off her ass, but thought it might be better if he had some more time to get used to the idea. She knew without a doubt he'd be rubbing the cool into the skin of her cheeks. If she got lucky, he might dip between those cheeks and…

"Probably should do them, too," he muttered. This was a whole other side of Red she hadn't seen before. He was hesitant. Indecisive. Not at all confident and surly. Which was why she believed he wanted her. If she didn't affect him at all, he'd have tossed a shirt at her and told her to get her ass back home. But he hadn't.

Again, she heard him flip the top and squirt aloe vera gel into his palm. Again, he rubbed his hands together before placing them on her skin. One hand on each thigh, Red slid his hands up and down her legs. He stopped just at the crease of her ass, his thumbs slipping high on each side of her pussy. There was no way to stifle the little whimper she had this time. She tried to keep it soft and gripped the sides of her chair tight to keep from making any more noise.

Up and down he went, covering her from just below her ass to her ankles and back. It felt so fucking good! How had she lived without this her whole life? Where were all the men like this in the world? She'd been at Salvation's Bane for six months now. Sure, there were some good-looking guys, all of them ripped and heavy with muscle. Some of them had women. Others didn't. Most of them were really good to her, never pressuring her for anything. It was as if they knew what she did for the club and considered her mechanic ability her way of helping the club. Of bringing in her share of the money. They didn't hit on her. They didn't expect her to perform sex acts of any kind for them. And *none* of them appealed to her anywhere as much as Red.

One last time, he slid his hands up her calves to her thighs to sit just below her ass. Again, his thumbs were so close to her pussy she wanted to shift just that little bit to get him to touch her. But she didn't dare. He removed his hands and picked up the bottle again. This time, instead of putting it in his palm first, he squirted some on each cheek of her ass. Probably to see what she'd do.

Rosanna tried to keep her gaze on him, though it was difficult in her position. He glanced back at her and she struggled to keep her expression neutral. She absolutely could not fuck this up or he'd bail. Finally, he sighed and indicated her ass. "You good with this?"

"Wouldn't have put you in a situation where I wasn't good."

He nodded crisply, then laid one hand on each cheek of her ass. He kneaded slowly, squeezing gently, then seemed to remember himself and just rubbed the gel into her skin. Over and over, he moved his hands over her ass and sides. Even the crease at her thighs wasn't forgotten. When the gel absorbed, he got another dollop. "Might have missed a spot," he muttered. Then he started all over again. This time, however, his thumbs dipped slightly into the crease, stroking from top all the way to the bottom. Then he gripped her cheeks from the bottom and squeezed, his thumbs slipping between the crease again, perilously close to her weeping cunt.

Rosanna didn't dare move. She wanted to spread her legs but was afraid to break the spell. Over and over, he rubbed her ass, gripping and kneading. Always he cupped her cheeks on his way back up. When he stopped, Rosanna dared another look at him. Red was breathing hard, the tendons standing out at his neck.

"You'll need it on your front too." God, his voice like this was sexy. When he wasn't yelling or growling at her, he could cream panties from a hundred paces.

She turned over, looking up at him as she did. The sun was still shining on them, but it was sinking low. Red knelt in the sand beside her. He wore a dark blue T-shirt that looked like it was two sizes too small. Muscles played under the material, and she wanted desperately to tell him to take it off but didn't dare.

As if he read her mind, he slowly peeled the shirt off his body. It was inside out when he tossed it aside. "Don't wanna get this shit on my clothes," he muttered.

"Can't have that," she whispered.

Red picked up the aloe vera bottle again, pouring a generous amount in his palms, then started on her legs. Rosanna nearly groaned. Of course, he'd start with her legs. Probably would insist on doing her arms too. She wanted him to get to the good stuff already! But when he got to the tops of her thighs, he ran his thumbs deep into the crease of her inner thighs. There was no way to control the shiver. She did widen her legs slightly before she could stop herself. He glanced up at her but took two more hard swipes up her legs before he stopped.

Her arms were indeed next. Aloe vera gel was coated liberally up her arms and her collarbone, just above her breasts. Red pinned her with his intense gaze, not letting her look away. Rosanna's breath caught. She was truly mesmerized by him. She wanted this like she wanted her next breath, but she couldn't open her mouth to tell him.

Finally, he took one last handful and a deep breath. As he rubbed his palms together he stared at her, like he was trying to give her every opportunity to indicate she didn't want him to touch her. Instead, she nodded at him. It was all she could manage.

With a resigned sigh, Red put his hands on her belly and slid them up to her breasts. They were really only just small bumps with nipples, especially when she lay on her back, but he cupped and massaged them like they were the most exquisite tits in the world. He had this look of near bliss on his face as he palmed them, gripping and squeezing them with a firm pressure. His hands were so big they spanned her chest easily, and those long fingers curled down the side of her ribcage.

Rosanna couldn't help but arch into him, calling his name softly before she could bite her lower lip. He grunted and continued massaging her breasts and torso. Her nipples were hard peaks, sensitive to his touch. When he finally stopped, he pulled her nipples, elongating them and rolling them between his big fingers. That was all she could stand. Rosanna arched her back and moaned out a long, low, needy sound.

The next thing she knew, Red had latched onto her nipple with his mouth and was sucking gently. Her hands flew to his head and she cradled him to her, arching her back and her hips in a needy undulation.

Red let go of her nipple with a little pop before opening his mouth wider and taking more of her breast into his mouth. His tongue flicked and circled her nipple while he pinched and stretched the other with his fingers. Then he moved to the other breast with his mouth and picked up the nipple play with his other hand while the free one moved down her body to find her bare sex.

Rosanna spread her legs eagerly, thrusting up to meet his hand. God, she needed him inside her! If he led her down that road, she was following as far as he'd take her.

"Such pretty tits," he rasped against one. His beard tickled her skin in the most erotic way. "Could suck on them all fuckin' night." His tongue stroked a hot path over the same nipple before he switched back. "So fuckin' sweet! Gonna eat you up, little girl."

"You just gonna suck my tits? I've got more for you."

"Oh, I'm gettin' there. Ain't rushin' this. When I'm done, I'll have my fill of you."

"You think so?"

"Know so. This is it, Rosanna. Just this. Nothin' else." He stopped and caught her gaze. She was so afraid he'd snap out of whatever spell had been cast over him, but he just waited for her to nod several times before he trailed his beard down her body until he settled between her legs. "Gonna eat you out. Gonna suck this little pussy dry. You ready?"

"Fucking do it, Red!" She gasped out her command, and he just chuckled. But he lowered his head to her, parted his lips, and covered her pussy with his mouth.

If there was a sweeter pussy this side of heaven, Red would like to know who had it. The green shit she'd had him rubbing all over her body didn't stop him tasting every inch he could. The scent was clean and fresh, mixing with the coconut scent of the tanning oil. Underneath it all, though, was an intoxicating fragrance unique to Rosanna that had plagued him since the day he'd met her six months before. He dreamed of that fucking smell every fucking night. Now, he had her beneath him. Her sweet pussy quivered beneath his tongue, weeping for him.

She writhed beneath him, and her thighs, though his arms were clamped around them, slipped through his grip and let her move when he wanted her still. He wanted to be able to drive her up at his leisure until she was so desperate for release she was begging him to let her come.

Fuck. Who was he kidding? He wanted her to beg him to fuck her. He wanted his dick buried so deep inside her she still felt him in the morning. But he couldn't have that. Not tonight. Not ever. But the more she responded to him, the more she wiggled and gripped his hair with her little hand and tried to force him harder against her cunt, the more the reasons why he couldn't have her became murky. Other than her age and his ex, he couldn't think of a single reason.

Red had never wanted a woman of his own. He'd never met one he could relate to. Sure, Joy had been decent in bed, but she was more of an excuse to keep other women at bay. Even after she left, he only fucked the occasional club girl to get his rocks off. There had never been this all-consuming need to mark a woman as his. Right now, all he could think about was straddling that lounging beach chair she sat on, pulling her thighs over his, and sinking himself into her tender pussy as deep as he could go. Then he wanted to come in her. Hard. Long. Repeatedly. It was madness. Yet, he couldn't shake it.

When she screamed out his name, her other hand going to his hair, he knew she was close. So he pulled back.

"Red! What the fuck?" She sounded like she was somewhere between a screech and a sob. Red managed a chuckle.

"What's the matter?"

"You know I was getting ready to come! Why'd you stop?"

"Because your orgasms are mine, girl," he said, giving her inner thigh a sharp smack. Mostly he just wanted to see how she'd react. When she sucked in a breath and met his gaze with a wide, shocked one of her own, he did it again. Her cunt gave him more of that liquid honey he was growing addicted to. So he smacked that little, quivering pussy with the flat of his fingers. Once. Twice.

Rosanna's eyes got wide, and her mouth opened in a little "O" of surprise. But she widened her legs farther, thrusting her hips at him.

"Fuck," she whispered. "Fuck! Red! Oh, God!" She seemed to lose the control he'd watched her fighting so hard to maintain since he'd first started touching her. He wasn't sure why she thought she needed it, but there was something inside him that just wouldn't let her keep that control when she was with him. He wanted everything from her but wasn't sure how much of himself he was willing to give her in return. That made him the worst kind of bastard, but he just couldn't help it. It was only Rosanna, though. Never any other woman he'd been with. He'd never wanted this kind of control over any other woman he'd ever met. Only Rosanna. Always Rosanna.

Knowing she was nearing the point of no return, Red slid three fingers inside her. She was impossibly tight. Not a virgin, but certainly not a woman having sex regularly. Which just called to his animalistic side even more.

"How's that feel, baby?" he asked, moving his fingers in and out while tonguing her clit.

"Fucking wonderful! Fuck!"

"So fuckin' tight." He went back to licking her clit, milking every bit of juice he could from her. He wanted her to be fucking soaked. When he pulled his fingers from her cunt, she sobbed out a protest. "Shh. I'm not done, baby." He slid his fingers down farther, to use the middle one to circle her anus. She jumped, gasping and whimpering. "Anyone ever take you here?" She shook her head, her eyes wide.

Without saying anything else, Red eased that middle finger inside her back hole, giving a couple of shallow pumps before adding a second finger. She did scream then, but not in pain. She rode his fingers with undulations of her hips. Red slid two fingers of his other hand back inside her pussy, filling her as completely as he could without fucking her. God knew he wanted to fuck her, but this wasn't the time. Mainly because he knew that, if he fucked her, he wasn't pulling out when he came. And he wouldn't let her go.

"Do it, baby," he hissed. "Come for me. Right fuckin' now!"

She did. Her body clamped down around his fingers and she let out a loud, long scream of pleasure. Red continued to tongue her clit, sucking and slurping everything he could from her. Her pussy quivered and pulsed with her orgasm, soaking his fingers with her juices.

When she finally stopped, Red pulled his fingers out gently and sat back on the sand. "Goddamn, I've never seen such a fuckin' beautiful sight." He hadn't really meant to say it, but there was no denying the truth.

She sat up, moving toward him. On instinct, Red

stood, grabbing her by the waist when she followed. Only she sank to her knees without a word and reached for the waistband of his jeans. Deftly, she unfastened them and pulled his aching cock free.

In his most fevered dreams, she'd done this. Sank to her knees and blew him good. Nothing could have prepared him for how good it felt for her to take his cock into her mouth and suck. It was like she sucked on her favorite flavor of popsicle. What she couldn't fit in her mouth, she worked with her hand. Faster and faster until she finally just let go with her hands and slid them around to clutch his ass.

Red let his head fall back, and he breathed in the clean ocean air. If he lasted beyond thirty seconds like this he'd be surprised. He thrust, and she took all he had to give her. Her mouth was stretched wide, and she could barely fit half of him. She gagged, but she didn't pull back. She clutched him closer, gripping his ass, then sliding one hand to his thigh to knead and grip the muscle there.

"Fuck, Rosanna! Goddamn! Fuck!"

"Mmm." She hummed around him, opening wider so he could fuck her mouth at his leisure.

Red slid his fingers through her abundance of hair, pulling it into a ponytail with his fist. He held it up and guided her the way he wanted her to go. She took him eagerly, opening her eyes and looking up at him with her mouth around his cock and tears streaming from her eyes at his vigorous use of her mouth. If there was a sexier sight, Red had no idea what it would be. Maybe his cum in her pussy? Yeah, that would be a sight to behold.

"Gonna come, Rosanna. Gonna shoot my cum all over your face. You don't want that, you say so now."

She pushed back so she could speak, and Red

had to grind his teeth in frustration. If she rejected him...

"Come in my mouth," she demanded.

"No," he said, more relieved than he cared to admit she hadn't told him to come on the sand. "I want to paint you in my cum. Want it all over you. Want to see you covered in it."

"Fuck, that's hot," she whimpered. "Yes. Do it!" She sat back on her heels and cupped her little tits. Opening her mouth, she stuck out her tongue, ready to catch what she could of his spunk. The sight was Red's undoing.

With a brutal yell to the stars appearing overhead, Red let go. His cum splattered her face and chin -- long, thick ropes of the stuff. She caught several drops of it with her tongue and swallowed it. White, gooey ribbons slid from her chin to her tits, and she rubbed it all over herself. She scooped the stuff from her face and sucked her fingers clean of his cum.

Red shook his cock, wanting every drop he could to land on her lithe body. In his mind, he'd marked her. It was a primitive, ridiculous notion, but he latched on to that. It wasn't a healthy thought, but he couldn't shake it. He'd marked Rosanna. She was his. He hadn't fucked her yet, but he knew it was only a matter of time. No matter what he tried to convince her of. He'd try to push her away. Try to make her see reason. But he knew the countdown had started. He would fuck Rosanna, and she'd be his.

Fuck. Who was he kidding? She was his already.

Chapter Four

Rosanna was more than a little stunned at the turn of events. After the frenzied orgasms, she let Red carry her to the ocean. He set her down in chest-deep water and helped her rinse herself. He didn't say a word but cleaned her like it was important to him. Like she was important. He watched her steadily as she splashed water over her face, even ducking under and scrubbing lightly with her hands. Once she'd finished, Red wrapped his arms around her without a word and just held her for several long moments. Rosanna wished she could stay right there forever. Naked, in his gentle embrace. It was the first time in her life someone had actually hugged her like this. It wasn't like the brief, affectionate hugs friends gave one another. It was a full-body, enfolding-her-in-his-arms kind of hug. She wanted more.

All too soon, he let her go and led her back to shore. She toweled off before tossing the towel to Red to do the same. They dressed in silence, and Red helped her gather up her bag and chair.

Finally, he asked, "You good?"

"Yeah," she said, looking up at him from under her lashes. She wanted to go to him, for him to hold her again.

"You got plans for the rest of the night?"

That surprised her. What did he want? Her heart raced at the thought of spending more time with him. God, she was pathetic. He was a man who'd barely said two kind words to her, and here she was fawning over him.

She shrugged. "Thought I'd find something to eat, then chill out with a beer or something."

"Come back to the garage with me. You can help

me finish a project in the basement. We'll talk." That was as close to asking her to do anything as she was going to get.

Rosanna nodded, trying not to grin like a loon. If he thought she was trying to take too much, he'd snatch away his offer. "Guess that means I finally get to work with you."

"Guess so," he grumbled. "But don't think you can all the time." He pointed a finger at her in warning. "Just thought I might see what you've been holdin' out on. Uh, mechanical-wise."

She grinned. "Of course. I'll meet you there."

"No," he said abruptly. "I'll have one of the brothers get your bike and stuff. How'd you manage to get all this shit here on a fuckin bicycle anyway?"

"Backpack," she said. "Biiiig fuckin' backpack."

That actually got a bark of laughter out of Red before he shook his head and chuckled. "You're a rare gem, Rosie. Don't ever change."

That caused her to start. She took a couple of steps back from him. "Who are you and what have you done with Red?"

"Brat. Pack up your shit. I've got Styx and Tinker comin' for your ride." He tossed her a helmet. Get on."

"I don't want to leave --"

"Someone steals it before they get here, I'll buy you new shit. Get on."

Wasn't this just the place she always wanted to be? On the back of Red's bike? She had to remind herself that Joy had been there too, and it hadn't gotten her anywhere. Though, honestly, it seemed like Joy hadn't deserved Red. With her past, it didn't mean Rosanna did, but she sure as hell wanted him.

She only hesitated for show before putting on the helmet and climbing behind Red. He started his Harley and revved the engine. Immediately, Rosanna felt a shiver of desire. Bikes had always been sexy, but she'd never had the occasion to be on one. She hadn't wanted a lover at Salvation's Bane other than Red, and, typically, women who rode on the back of a man's bike were screwing him.

They sped off down the road and she squealed, wrapping her arms tighter around Red. She felt his chuckle where her body pressed against his and was glad of it. He didn't laugh or even smile nearly enough. If she accomplished nothing else, she wanted to make him do both as often as she could while she was with him. Even if it was only tonight.

Red took the long way back, and Rosanna thought it might have been for her because, at one point, she threw her head back and howled at the moon for the sheer joy of the experience. She now understood why the men liked it so much. Hell, had she known how freeing it felt, she might have tried to buy her own instead of saving every penny she could in case she had to make a quick getaway. The ocean breeze and balmy night air were a whole other level of wonderful when speeding down the road on the big Harley. It was fun… and sexy as fuck.

All too soon, the ride was over. Red pulled into the garage and turned off the engine. He held out a hand for her to steady herself as she got off before he put the kickstand down and swung his long leg over the seat. He took her helmet, fastening it to the back, then led her to his office. Once inside, he moved a filing cabinet. At first, she had no idea what he was doing, but then a door appeared, perfectly hidden as a wall.

"Holy shit! I didn't even see the seam!"

"And you won't. I'm the only one who knows

how to open it, and you're the only person in the garage who knows about this. The only other entrance is the tunnel where we bring the cars in, and only a handful know about that. Consider yourself in an elite club, Rosanna."

He led her down a dark tunnel. She fisted her hand in his shirt when the door shut behind them. Again, he chuckled. "Afraid of the dark?"

"It's a creepy tunnel. Of course, I'm scared!" That carefree sound from him was worth any embarrassment on her part.

"Well, hang on to me. I won't let the boogie man get you."

The tunnel seemed like it went on forever. By the time it opened up into a larger section, she'd started to get claustrophobic. It sounded like Red fumbled with something on the wall, then lights flickered and came to life, lighting up an underground garage at least the size of the one above ground.

"Woah," she said in wonder, finally letting go of his shirt and looking around her in awe. "This is… this is fucking amazing!" All around the place were high-end, exotic cars. There was a Lamborghini and a Ferrari, an Aston Martin, and more than one Mercedes. "Holy fucking shit! Red… wow! You sure know the way to a girl's heart."

"Calm your tits, babe. They ain't yours."

"Can I drive one?"

"Nope. What you can do is tell me what you know about them and if you can erase any digital footprint of them."

"No one can do that," she said. "Not without some serious reprogramming. But you don't need to do that."

"Explain," he snapped, all business now.

She turned back to him. The old Red was back, and he was intensely focused on her. Much like he had been at the beach. She shivered but tried not to look like that attention affected her.

"Well, every single one of these cars has a sophisticated computer system. They control everything from the fuel injectors and braking system, to security. They have to be updated periodically, and most of them do it by satellite."

"Continue."

"Jesus, Red. I can't give you all my secrets." She grinned up at him, trying to sound cheeky, but the fact was, she really *didn't* want to give away all her secrets. Sure, other people around the country could do what she could, but she doubted there was anyone else close or Red would have them in his employ.

"Rosanna…" It was a clear warning.

"Look. I only use my powers for good. Besides, if it gets out you can bypass all that shit, it will bring the police straight to your door and this place will be shut down quicker than a motherfucker."

"Ain't interested in how you do it, just if you can do it and what you do. And no one will find out unless you tell them. Only other person in on it is me. Possibly Beast or Thorn because it affects the club, but that's it. And they ain't tellin'."

"OK, so I can change the VIN number. Like for everything other than engraved parts, and they can only be traced to the manufacturer production and assembly factory. Not to the specific car." When he said nothing, she added, "But you already knew that. Anyway, with the clean VIN, any dealership can do regular maintenance and such without risk of them finding out the car's stolen." When he still said nothing, she said, "I can also make my own fobs unique to whatever car I need to. I can unlock it, get in, and drive away." He just looked at her, his expression neutral, but his neck and cheeks were getting red. "I'm not lying, Red. I can --"

"Prove it."

"What?"

"If you can really do that, prove it." He crossed his arms over her chest, looking like he was pissed as hell.

"And there's the Red I know and love," she muttered. "Fine. Which one do you want me to start with?" He pointed at a Mercedes. "Prove it," she muttered as she walked over to it. She pulled out a small, round device from her pocket. Since she'd made it, Rosanna never went anywhere without it. She'd only used it once or twice to verify she could do exactly what she'd said she could do, but it had worked like a charm.

It worked with her phone on a special app she'd programmed. Which was why she never, *ever* turned on her GPS. In fact, she'd completely disabled that feature on her phone and installed the latest VPN for extra security. A few seconds later, she'd simulated a fob and unlocked the doors. Then she unscrewed the front panel to get to the vehicle's computer. A few seconds later, it was done. She saved the number, then turned to Red and showed him.

"This is the new VIN number for this vehicle. You'll have to replace it on the windshield and the driver's side door, but that's simple enough. I don't have the physical fob to program here, but that's easy enough, too. I can program it with the app. If you look up that VIN number, it will match this car exactly, except it's clean. Never been sold and was manufactured at the busiest plant that makes this particular car. The only way to actually prove it's wrong is to go through each manifest and track it by hand. Even then, there would be room for error, even with luxury cars like these. While all of them are expensive, they aren't that rare. Sold all over the world. You get them shipped from someplace in Europe, anything could have happened between here and there."

Red looked at her as if he were about to explode. "Dozens of men in Bane would kill to have this job cause the money's fuckin' great. None of them can do this. How the fuck did you figure it out?"

"'Cause I'm fuckin' smart, that's how," she snapped.

He closed his eyes and took a deep breath, letting it out slowly. "Anyone else know about this? Did you have help developing it?"

"No. I did it all by my little self."

"Relax," he muttered. "Didn't mean to insult you."

"Then exactly what did you mean to do?"

"I just… Fuck, Rosie!" He lunged for her and pulled her against his hard body. His equally hard dick pressed into her belly. "You have no idea how much that fuckin' turns me on." He wrapped his arms around her and lifted. Rosanna squealed, her arms instantly going around his neck. Red's big hand fisted in her hair, then he pulled her head back and took her mouth with his.

Rosanna wasn't sure what she expected, but having Red set her on the hood of a Mercedes while fucking her mouth with his tongue was not it. Not that she was complaining. The second his tongue flicked hers, she was a goner. His hand tightened in her hair, moving her exactly where he wanted her. He thrust his tongue boldly, deepening the kiss until all she could think about was kissing him back, giving him as much pleasure as he gave her.

With a growl, Red whipped her shirt off. She'd left her bra off and was now glad of it. He lunged for her chest, taking one nipple into his mouth to suck. Stretching it out, he finally let go with an audible "pop" before giving the other tit the same treatment. He cupped the other breast, pulling and tugging, rolling the nipple between his fingers mercilessly.

"Fuckin' love these little tits," he growled at her chest. "Love suckin' on 'em." As he did exactly that, he unfastened his jeans, then her shorts. Before she realized what he'd done, Red had her shorts and panties off and shoved her back so she lay sprawled over the hood of the Mercedes.

He wrapped his arms around her legs and tugged her forward until her ass hung off the edge before lowering his face between her thighs. She cried out when Red's mouth covered her pussy, his tongue fucking her much as he had her mouth. Only now, he flicked her clit instead of her tongue.

An orgasm hovered just out of reach and Red, the bastard, seemed determined to hold her there, not letting her crest that wave. Her whole world narrowed to his mouth on her cunt. All she could concentrate on was the feel of his lips and tongue playing along her sex. He sucked each delicate lip into his mouth several times before once again covering her pussy with his mouth and stabbing his tongue inside.

She screamed in frustration before Red lifted his head. She sat up on her elbow then, needing to see what he was doing. One fist pumped that big shaft, his hand barely spanning it. The second she saw it, she wrapped her legs around him, pulling him to her. Red didn't argue, simply aimed his cock at her entrance and surged home.

Rosanna screamed again, this time in pain. It was more the shock than anything else. She wasn't a virgin, but he was big, and she was still very tight. "Hold up! Hold up!" She panted for breath, the pain manageable, but only if he let her adjust.

He stopped, but didn't pull out, just held himself deep inside her. "Talk to me, Rosie."

"Just… just give me a second." She winced and gripped him tight, needing a few more seconds. "It burns."

"Breathe through it," he said. "You can take me. You're not a virgin."

"No, but you're not exactly small."

He leaned forward, careful not to move too much inside her, and took her mouth again. This time, his kisses coaxed her. Teased her. His hand found her nipple again while the other hand found her clit. He pressed on the little nub of flesh at the same time he twisted her nipple gently. The result was a rush of pleasure, easing his movement inside her cunt.

Rosanna gasped when he slowly withdrew, then eased his way back in. The pain was much better. And she was soaking wet. It still wasn't comfortable, but she could see it getting there.

"Love how tight you are," he murmured. "Don't want to hurt you, though."

"It's better," she said. "Just need time to adjust."

"Got all the time you need, baby."

Again, he slid out, then back in. Several times. Finally, the pain faded to be replaced by an altogether different burn. When she started arching her hips back at him, he praised her.

"That's my girl. See? You can take me."

"So good," she whispered. "Fuck! What are you doing to me?"

"Fuckin' you. Gonna fuck you hard in a minute."

"Yeah?"

"Oh, yeah, baby." He kissed her again, starting to move in more rhythmic thrusts. When she began to move with him, he situated himself more comfortably between her thighs and started a hard, driving rhythm.

How had she lived without this? The pleasure on the beach had been the stuff of fairy tales. This was... unimaginable. Her whole body was alive with sensation. The cool metal of the car's hood. The hair-roughened body of the man fucking her. The sense of invasion of Red's cock inside her tight cunt. All of it added to her pleasure, making her need more and more until she spread her legs wide and brought them to her chest.

"Fuck me, Red! God! That feels so fucking good!"

"That's it. That's my little needy girl. You like this, don't you?"

"Fucking love it! Harder!"

He gave her what she asked for. Red pounded into her, sweat starting to bead on his forehead and drip down his face. Her body was slick with it. He adjusted his grip around her thighs, looping his arms over them to have leverage to pull her to him as he slammed into her. It wasn't enough.

With a frustrated grunt, Red yanked her off the car, spun her around, then shoved her chest back to the hood. He gripped her hips and shoved himself back inside her from behind. Rosanna cried out as he started fucking her again. This new position put him deeper inside her. She could see him reflected in the windshield of a nearby car. His large powerful body behind her, taking her like an animal. Muscles stood out in his thighs and his arms. His abs rippled with every movement he made. He gripped her hips and pulled her to him hard. Fast. The tendons stood out in his neck as he strained.

Rosanna braced herself on the car and pushed back to meet him as best she could. It was a rough, teeth-clattering ride, and she couldn't get enough.

"Fuck!" she screamed as he pounded inside her. "Goddamn, motherfuck!"

Red growled, then shoved one of her knees up onto the hood and moved in closer to her, his balls slapping her clit with every thrust.

"Gonna pump you full of my cum, Rosanna. You're gonna take every fuckin' drop. Understand me?"

"Yes! Fuck yes! Fill me full of it!"

What the fuck was she saying? *Come in her*? Why had she... Oh, God, he was doing it! And she was too. Unable to think past the overwhelming pleasure, Rosanna screamed out her orgasm just as she felt Red's cum explode inside her. She backed against him, trying to get as close to him as she could. Red's grip on her ass as he held her to him bordered on pain, but it only enhanced the experience for her. Never had she felt anything even close to this mind-numbing pleasure.

Red's cock pulsed inside her for long seconds. Even after his frenzied fucking stopped, he held himself inside her, bending over her to kiss her neck and shoulder. After a while, he slowly raised himself off her and let his cock slide free. Rosanna was unsure what to do but couldn't move anyway

She heard him move away. As she stood, he dipped a wet cloth between her legs and cleaned her gently. Rosanna turned around to find him wiping his cock before tossing the material into a trashcan.

"You good?"

Was she? Red had just fucked her brains out and… and come in her. He didn't acknowledge that he'd come inside her, and she wasn't about to. So, was she good?

"That's the second time you've asked me that tonight."

"I seem to be doing things to make me have to ask you." He sighed and picked up her panties and shorts. "Here," he said, dropping to his knees to help her into her clothing and slide them up her legs. She fastened the jeans and slid into the shirt while he pulled up his jeans and zipped them, leaving the button undone. "Come on," he said, taking her hand and leading her to an office.

He led her to a leather couch before going to the fridge and getting her a can of Coke. He had a beer. Sitting next to her, he sighed. "We need to talk."

"Yeah," she agreed. "Looks like it."

"I already told you my son is likely to go after you. I know Thorn knows your story, but, if I'm going to be able to help you, I need to know exactly what he's likely to find."

Rosanna's head snapped up, her gaze meeting his. This was the last thing she expected. "What?"

"Tell me about your past. Why'd you show up here in the first place? And where'd you learn so much about cars?"

Chapter Five

Red watched as Rosanna's expression closed off. She didn't want to do this, and he had a feeling it was going to be very painful for her. While he had no desire to cause her pain, he needed to get the truth if he had any hope of helping her.

When she lowered her gaze, he gently grasped her chin and tilted her face up to meet his eyes. "I can get it from Thorn because of the circumstances, but I'd rather have it from you."

She closed her eyes and let out a slow breath. "It's not pretty."

"Then we'll start easy. Tell me about cars. Who taught you? When did you learn?"

"It's all kind of related," she said softly. "Red?" She glanced up. "I don't really want to tell you."

"Baby, I'm not here to judge."

"It'll be hard for you not to. I'm not a good person."

He gave her a slight smile. "Honey, I guarantee you, you're a much better person than I am. No matter what you've done. Now, just start. The quicker you do, the quicker it will be over with."

"Not sure you're gonna feel that way when you hear this." She straightened on the couch, half turning to him so one leg was hiked up on the seat, her knee bent. She clasped her ankle and rubbed nervously. Rosanna seemed to be pulling her thoughts together, but she was going to tell him. Red could see that. "So," she said. "Cars." Clearing her throat, she began.

"One of my mom's boyfriends taught me. I was thirteen when he moved us in with him. Sixteen when he kicked us out. Seventeen when I split." She sighed. "And, yeah, I'm eighteen now. Not twenty-three."

He snorted. "Figured. Thought you'd at least be twenty, though. Continue."

"So, it's always been my mom and me. I never knew my dad. Probably because they were both druggies. She wasn't a loving mother. Hell, she used to blame me for my dad leaving and would lock me in the closet most days. Sometimes, she'd beat me. Other times she'd just not let me eat. Hell, most of the time, she forgot to get food. Mom never told me who my dad was, and I never asked because I knew, even early on, that it wouldn't do any good. My whole life, there was a string of men lasting from a few weeks to a year or more. Until Davies."

"That the man who taught you cars?"

"Yeah." Rosanna readjusted her position before continuing. "He'd worked in a chop shop in New York City when he was a teenager. When he let me and Mom move in with him, he was twenty-two. She was thirty. I have no idea why he was with her. God knows she was pretty used up by then. I was only nine years younger than him. Mom was eight years older than him. Davies was right in the middle, so I'm not sure if he felt like I was a daughter or a younger sibling. Same with my mom, only he was fucking her. At least, at some point. The main relationship I remember between them was more like brother and sister than lovers. Whatever their deal was, Davies took me under his wing."

She smiled, obviously remembering something amusing. "We lived in Charlotte, North Carolina. Home of NASCAR. Davies was fascinated with speed. He was always looking for ways to make a car go just that little bit faster. He worked at a garage. Yours reminds me a lot of that one in some ways. There was nothing he couldn't fix. I suppose, his years in the chop shop taught him more than just tearing cars apart. He had a reputation of taking the hardest jobs in the city. The cars everyone said were too far gone to do anything with other than to scrap them or rebuild them from the ground up. He took them and fixed them. I'm not talking about restoring them or anything. He used what he had and somehow made it work.

"Anyway, he'd bring me to the garage with him as often as I wanted to go. I cut class a lot to hang out with him. Not because I wanted to be with him, though he was nicer to me than my mother ever was. I wanted to work on cars. I could rebuild a transmission faster than anyone in the place. I was so good, the owner started paying Davies extra when I helped so I could make a little money. Davies always said he took a cut because I worked for him and he worked for the garage. That made me contract labor. But he gave me extra allowance when I worked with him. I never actually counted, nor did I really care, but I suspect he gave me his cut."

"Sounds like a decent guy."

"He was. Mostly. He was the first person in my life to give a damn about me. No idea why he did, but he was really good to me." She cleared her throat. "Sometimes, at night when he didn't have to work the next day, we'd scope out the countryside. We looked for old cars that appeared to be in decent shape but hadn't been moved in months. Junkers people just parked and did nothing with. We'd steal them. Put them on a rollback we'd 'borrow' --" She made air quotes. "-- So no one could link us to the theft. We'd fix them, soup them up, then take them back and park them right where we left them. He'd leave a note on the dashboard that said, 'You're welcome. Enjoy.' It was the best game ever."

"He actually put money into cars he didn't get paid for?"

"Oh, no," she laughed. "We'd steal parts from junk yards and such. Almost got bit by more than one junkyard dog. I have no idea how mean Leroy Brown was, but junkyard dogs are pretty fucking mean."

Red couldn't help but laugh at that. "Thanks for the earworm, but you're not getting out of finishing." He laid a hand on the back of the couch. His finger found one long curl. Threading his finger through it, he tugged gently. "Keep going."

"That all lasted until just after I turned sixteen. We were working at the garage. Putting together an engine or some shit. I can't remember. Anyway. One minute things were going fine. The next, my mother storms in and accuses me of sleeping with Davies. I thought she was gonna kill me. She destroyed a bunch of shit inside the garage, and Davies got fired. He wasn't fucking me, but he did have a woman on the side. She was only a couple years older than me, but then, there wasn't really that big of an age difference between the two of us. Not really."

"I take it your mom moved out?"

"Are you kidding? She fought tooth and nail for that place. She had no ground to stand on, but she tried. Davies told her she had to leave, but said I could stay if I wanted. Only his new girlfriend didn't want me around. Looking back, I could see why. She didn't want there to be temptation in the way. So, I helped get Mom to leave. We got a little crackerjack house in the shittiest part of town imaginable. Mom, already deep into drugs and alcohol, was in a stupor most days. She had no money, so she prostituted herself. I came home more than once to her having sex with a man or two for crack or meth. She did whatever she could to get her fix."

Red hated to ask his next question, but it had to be done. "She sell you out?"

Rosanna shrugged. "She tried. Once. I fought them off. Stabbed one of them. Mom was pissed she didn't get her fix, but she wasn't in any shape to do much about it. All she could do was yell at me from the couch. I went to my room and locked the door. Later that night, something woke me up. To this day, I have no idea why I woke up. Mom was silent as death when I spotted her creeping up to my bed. I watched her get closer and closer. When she was almost to the edge of my bed I just said, 'Mom?' And she pounced on me. She had a knife, and it scraped over my shoulder when she tried to stab me. I was too slow, but thankfully, she was either too weak or too high to get her aim right. It was just barely a scratch, then I tried to grab the knife, but I knocked it out of her hand. It went flying into the corner out of reach." She trailed off, looking away from Red. He saw pain and shame in her eyes. Whatever had happened next hadn't been pretty.

"You can do this, Rosanna," he said softly. "Just give it to me."

"Red, it's not that simple."

"Did you kill her?"

She blinked but nodded slowly. "It's not what you're thinking, though."

"What do you mean?"

"I didn't just kill her, Red." She shuddered, wrapping her arms around herself. She was pale now, chill bumps rising over bare arms and legs. Red pulled her into his lap and wrapped his arms around her.

"What did you do?"

"I… I fought her. I fought her to the floor, then I straddled her on my knees. We were close to the wall and an old radiator. I wrapped my hands around her throat and I squeezed. When she fought me, I shoved her head against the radiator. Several times. In my mind, I relived every single time she'd hit me as a child. Every time I'd been hungry because she either didn't get groceries or just wouldn't let me eat. Every name she'd ever called me. For being so wrapped up in drugs she didn't even try to make Davies want to stay with us. I knocked her silly, then squeezed her throat until she stopped moving, then I let up. I smacked her face a couple of times, and she wheezed in a breath." Tears streamed down her face now. It was killing Red, but he had to let her get this out. He stroked her arm gently, saying nothing. "I… Red, I tortured my own mother."

"That's not torture, honey."

She shook her head hard. "I didn't just do it once. I did it over and over. Each time, I'd let her come back to herself before I started again. The whites of her eyes turned red. There were mottled bruises around her throat. I have no idea how many times I did it, but each time I'd start again, Mom would look me in the eyes and there was terror. If she moved, I shoved her head against the radiator. There was blood everywhere. I have no idea how she didn't die from the head blows alone. She probably would have if I'd left her there. I kept my eyes focused on hers. Mom knew I was going to kill her. She just didn't know when it would end. When I finally let her die, I was looking straight into her eyes. I didn't really decide to finish it. I was just tired. My arms and hands hurt. Because of her meth use, she was only about ninety pounds. Sure, she was probably high, but she also used alcohol and benzos to counteract the tweaking from the meth. I worked on cars for a living. I wasn't bulky, but my hands and arms were strong. My strength and the blows to the head meant she had no chance whatsoever."

"Fuck," he muttered, unable to keep it in. "How'd you get away?"

"I didn't dare leave the house. Once the homicidal rage passed, I was scared out of my freaking mind. If the cops found me, there was no way I could avoid prison. Not even if I proved self-defense. Not the way I'd killed her. It stopped being self-defense after she lost consciousness the first time.

"I packed a few things I couldn't live without. Wasn't much. I took my stash of cash and a change of clothing. Mom was on the floor of my bedroom. I didn't want to touch her, but I didn't want her to be readily seen either. I had a little trap door in the floor. I'd used it to sneak out of the house many times when she had men over to fuck for drugs or alcohol. I was always afraid she'd try to drag me into it. It took some doing, but I dragged her down under the house and covered her with a blanket. Then I pulled all the blinds in my room. They mostly stayed closed anyway. I locked my bedroom door, then turned on a light in the kitchen. I left a radio on a talk radio station. Kinda low so someone outside could mistake it for voices. Then I pulled the rest of the blinds, locked all the doors and windows, then just got on my bicycle and left."

"Where'd you go?"

She shrugged. "Just out of Charlotte. I took every back road I could find. Cut through old dirt roads and generally stayed off the main drag. It was warm out so, though uncomfortable, sleeping outside in wooded areas wasn't all that bad. I stole a sleeping bag and a couple of pots. Managed to score some canned goods at food banks and ate pretty good for the most part. Better than I had at home except when Davies was there.

"I made it across the North Carolina border to Fort Mill, South Carolina. I always kept an ear out for anything out of Charlotte, but I didn't have a radio or a phone or any way of really keeping up with what was going on. I found a bus going south and bought a ticket. It brought me here. To Palm Beach. I found your garage and the rest is history."

"Yeah. I gave you a job because you had sass and knew what the fuck you were doin'."

She sniffled out a small laugh. It wasn't much, but he'd take it. "Stupid Julio. Why do you even keep him on? If it hadn't been for him being such a dumbass, you could have been spared all the fucking trouble I cause you."

"True. He was about to take a hammer to Marge's Pinto when you marched up to him, grabbed it out of his hands and shoved him away from the car. Then fixed that old bucket of bolts so it ran like a brand-new car. Only took you an hour that first time. If I hadn't had Julio, Marge wouldn't have her prized car."

They were silent for a while. Red just held her. She was with him, with the club, because she was hiding out. The fact was, there was a very good possibility Rosanna wasn't in any danger at all. Sure, Anthony could dig up the fact that her mother was dead, but there were many possible explanations for why she left. Starting with the abuse. She'd been sixteen, so she hadn't been an adult, but being a runaway didn't necessarily mean she would be suspected of murder. When they'd found the body and if anyone saw her leave would go a long way toward determining whether or not she was a suspect in her mother's death. This was something he'd have to talk to Wrath at Black Reign about.

In the meantime, he needed to figure out what he was going to do with her. Red should be acting as her guardian. Not fucking her.

Fuck. He was in way too fucking deep. And he was going to hell. Because he wasn't sure if he could give her up now that he'd had a taste of her.

"So, what now?" she asked. "You gonna want me out of the way? I can stay at the clubhouse if you want. I don't want to cause you any more trouble."

"Ain't you causin' trouble. And no. You'll come with me to the garage every fuckin' day. You still got work to do whether we're fuckin' or not." He'd meant that to be funny, but she didn't laugh.

"I don't expect anything from you, Red."

"Don't worry about that right now," he said, anxious to avoid that subject for now. "We'll just get through one day at a time until we figure out exactly how much danger you're in. I'll be honest with you, Rosanna. I think there's a very real possibility nobody gives a shit about a dead crack whore. You may not be in any danger at all. At least, not from Anthony."

She nodded slightly, looking up at him with those big, green eyes. "OK."

"Fuck," he whispered, trailing a finger down her jaw. "Why are you so Goddamned beautiful?"

She sucked in a breath, and Red had no choice but to kiss her. He took his time, just savoring her taste. Her little mews and whimpers, the way she shivered in his arms, gave him courage he hadn't known he needed. Red knew he was no prize. He had baggage and wasn't sure he had anything left in his cold, empty heart to give a woman like Rosanna. She deserved a man who could give her everything. He'd long ago thrown out all the good inside his soul.

Her mouth was wet and slick, her tongue still tentative even after the two wild interludes they'd already shared. She hadn't been a virgin, but he knew she hadn't had much experience with sex. That was both a blessing and a curse. He wanted to be the one to teach her new things. Wanted to be the one she turned to when she wanted something she'd never experienced. At the same time, it gave him this deep-seated need to keep her close so no other man could have what he'd claimed. Even if he had any intention of doing just that, he couldn't. Joy and Anthony would just make both their lives miserable.

Ending the kiss, Red pressed his forehead to hers and sighed. "What am I gonna do with you, girl?"

"You could kiss me some more," she said, giving him a hopeful look that nearly broke his heart.

"Rosie, we can't do this. Shouldn't have started it in the first place."

"Why? Because you still love your ex?"

He jolted back slightly but still threaded a hand through her hair to hold her still. "What? Hell, no! She's a pain in my ass. One I'd love to be rid of."

"Then… Is it because I don't know how to please --"

He put a hand over her mouth before she could finish. "Stop right there, Rosie. We can't because you're younger than my son. Christ! I should be adoptin' you instead of fuckin' you!" She giggled then, ducking her head slightly. Red saw her shy grin and knew this wasn't a battle he was going to win with her. "You think that's funny, do ya?" He dug his fingers into her ribs slightly and tickled her until she squealed with laughter.

"Stop! Red!"

"Little witch. Gonna tickle you 'til you pee."

They wrestled around the couch, him tickling her and Rosanna trying to escape. Red had no idea what possessed him other than her pain and his need to soothe it. He wanted all those negative memories gone and for pleasure to take their place. He lifted her shirt and tickled her bare skin, sliding his palm ever upward until he cupped the weight of one small breast. Her breathless smile was all he could take.

Red pushed her shirt above her breasts, exposing them to the cool air of his office. They were already pebble hard. Taking one into his mouth was a compulsion he didn't try to resist.

With a happy sigh, Rosanna arched her back and cradled his head to her. Her acceptance was like a balm to his lacerated heart. It wasn't that Joy had hurt him. It was that he'd never opened himself up to her in the first place. He'd honestly never thought he'd ever find a woman to love. He wasn't sure Rosanna was that woman, but he wasn't sure she wasn't, either.

He looked up at her and she smiled at him. As she watched, he licked one nipple. Then the other. "You're delicious," he said in a husky voice. "All over."

"You like the way I taste?"

"I do. Ain't never tasted nothin' sweeter."

"Could you -- I mean -- would you want to taste my pussy again?"

"More than anything." He didn't wait for a better invitation. He unfastened her shorts and slid them off those firm legs. She was truly a work of art. Lean and finely muscled. He unzipped his jeans and pulled out his cock. If he was doing this, he was jerking off while he did. Red couldn't remember the last time he'd felt the need to come three times in a single night. Yet, here he was.

Sliding down her body, Red covered her sex with his mouth and stabbed his tongue deep. Instantly, her needy honey hit him like a drug. The lust exploding inside him was literally that hard. Unimaginable hunger swamped his good sense, and the instant her juices hit him, Red knew he was fucking her again. The only way to stop it was for Rosanna to back off. 'Cause he couldn't. Not in a million years. He knew that, as long as she allowed it, he'd want to be buried balls-deep inside her. He'd always have this driving need to fill her with his seed and keep her tied to him in the most primitive way possible.

He thrust two fingers deep inside her, working her pussy while he flicked her clit with his tongue. He used the thumb of his other hand to rim her asshole, wanting to claim every single part of her he could.

"Red!" Rosanna screamed his name, thrusting her hips to meet his hands. Red continued to drive her closer to the edge, wetting his thumb with the abundance of moisture flowing from her pussy. Then he eased his thumb inside her asshole to the first joint. She gasped, her body instantly breaking out in a sweat.

"Hurt?"

"No!" She gasped again, then carefully tilted her hips and worked his thumb deeper inside her. "So good!"

Red let her continue to move, holding as still as he could while she adjusted. God, she was a wild one! Had any woman he'd ever been with been so genuinely turned-on by everything he did to her? Not even close. Not only did Rosanna pick up on what he liked, but she was eager to try new things with him. She didn't balk, just jumped in with both feet. When something wasn't to her liking, she didn't pretend to like it just to get him off, or give up without giving it an honest shot. She told him how to fix it. Because of that, Red knew they could add a whole other level to sex if he dared take her there. God, he wanted to so bad! But not just for the experience himself. He wanted her so addicted to him she never wanted to leave.

"Love this fuckin' little pussy." He bent to lap around his fingers and catch the moisture leaking from her cunt. In the process, he licked below her pussy, across the perineum, between his fingers and thumb. "Love this little asshole, too. Want to fuck it. Put my cum in it."

"I don't know if it'll fit," she said, raising up on her elbows. Her eyes were wide and glazed. He loved that look. A sex goddess at his mercy.

"Oh, it'll fit. I'll get to stretch you first. By the time I'm done, you'll be begging me to stick my cock in there."

"Put it in my pussy now, Red," she whispered. A devil in his ear. He'd known it would happen the second he kissed her. But he honestly thought he could hold out longer than this. "I liked it when you fucked me on the Mercedes." She cupped her tits, squeezing and kneading them as she seduced him. "That was so fucking hot!"

"You were fuckin' hot." Red continued to pump her cunt with his fingers. He kept his thumb in her ass, letting her move on it as she needed to. She'd nearly worked all of it into her body. Carefully, he inserted another finger. She let out a long groan of pleasure.

"Feels so fucking good. God, Red. I need you to fuck me. Please."

"I will, baby. I will. Gonna pin you under me, slide into that tight little pussy. Then I'm gonna take you nice and slow."

"But what if I don't want slow?" She was panting

now, her little body writhing on his fingers. Those little tits of hers were squeezed tight in her hands.

Red pulled his fingers from her cunt and slapped it sharply. "You'll take what I fuckin' tell you to take," he growled.

With a scream, Rosanna came the instant his hand slanted on her clit. Her body contracted around his thumb, and her pussy quivered with each pulse of her orgasm. "Red!"

"Goddamn!" He swore as he withdrew his thumb from her ass and climbed up her body. With a quick thrust, he shoved his dick inside her still-coming pussy. He wanted to feel her orgasm milking him. "Motherfuck, you're tight! How can you be so Goddamned tight?"

For long seconds, Red held himself still inside her. The way her body clamped down on him nearly made him spill his cum the second he sank into her. He held on by sheer force of will as he watched the pleasure on her face.

When she finally floated down from her orgasm, Red pulled his hips back, then thrust forward, sinking into her in a slow, steady movement. He had one knee bent on the couch with her thigh over his, the other foot on the floor. He was fully dressed, while Rosanna was minus her shorts and had her shirt above her tits. Red raised up as he fucked her, looking down at where they were joined. He loved how he stretched her. Loved the way his cock looked sinking into her cunt.

Rosanna bucked against him, trying to drive him deeper. Faster. So he smacked her mound. "Hold fuckin' still," he snapped, giving her his sternest look.

"No! Need you fucking me hard!"

"I said no!" He smacked her pussy again. She cried out, arching her back.

"God! Do that again!"

"Motherfuck," he bit out. "You're gonna get a hot ass if you don't hold still."

"You gonna spank me?" She looked up with wide-eyed innocence. Just like a little girl who'd been caught being naughty. She grinned then. "Will you spank my ass? Or fuck it?"

"Rosie, you're in so much fuckin' trouble…"

"You could do both at the same time."

"Goddamn it!"

Red gripped her thighs and started fucking her in earnest. Their skin slapped together loudly, mingled with her sighs and his grunts. Red wasn't sure he had any control over his body when she wanted this. His Rosanna. She liked him raw and dirty. He'd planted the suggestion of taking her ass, and she turned it into a fantasy. Just like he'd wanted. Now, he was hard-pressed to think about anything else.

"Fuck! Fuck!" She chanted the word over and over while he drove into her. When he didn't slap her pussy again, she did, bringing her hand down sharply over her mound.

"Holy shit! Do that again, Rosie girl!"

She did. Then again. It wasn't long before her bare mound was pink with her slaps. Red pulled out and dove between her thighs, latching onto her pussy lips. He sucked each one before lapping at the cunt he'd been fucking so vigorously. "Still fuckin' sweet," he muttered before spitting on it and rubbing the saliva down to mingle with her own moisture.

Red gripped her hips and flipped her over. He positioned her the way he wanted her, pressing a hand down on her back to force her head down while keeping her ass in the air. He aimed his cock and jerked her hips back onto it. Red fucked her hard, occasionally bringing his hand down on her ass. Every time he did, she screamed, and her pussy squeezed his dick in a strangling grip.

"That's it, baby. You need to come?"

"Yes!" she screamed and pushed back against him, moving with him, taking him as deep as she could. "Fuck my pussy! Fuck it!"

"One day soon, I'm gonna fuck this little asshole," he said, easing his thumb back inside even as he continued to fuck her pussy. "Gonna fuck it as hard as I fuck your cunt. And you're gonna fuckin' take me. You hear?"

"I will! I will! Spank me again, Red. Please!"

He did. He fucked her at her pace. She rocked back against him, taking him fast and hard while Red fucked her ass with his thumb and spanked her cheeks with the other hand. Just before she came, he snaked his arm around her waist and lifted her up. She screeched her displeasure, but soon settled when he sat on the couch with her facing away from him, his cock still buried deep inside her.

Rosanna braced her feet on the couch and immediately began to ride him. Red found her nipples and rolled them between his fingers. "Yeah, baby. Fuck yourself with my cock."

"I'm gonna come this time," she said, glancing at him over her shoulder. Red grinned back at her.

"You bet you're gonna come." He caught her lips with his and kissed her as she fucked him. Her legs were spread wide, and he found her clit with one finger, circling it over and over.

"Fuck! Oh, God, Red! I'm coming!" She screamed long and loud. Red grabbed her hair, bunching it tightly in his fist as he kissed her, catching her screams in his mouth. She clamped down on him hard, and Red knew it was over.

Seconds later, he erupted inside her, his cum shooting out like a bullet. He was buried deep, her full weight settling on him as she orgasmed. Through the blinding pleasure, Red registered they weren't alone, but he couldn't focus enough to do anything about it. Rosanna lay limply across him, her legs spread wide while he impaled her. His cum was probably overflowing her pussy to drip down his balls to the leather couch.

"Whoa there, Red. Nice show, but warn a guy next time, will ya?" Styx had opened the office door, obviously not expecting the show he was getting. Rosanna squeaked but froze.

"Still," he said at her ear. "Don't you fuckin' move."

"But --"

God, he was a bastard! Instead of covering her, or pulling out and getting in front of her to shield her from Styx's gaze, Red smacked her pussy yet again.

"I said still," he bit out. Her eyes were wide as she looked at him. "Just look at me," he added. "You're fine. Ain't lettin' no one touch you but me. You get me?"

She gave him several little nods. And he kissed her, his tongue sliding between her lips briefly. Then he turned his attention to Styx.

"You ever hear of knocking?"

"Well, yeah. But if I had, I'd have missed this lovely sight. Take it you finally lost the battle?"

"Don't need comments from the peanut gallery, Styx. Why you here?"

"Just wanted to tell you the boys are startin' our run. I'll meet Poison and his crew in about two hours. We'll bring the cars here from three different routes."

"How many'd you get?"

"Three. Coulda got four, but Poison said they ran out of time on the Corvette."

"That one shoulda been easy."

"Yeah. Owner had some kind of aftermarket security system Grease wasn't familiar with. Decided it was better to let it be than to get caught."

"Always the better option." Red petted Rosanna's pussy while he talked to Styx. The blatant show of their fucking was turning him on mightily. Already his cock was hard inside Rosanna again. She whimpered, squeezing his dick when it pulsed.

Styx nodded in their direction. "You sure that's a good idea? Most women don't like being shown off like that."

"Her pussy's strangling my dick she's squeezing so hard. I think it turns her on."

"Red," she hissed. "Stop it!"

He chuckled. "What? You don't like one of my brothers watching us fuck? Ain't like he's gonna try anything."

"No, honey," Styx said. "You're all Red's. Ain't no one, including that fuckwit Julio, gonna make a run at you while Red's your man. We respect his claim." He grinned then. "Besides, I enjoy the show as much as Red likes showin' you off."

"I'm never gonna live this down," she groaned. "Fuck."

"Ain't no one gonna harass you either," Styx said. "Red would mutilate us and throw the bodies to the gators if we did. No judging here. Do what you want. Ain't promisin' no one will watch, but this is an MC. We have sex all over the place on club property. It's just one of the perks of being in an MC."

Styx must have said the exact right thing,

because Rosanna barked out a laugh and turned her head to look at him. "You're all fucking crazy."

"You got that right, honey. But your man there? He's the craziest of all. He'll show you a wild time, but he'll protect you when you need it. Don't be afraid of exploring sex with him. He's got your back."

It was Red's turn to laugh, considering the position they were in currently. "Yeah. Literally."

"Go on then," Styx said, turning to leave. "Fuck the shit outta her, Red. You got a few hours. I'll warn the guys to knock before entering."

Chapter Six

Even in the days when Davies had been with her, the two of them stealing and souping up cars for fun, Rosanna was never as happy as Red had made her the last three weeks and four days. They'd played as hard as they'd worked, and Red believed in working *very* hard.

He'd put her little app to good use, going with her to Miami and Fort Lauderdale to get a choice car or two and bring them back to his hidden, underground garage. Everything had worked like a charm. Of course, Red had made sure there was no way to track her through the app before they'd gone. Apparently, he knew some very tech-savvy, very rich people in very high places. They'd found a weak spot or two in her app, or more correctly her phone, and fixed it. Red said she'd received an awed fist-bump from a woman named Suzie who said it was the awesomest thing she'd ever seen, and a grumbled "good job" from someone called Giovanni. Apparently, Giovanni was the big-shot tech genius. Giovanni said some of Rosanna's workarounds were "highly irregular" but "nauseatingly brilliant." Rosanna wasn't sure if it was a compliment or not. All she wanted to do was break the tech so Red could do whatever he did with the cars. Besides, if it helped the club out, she'd do whatever she needed to. Salvation's Bane had been more than good to her.

Right now, they were working on a Ford GT40 MK II. How he'd come by it, Rosanna didn't much care. It was just fucking cool!

"I can't believe you got this," Rosanna said, bending over the open hood. The engine was located behind the cockpit so the hood was actually in the back of the car. She inspected it with awe, her heart fluttering with excitement. "You keeping it? I'd keep it." She knew she was talking a mile a minute, but she couldn't help it. The thing was a brilliant sunset red with a chrome racing stripe and accents. She didn't give a shit about the interior, but it was as opulent as the sixty-thousand-dollar Roush motor.

Red scowled at her. "No, I ain't keepin' it. It goes to a buyer overseas. We just need to clean it up."

"And by 'clean' you mean make sure identifiers are altered. Does it matter about a VIN number?"

"No. This buyer won't be selling it, and he knows it was procured in a less-than-reputable fashion."

She snorted. "That's a good way to put it. You sure we can't keep it?"

"We can't keep it, Rosanna."

"Party pooper," she grumbled.

Red smirked, then went back to work.

The car was at the back of the garage. Though there were a couple other cars in there with them, this car was a little apart from the others. Probably so there were no accidents with the paint job. Rosanna worked on one side of the car while Red worked on the other. There wasn't a whole lot to do mechanical-wise, but Red always went over every car before he sent it out. In the short time she'd been allowed into the clandestine garage, she'd learned that in no uncertain terms. Before a car left this particular garage, he personally inspected it. No judgment. Just double- and triple-checking everything. He'd grudgingly agreed to let her help him, though he still kept a close eye on the preventive maintenance she did, and she had to run any changes by him first.

The GT40 was the last in this series to be

completed. Red had just brought it in today, though he'd had it stashed a few days before the other cars had been brought in. Getting to see a machine like this, let alone touch one, wasn't something Rosanna had ever thought she'd do. Davies would be shitting himself if he were here right now.

Red moved around to the side of the car he had closest to the back wall. He was concentrating heavily on making sure the expensive engine was sealed properly and had the grease inside the appropriate parts. He was so engrossed in his task he hadn't even glanced up at her once. True, she wasn't doing anything but *oohing* and *ahhing* over the car, but she still wanted him to pay her *some* attention.

A wicked idea formed. Testing her theory, she stepped back slightly from the car and crouched on the floor. Red kept at his task, not saying a word. He was bent over the engine, his body slightly away from the body of the car. Rosanna crawled between him and the car and carefully unzipped his fly. She reached in and grasped his cock, pulling it out, and slid her lips around it before he could say anything.

"What the fuck, Rosie?"

"Something wrong with the GT, boss?" Styx called to them from across the room where he worked on a Ferrari. He sounded genuinely concerned, but knowing Styx, he probably knew she was on her knees with the boss's dick in her mouth.

"No!" Red said immediately. His hand fisted in her hair and held her still. He didn't seem to be able to stop the subtle thrust of his hips, though. "Stay there!" Then he cleared his throat and said more calmly, "I mean, everything's good. We're all fine here."

"Fuck," Styx said. It sounded like he threw a wrench to the floor. Rosanna heard his heavy boots stomping across the room. "Goddamn it, Red! I know she's good, but if she's done something to fuck… uh… well, shit."

Rosanna looked up to see Styx, who'd just come around the corner, hold his hands up in surrender when Red growled at him. Red still had her hair gripped tightly in his hands, and there was no easy way she could gracefully slide her mouth off him and get to her feet. Instead, she just looked up at Red who, for the first time since she'd known him, seemed to have no idea what to do. A quick glance at Styx told her he was just standing there in shock.

With a shrug, Rosanna gripped Red's ass with both hands and continued to suck him off. The death grip he had on her hair made it difficult, but once she bobbed forward and back a little, he let up on his grip and groaned.

"Fuckin' girl's gonna be the death of me."

"Yeah," Styx said. "But what a way to go." Rosanna heard more footsteps approaching and men mumbling, but Styx recovered and waved them off. "Nothin' to see over here. They got it under control."

"You sure, man? 'Cause that GT's got a lot ridin' on it."

"Yep," Styx said, stopping the two men headed in their direction.

"You think I'd let anyone fuck up anything in my shop?" Red growled. "Get your punk asses back to work before I retire all a ya! Permanently!"

He let up a little, and Rosanna pulled his dick out of her mouth. "Should I stop?"

Immediately, he grabbed her hair and pulled her back to him. "Don't you dare!"

With a happy sigh, Rosanna took him deep again, gagging slightly on his length. Red urged her faster and faster, his thighs quaking. She rested one hand on the back of one leg while the other still gripped his buttocks. His cock swelled and pulsed as she worked it, doing her best to drive him mad with wanting her. They might not fuck here with his men around them, but he'd fuck her silly when they got home. Would probably spank her ass for this little stunt. But it was worth it.

It wasn't long before he let loose a stream of hot cum down her throat. Rosanna swallowed every drop, not spilling any even when he shoved himself as far down as he could. She let her throat muscles massage the head of his dick when she gagged a little. He seemed to appreciate it as he shuddered and gripped her hair harder.

Once he was spent, Rosanna tucked him back in his pants and zipped him up. He looked down at her with a blank expression. It was like he wasn't sure what he wanted to do with her. His gaze darted up, sweeping the room. Rosanna heard the others working and talking. Nothing seemed amiss.

Red pulled her up by her hair and looked her over once. "Keep going. I'll be back."

"Did I do something wrong?" He was pulling away from her. He'd been doing that after sex for days now, and Rosanna wasn't sure why.

"No. Get back to work."

She watched him walk away. "You're welcome for the blow job," she muttered, then turned her attention back to the GT. If her man wasn't getting her off, maybe the fucking car would. "Moody fucker."

* * *

Motherfuck, that woman got him every fucking time! Red could give two shits if everyone in the whole motherfucking place saw her giving him head, but he didn't want them to get the idea they could get in on the action, especially when she was no longer with him.

That thought sucked. But, Goddamn it, he was too fucking old to start over now. She'd want kids and shit and, even if he hadn't done anything to prevent her getting pregnant, his kid was already grown. He didn't want more kids. Did he? Since the first time they'd had sex, Red had made a point to never use a condom. He wanted her tied to him, but he knew he could never keep her. He was one sick, fucked-up bastard.

Red stayed locked in his office the rest of the day. The only thing left was the GT, and Rosanna had that well in hand. She could check off on it as well as he could. It surprised him how implicitly he trusted both her and her abilities, but there it was. He didn't even trust Styx, and he'd known the man for twenty years. Yet, here he was. Trusting both his and the club's reputation to a little slip of a girl he'd known less than a year. What the fuck was wrong with him?

There was a knock at his door. Red thought about not opening it, afraid it was Rosanna. Instead he braced himself for the hurt look he knew he'd see in her eyes after his abrupt departure earlier. Surprisingly, Styx stood there.

"We good to roll?"

"If Rosanna's done with the GT, then yeah. Load 'em up."

Styx turned to leave, then hesitated, looking back over his shoulder. "You know, if you're not careful you're gonna get what you're trying so hard to accomplish."

Red felt every single one of his forty-eight years in that moment. "And what's that, wiseass?"

"You're gonna run her off. She's gonna either leave or move on to someone else in the club."

"Good. Girl needs a man closer to her age. I'm too set in my ways to take on a kid."

"You sure about that? Really sure? Could you see her with Grease or Doc? Hell, I'd take her on if she was interested. She's beautiful, passionate, and giving. And wicked smart with cars. You think that ain't a turn-on to every fuckin' man in this place? And she's chosen you."

"Well, she needs to fuckin' choose again!" he snapped. "You want her? Take her."

Styx glared at him, anger showing. But he nodded. "I might just do that, Red. If it happens, if you say a fuckin' word negative against that girl, I'll fuckin' kill you. Might anyway just because you're fuckin' stupid." Then he left.

Red knocked his forehead against the door frame several times, trying to knock some sense into himself. Styx was right. He was liable to kill any man trying to take her on as their woman. Because she was his. Except she couldn't be his because he was a bastard and because he was more than old enough to be her fuckin' dad!

God! This was fucking madness!

"Hey, Rosanna!"

Red's head shot up, and he scanned the room with a hawk's eye. That was Styx, and he definitely approaching Rosanna. She looked up from the GT but didn't stop her work.

"Whaddaya want, Styx? I got work to do."

"Hey," he raised his hands in a non-threatening gesture. "Ain't lookin' to piss you off. Just wondered if I could give you a ride home tonight."

Rosanna had ridden with Red. Hell, she'd been

on the back of his bike for weeks now. He knew she
wouldn't ride with anyone else because they'd asked
her before.

From across the room the two other men
guffawed, taunting Styx.

"Red'll beat your ass, man. Tryin' to fuck his
woman."

"It's your funeral, man. But hey. If any woman is
worth it, it's our Rosie."

Wait. Their Rosie? What the fuck?

"Y'all shut the fuck up. This is between me and
Rosanna." Styx threw over his shoulder.

Rosanna looked shocked as she glanced at the
other men before turning back to Styx. "I -- I suppose
it's fine." She glanced down at her feet. "Might as
well." Then her gaze shot back to his. "But I ain't
doing... you know." Was she embarrassed because
Styx had seen her sucking Red off? The fuck? "I don't
do it for just anybody."

Red barely caught those last words, but Styx
grabbed her chin and tilted her head up. "Hey. Look at
me." When she did, he continued. "Just cause Red's an
ass doesn't mean the rest of us are. You never have to
do anything you don't want to do. And this is a ride
home. A way for you to be comfortable. Nothin' else.
You decide you want to make it something else, well,
I'm always game for that." He gave her that cocky grin
Styx was known for. Red wanted to punch it off him.

"OK," she said softly. Then she ducked her head
away again. For some reason, Styx stepped into her
space and pulled Rosanna into his arms. Surprisingly,
she let him. Then it occurred to Red. She was crying.

"Son of a bitch," he muttered, banging his head
some more for good measure. If he was any kind of
man, he'd give Styx his blessing and let him take care

of Rosanna. But Red knew he was a bastard. Before he even realized what he was doing, Red stormed out of his office and moved to Rosanna and Styx. He could hear the others calling out to Styx and laughing at the predicament. They probably had no idea how distressed Rosanna was.

When he came up behind Styx, Red reached for Rosanna. "I got this."

Styx held her tighter, turning away from Red. "You lost that right after we talked," Styx said.

"Give her to me. You don't want to fight me over her 'cause I will fuck you the fuck up."

"Give me one good reason, Red. She gave you a gift, and you threw it away." Styx's voice was quiet, but he meant business. "You said yourself she deserves better. Ain't sayin' I'm better, but I damned sure won't treat her like you did today."

Red didn't say anything. He couldn't. Everything Styx said was the fuckin' truth. Didn't mean he was letting Styx have her. He pulled Rosanna away from Styx, who only let go when Rosanna did. She ran her forearm over her eyes and stomped away from them both.

"Where you goin'?" Red barked.

"Back to the clubhouse."

"Good. Bike's parked where it always is."

"Ain't going with you," she said, not turning around. Instead, she kept walking toward the exit.

"You can't walk home. It's too far. And you can't catch a cab."

"Never said I was going straight home," she said. "I'll get there. Eventually."

"Like hell," Red said. "Get your ass back over here." He knew of several bars in the area she could walk to, then call a cab. That wasn't happening.

She whipped around, jabbing her finger at him from across the room. "Fuck you, Red! I'll do whatever the fuck I want. Go wherever the fuck I want to go!"

He took a threatening step toward her. "Don't push me, girl. Now, get over here. We're going home."

She flipped him off. "I'm outta here. Don't forget to lock up, boys."

"Red, let her go." Styx put a restraining hand on Red's shoulder, but Red shook him off.

"Like hell! She's headed to a fuckin' bar. You want her goin' in one of those places without one of us?"

Styx grinned. "No. So I'll just follow her there and buy her a drink."

Red took a swing at Styx. The other man ducked it but let Red go. It took him a couple of seconds to catch up to Rosanna and when he did, he simply scooped her up and carried her to his bike.

"Let me go, motherfucker!" She fought, squirming and hitting at him as he carried her. When he put her on her feet beside his bike, she launched herself at him, screaming and slapping him. She was a little thing, and her blows were easily either blocked or ignored. Until she hiked a knee into his groin. That got his attention.

"Rosanna, stop it!"

"You stop it! You don't want me, but you don't want anyone else to have me! Are you fucking insane?"

Red was losing his grip on his temper. This had been building for days. The longer they carried on with the sexual relationship they'd forged, the more pressure he was under. "Just stop it and let me take you back to the clubhouse."

"Go fuck yourself!" She kicked at his shin, but he

sidestepped it, snagging her arm. He didn't want to hurt her, but he needed to get her on his bike and get going. She always mellowed out when he got her on the bike. Girl loved the wind in her face as they sped down the highway.

"Stop fightin' me and get on the bike, Rosie. I'm takin' you home."

"Like hell! I managed on my own a long fucking time. I can manage without you!" She kicked out again, this time landing a stinging blow to the shin.

"Goddamn it, Rosie! Would you fuckin' stop!"

This time, she launched herself at him with a rebel yell. He caught her in mid-flight. Then things just kind of happened. One second she was fighting him tooth and nail, the next they were kissing. Red groaned, needing this. He needed the taste of her. The touch of her skin against his. Her hair tangled in his beard.

Fuck! Why did he have to feel this for her? Why couldn't he see her as a daughter or just a young woman in need of protection like he had in the very beginning? This all-consuming attraction to her was killing him. He needed to distance himself from her. If not, she could really be in danger from his son. Wrath was supposed to contact him any day now, but the wait was yet another thing working against him. Red hated waiting.

The longer they kissed, the more aggressive Red got. Rosanna followed him, just like she always did. They spiraled downward into a dark, troubled den of desire and iniquity he had no hope of protecting her from.

With a sharp grunt, Red unfastened the waist of her jeans and slid his hands around underneath the fabric to cup the bare cheeks of her ass. One hand slid down the seam of her ass to find her pussy and finger her from behind. As he expected, she was soaking wet.

"Fuck me," he muttered between kisses. "So fuckin' wet!"

"Why are you doing this to me?" Rosanna's sob was heartbreaking. He wanted to answer her, but he just didn't have the words. "If you don't want me, why won't you let me go? Why do you keep showing me what I'll never have?"

Red was desperate now. He couldn't do this conversation. Not like this. Maybe if he were inside her he could manage. He reached between them and opened his fly, taking out his cock. Of course, he was fucking hard.

He spun her around, pulling down her shorts. Shoving aside her thong, he found her entrance with his dick and shoved home. There was so much he needed to say to her. So much he needed to figure out for himself. But how to do it when all he could think about every time he saw her, heard her voice, was this all-consuming need to be inside her? To make her his when he had no right to claim her?

She cried out, trying to balance herself on the seat of his bike, but Red pulled her upright, his hand circling her throat. He held her tight against him as he put his mouth right by her ear. His voice was gruff, angry. Red knew he needed to tone it down, but these were his rawest emotions. What he felt for Rosanna went beyond his experience or anything he'd ever expected to feel, and he was running on blind instinct.

"You listen to me and listen well, girl. You will never belong to another man. You're mine."

"But you don't want me," she sobbed. "Don't you get it? There's no one in my life I'd want to belong to other than you! I love you, Red! I always have! Since the first day I met you! Why won't you love me back?"

Licking up her neck and the side of her face, Red tasted her tears. He turned her head to him so he could kiss her once again. Just like before, she opened to him willingly. Eagerly. He wanted to tell her that he wasn't good enough for her. That he was a pervert for having taken things as far as he had with her. The words just seemed to stick in his throat, as if saying them would make them true.

"You're just gonna have to make do, Rosanna. I can't give you what you need, but I'm keeping you anyway."

At his declaration, she let loose another little sob. Red wrapped one arm around her chest and the other around her waist, holding her still as he moved inside her. Fucking Rosanna was always a revelation. Just when he thought it couldn't get any better, she brought him new pleasure he'd never imagined. She tried to move with him, thrusting her hips back at him. She arched her back, trying to bend over so he could have better leverage or maybe use her hips to fuck him harder. But Red didn't want that. He wanted her just like this. His arms tightly around her, her body at his mercy. They weren't even naked, and they probably had an audience, but Red had no self-control. Not now. Not with Rosanna trying to run from him.

"Who do you belong to, Rosanna. Who?" he growled beside her ear in harsh grunts.

"Not you," she spat even as she reached back to grip his thighs, her little nails digging in like kitten claws. "Never you!"

"Really? Who makes you scream? Who makes you come?" She shook her head, not answering even as her breath quickened just like it always did just before she came. "Say my name, Rosie. Say it!"

She still shook her head, but when he reached down to find her clit with his finger, she gave an ear-piercing scream. "RED!"

Her pussy clamped down on him, squeezing the life from his dick. "That's it," he bit out as he fought off his orgasm as long as he could. "Take my cum from me. Take it inside that little body of yours."

"Yes! Oh, God! Yes!" She screamed as she came, milking him as she did. Red exploded inside her with his own insane bellow. Some of the frantic pace slowed, but there was still a need inside Red to make sure she knew who she belonged to. Though he kept telling himself it could never be him, apparently his body thought otherwise. So did his fucking mouth. Because he was fully aware of what he'd just done.

He glanced behind them to see the place empty. Styx must have hurried the boys out. Rosanna had gone limp against him, still impaled on his cock.

"Come on," he said. "Let's get home and I'll clean you up." She just nodded, making no effort to straighten her clothing. Red did it for her, handing her a helmet. "Can you hang on to me long enough to get home?"

She put on the helmet and nodded her head. "Yeah. I'm good." She wasn't, though. He could tell. This stupid indecisiveness was getting to her. He needed to shit or get off the fucking pot. Either embrace her as his ol' lady, like he wanted to, or let her go completely.

Chapter Seven

Your love is like a rollercoaster baby, baby...

Yeah. Ohio Players and the Chili Peppers had it right. Rosanna couldn't get the song out of her head as she and Red continued on their roller coaster ride. In private he was one way. In public quite another. Hell. Who was she kidding? He never opened up to her like she did to him. He still hadn't told her what had happened to him and his ex, Joy. Or why his son seemed to hate him so much. And why he wasn't trying to make it better. He just took and took, and Rosanna was nearly at the end of her rope. Had she been a stronger woman, she'd have left weeks ago. Yet here she was. Back in the main garage. Back on Marge's Pinto again. If she made enough money to get out of Palm Springs and still have enough left over after the cars were sold, she was buying Marge a Fiesta and scrapping this fucking Pinto.

The shit of it was, Rosanna was convinced Red needed her to be whole himself. Maybe he was just so set in his ways he couldn't see that, or at least couldn't recognize it. But Rosanna did. She knew he needed her as much as she needed him. No matter what she did or where she went, Rosanna would always need Red. Healthy? Not at all. Not unless he finally opened his eyes and realized they were better together than they were apart.

She was just finishing up the Pinto -- again -- when she heard a commotion at the front of the garage. Her station was in the back, away from the comings and goings of patrons and club members. For which she was grateful. She got more work done when no one bothered her. But some part of her wondered if there was another reason Red had put her so far from prying eyes.

"Ian!" A male voice called out loudly over the normal din of the very busy garage. But if Rosanna heard it in her little corner, so did everyone else. Including Red. Even if he was in his office, he never closed the door during business hours. Well, unless he was fucking her.

"Fuck," Grease muttered. "That prick, Anthony, again."

"His son?" she asked, wiping down a wrench she'd just finished using. "Wonder what's going on."

"Not a clue. But I'm sure it's not good."

She knew she needed to keep her nose in her own business. For whatever reason, Red didn't want her involved in his past. If he had, he'd have told her what was going on. He was supposed to be looking into how much trouble she was likely to be in if his son dug into her past, but he had yet to tell her what he'd found. That either meant he hadn't found anything or he just didn't care enough to follow through. Yeah. All signs were pointing to Rosanna needing to just get the hell outta Dodge and chalk it up to hard lessons learned.

"I'm on to you, old man," Anthony said, a big smile on his face. "When I'm done, you'll be in jail for the rest of your life."

"It's a fool's game you're playing, Anthony. Your accountants have my records. I've been keeping in touch and, from what I understand, I may be gettin' a fuckin' tax refund for the last three years where I broke even through my own accountant. Thanks for that, by the way. I'll be sure to use your accountants for next year's taxes. They seem to be better at it than mine."

"Bastard," Anthony hissed. "Don't you worry. I'll get you and your little whore, too."

That gave Rosanna pause. Yeah, she hadn't thought about her relationship with Red that way, but did others?

She laid down the wrench and started to move toward them. Grease stepped in front of her. "Don't, Rosie. He'll do his best to hurt you if you do."

"But Red…"

"Is being Red. He won't show weakness by defending you. You know that."

She stuck her chin up. "I'm the reason he's giving Red a hard time about me anyway. If I hadn't put on such a display when they were here the last time, he wouldn't be trying to use me to get to Red."

"You don't know Red very well if you think he'll defend you. He won't. Not like this. Just stay back here."

That brought her up short. If he felt as much for her as she felt for him, shouldn't he be proud of her? Defend her with his last breath? Some shit like that in romance novels? With a slow nod, she went back to work. Or, at least, pretended to work when she was really eavesdropping. She was finished with the Pinto.

Grease shook his head. "No, you don't. Get in there and start that thing up. Make sure it runs right."

Styx came over to them, probably because Grease had sent some silent male signal that indicated the little female was getting into trouble. He glanced over his shoulder at Red and Anthony, an angry expression on his face.

"Just ignore them," Styx said. "Most especially, ignore Red. When he deals with Anthony or Joy all he's concerned about is not letting them see how much they hurt him."

"Like I was supposed to know that," she muttered. "If he'd tell me things like he made me tell him, I could just flip them off behind their back and be content."

"Do that anyway," Styx said. "Don't let them under your skin. Neither of them."

She tried to just go back to work. She cleaned the buildup off the outside of the Pinto's engine and tried to just zone out. But she couldn't.

"No way that bitch isn't in on whatever you're doing," Anthony said, so loudly there was no way he hadn't meant for her to hear. "I'll go after her. She's probably got a rap sheet full of prostitution and drugs. I'll give her a choice. She can either cooperate with us or go to jail for the rest of her life. Drug charges are like that. Even one offense can land you in prison. Multiple offenses? Well, people tend to disappear in the prison system for shit like that."

"Why would I care if you go after anyone here? They don't keep their nose clean, that's what happens."

"You really are a cold son of a bitch, aren't you? Do you care about anyone?" Anthony sneered at Red, obviously caring more than he let on.

"I cared about you once upon a time. But your mother fixed that."

"Don't talk about my mother! It's all horseshit," Anthony spat. "You didn't care about her, and you never cared about me. You probably don't even care about your little whore, even though everyone says you do. They say you're inseparable. That you even protect her from harsh language."

"Everyone thought I cared about your mother, too." Red shrugged. "Believe what you want to believe and do what you have to do. Unless you require my cooperation with your investigation, I suggest you leave. We don't allow loitering here. Too fuckin' busy."

Anthony looked around the garage until he

spotted Rosanna. Then he made a beeline toward her. "You!" he called out. "The whore!"

"I'm gonna fuck him the fuck up," Styx said.

"Who?" Rosanna asked, the little laugh in her voice not humorous at all. "Anthony or Red?"

"Good Goddamned question," Grease muttered.

"You!" Anthony hollered again. Rosanna turned, her hands gripping the hood of the Pinto as she rested her ass on the edge.

He was looking right at her, so there was no way she could pretend she didn't think he was talking to her. "My name's Rosanna," she said. "And if you call me a whore one more time, I'll take a wrench upside your head. And before you can ask me if it's a threat, no. It's not. It's a fucking promise."

"Listen. I don't know what he's paying you, but that's all he's doing. You're a fool if you think he cares about you. He had a kid with my mother and still left her. You're nothing but a pleasant pastime to him." Anthony looked her up and down. "Shit, I doubt a little innocent thing like you can keep his attention much longer." He pulled out his business card and handed it to Rosanna. She didn't take it but couldn't help but look down at it. "Call me when he dumps you and you want to punish him. Turn state's evidence, and I'll see to it you get a good deal."

Rosanna didn't say anything, only pushed off the car and walked away. Through all that, Red never said a word. He didn't come to her defense. Didn't even come to support her. Even if he didn't love her, she'd have thought he'd have kept someone from harassing his employees. She'd never seen him interfere in anyone's personal squabbles, but this was different. Shouldn't he have taken up for her? Kicked Anthony out on his ass?

As she got her backpack, readying to leave for the day, she heard the conversation between Red and Anthony continue. "You've got a good lap dog this time, don't you, old man. Maybe when you get tired of her she'll make her way to me. Then I'll be the one fucking her. She'll be my lap dog. I'll make her testify against you in front of a jury, physically battered and broken using the script I'll write for her. She'll blame you. Sweet little thing like that? She'll have them eating out of the palm of her hand. Then your ass will be mine. I'll lock you up and throw away the key. That little whore will be my pet until I tire of her. After that? No one will care what happens to her. She'll be just another whore in an MC."

Rosanna braced herself for the backlash. No way Red let him get away with saying something like that.

"Have at her," Red said in a dismissive tone. "If I were involved in anything illegal, do you honestly think I'd trust some dim-witted whore with all my secrets so she could spill them the first time she got pissed at me? Your mother taught me that lesson." Then he shrugged. "Try to take her if you think you want her. I guarantee she'll never satisfy you and you'll have wasted all that hard work for nothing."

* * *

That fucking prick. Red was going to take care of Anthony one way or another. Killing his own kid went against everything he believed in, but he had it in him to do just that. Seeing the look on Rosanna's face when he'd lain it out for Anthony…

Try to take her if you think you want her. I guarantee she'll never satisfy you and you'll have wasted all that hard work for nothing…

Red knew the second he'd uttered those words, he'd just given Rosanna up for good. The girl had stuck with him longer than she should have. She did it not because she was weak or stupid or just couldn't take a hint. Rosanna did it because she loved him. Red believed her when she'd told him that in the garage a few weeks back. She hadn't said it again, but he knew she did. Red wasn't sure he didn't love her, too. But he hadn't said it back. Hadn't even thought it until this very second.

Now, Red knew he'd have to be content to stay in the background and just watch over her until she found a strong protector. Styx had indicated he might take her on. He could only hope Styx claimed her. Even that thought filled him with more grief and sorrow and rage than he'd ever experienced in his life.

Fuck it. Red knew he'd gladly give himself to the DA's office if it meant keeping Rosanna safe. He saw the way Anthony looked at her. Red knew his son would make a play for Rosanna. So help him, if Red had to kill the little bastard, he'd do it to keep him from getting a hold of her. Red had seen cruel men before. The boy he remembered was kind and gentle. The man Joy had raised was evil to his core. Eaten up with hate. All of it focused on Red. The boy knew he cared for Rosanna. He could see it in his eyes the same way the members of Salvation's Bane could see it. Red could deny it all he wanted, but the secret was already out. Anthony would use that knowledge any way he could to gut his father.

He watched her leaving the garage. She didn't look back at him as she got on the bicycle that had sat in the corner for months now. She got on and took off as hard as she could.

"Looks like your little whore's done with you, Red." Anthony sneered Red's road name like an insult. "I give her a day before she comes to me. We'll see how good the little slut is then, won't we?"

Red inhaled for patience. He couldn't kill the kid in front of witnesses, especially not his club. He'd never put them in that kind of a position. "I suppose we'll see, won't we?" he said, turning to Anthony. There must have been something unholy in Red's eyes when he looked at his son because the other man got a surprised look on his face and backed up three steps before finding his backbone.

"Anthony, we need to go. Now." Joy's voice registered in his brain where he hadn't even been aware she was here before. She had her phone out. From the glance at the screen Red saw, she'd been videoing the scene. Trying to get him to lose his cool. Well, they'd almost succeeded.

"Guess you're smarter than I gave you credit for all those years ago," Red said to Joy.

"Only ever saw you with that look on your face one other time." She motioned at Anthony. "Get in the car. I'll be right there."

"When you sold me out to who you thought were the cops?"

"Yes," she said softy. "Biggest mistake I've ever made in my life."

"No. But if it hadn't been for Thorn, it would have. He saved your life, Joy. I hope you realize that."

"You'd have killed me?"

"Without remorse. You might want to really think about that. Then think about what I'd do if someone I loved was threatened."

Joy looked stunned, blinking several times and actually looking hurt. "Are you... are you saying you... *love* that girl?"

Red shifted his gaze to Anthony's retreating form. "I am."

"Then why did you say all that stuff about her?" Joy looked like she was ready to throttle him. "You really are a stupid-ass motherfucker." She sniffed at him. It was the first time since she'd left she sounded like a club girl. "She's leaving you. You know that, right?"

"Fully aware," Red bit out.

"Why the fuck did you say all that?" Joy looked angrier now than she had since Red kicked her out of the Bane clubhouse. "*Have at her*? You actually called her a dim-witted whore!"

"No," Red said. "Everyone took it that way, including Anthony." His son was in the Escalade sitting outside the garage. Of course, the kid had a fancy ride.

"Oh, really." Joy looked exasperated as well as angry. Red just looked at her, not blinking or in any way indicating he was joking. Red saw the exact moment Joy realized exactly what she was dealing with. She covered her mouth with her hand. She shook her head, and glanced back over her shoulder, presumably at Anthony. "You're gonna kill him. Aren't you." It wasn't a question.

"Jury's still out, Joy. You know it's not up to me."

She nodded, a tear trickling down her cheek. "I'd ask you to go easy on him, but I know you'll do exactly what you're told to do."

It was telling to Red that she didn't mention Thorn's name. Apparently, she'd learned her lesson in secrecy well. She might tell Anthony but Red doubted it. She'd want her son to die quickly. Not suffer knowing it was coming. "If it comes to it, you know I'll make it painless," he said softly.

"Will you? Don't promise something you can't keep. If he truly tries to hurt her, you'll make him suffer. It's just how you are."

She had him there. "Then I'll do my best to make it quick and painless."

"I guess that will have to do." She turned to go, then turned back to him. "For what it's worth, I was wrong. About you."

"You said I was an egotistical maniac."

"Oh, no. I was right about that." She gave him a sad smile. "I was wrong when I said you weren't fit to be the father of my child. You were the best dad ever. I was just too jealous to let you continue. All this?" She waved her hand around in the air. "Is on me. I raised him to hate you. I guess I reap what I sow."

"You take care of yourself, Joy."

She nodded, then walked to the Escalade and got in. Red could see Anthony questioning her, but Joy just shook her head. He saw her mouth, "Drive." Anthony backed out of the parking lot and sped off.

It wasn't long before his phone rang. "Little busy, Thorn."

"Yeah, fuck you, too. Wrath wants a meet. Says he has an idea about your little problem."

"Figured he might. Tell him I'll be there in an hour."

"You sure about this?" Thorn seemed to be thinking along the same lines Red was. Would he have to kill Anthony?

"I am. He's making plans to hurt Rosanna, and I won't allow it."

"You have my blessing to take care of it as you see fit. I know you won't do anything you don't have to."

"Understood." He paused. "Rosanna's headed back. Probably to pack and leave."

"What the fuck did you do this time, you son of a

bitch?"

"Same thing I always do, only this time she's done."

"She say that?"

"Didn't have to. I didn't leave her much choice if she wanted any kind of self-respect. Just... make sure she has a safe place to go until all this is taken care of. I'll ask Wrath, but it would be better if you reached out to El Diablo to see if they would take her in."

Thorn sighed. "You're sabotaging your own happiness as well as hers. You know that?"

"Yeah. Didn't have much choice. I dealt with Joy and Anthony like I always do. Only way they leave me the fuck alone."

"You made it seem like you didn't care for her."

"The fewer people I care about in my life, the better off. Joy understands now, and I think she'll keep it to herself. Mainly because she's convinced I'm going to kill Anthony, and she doesn't want him to suffer knowing it's coming."

"You trust her?"

"No. But, in this case, I think she might keep her mouth shut. It was the first time since she was kicked out of Bane she thought like a club girl. She knows what's at stake and the lengths I'll go to keep the club and everyone in it safe. Including Rosanna."

"Well, maybe she did learn her lesson," Thorn mused.

"My thoughts exactly."

"I'll call Wrath. Let me know the second you decide what's happening. Me and Mariana will take care of Rosanna for you."

"Should be me," Red muttered. "I should be the one protectin' her."

"I know, brother. Just know we've got your back.

And hers."

"I owe you."

"Yeah? Next time I call, fuckin' answer with 'Hello.'"

Chapter Eight

If Rosanna had ever been more devastated in her entire life, she didn't know when. Not when she'd killed her abusive mother when she was sixteen. Not when she realized she was all alone in the world after Davies left. The way Red saw her -- as nothing more than a dimwitted whore -- shredded her heart into a million pieces. Anthony gave her the creeps, but even if he hadn't, even if Red hadn't just thrown her away like garbage, there was no way she'd put herself into a position to testify against Red. Rosanna loved Red with all her heart and soul, but she was done.

She rode around for a while, peddling hard to get all the raging grief under control. She thought about going to the beach, but even that solace wouldn't help this afternoon. She found herself riding by Tito's diner where Marge's Pinto sat in the corner of the parking lot, shining and sparkling like new. Piece of shit. The sight of the car brought on a fresh flood of tears, and she had to stop to keep from wrecking.

As if the day couldn't get any worse, Marge saw her and hurried out of the diner, Tito in tow.

"Rosanna? What happened? Are you all right?" Marge glanced over her, apparently looking for injuries. Tito steadied her bike and helped her off even though she didn't want to get off.

"Here," Marge said, putting her arm around Rosanna's shoulders. "Come inside where it's cool. I'll get you a glass of ice water."

"I'm fine," she said, swiping at her eyes. "I need to get back to the clubhouse."

"No," Tito said. "You need to come inside and rest. It's hot, and you're not sweating. How long have you been riding?"

"I -- I don't know. Couple of hours maybe? I left the garage at three."

"*Mierda*!" Tito rarely swore, so Rosanna figured this must be pretty bad.

"Sweetheart, it's seven-thirty," Marge said, urging her toward the diner.

The two of them got Rosanna inside, where Elena had a tall glass of ice water and a wet towel ready. She handed them to Marge, who set the glass on the table in front of the booth she'd forced Rosanna into, then blotted Rosanna's face with the cool, damp towel.

"Do you have any aspirin? My head's pounding." Between the crying and the heat, she was pretty fucking miserable.

"I got you, sweetie," Marge said. "You just sip on that water. I want it all gone, you hear me?" She left and returned moments later with two pills, laying them on a napkin on the table.

"She looks pale," Elena said. "She can't leave like this."

Tito nodded. "I'll take her back to the clubhouse. Thorn wouldn't like it if we left their girl on her own."

"Ain't nobody's girl," Rosanna muttered. Which just brought on a fresh wave of tears. She buried her face in the towel and pressed it close to her eyes.

Elena gently urged her to drink more water. Thankfully, for first time Rosanna could remember, the place was empty. No one but the three of them was there to witness her breakdown. None of them pressed her to tell them what was wrong. They just tried to make sure she was physically OK.

When her tears finally stopped, Marge gripped her hand. "We got your back, sweet girl. Just you remember that."

What could she say? Rosanna nodded, then

drank the rest of her water. She felt better after the glass and, thankfully, Elena refilled it without asking.

"Drink more if you can," she said gently.

The adrenaline was starting to wear off Rosanna. She was shaking and exhausted. It wasn't too far from the diner to the clubhouse, but she doubted she could make it on her bike.

Tito nodded his head once. "OK, then. You'll let me take you home?"

"Did I say that out loud?" Rosanna looked up at the older man in confusion.

He smiled gently at her. "No, *chica*. But you didn't have to. You're exhausted and upset. Not a good condition for riding." He looked at Elena. "I'll put her bike in the back of the truck. You call ahead."

Somewhere in the back of her mind, Rosanna knew he meant that Elena was to call Thorn and tell him they were coming in with her. The fact that they didn't actually mention Thorn by name let her mind discard it. If they had called the name of any member of Salvation's Bane, Rosanna was sure she'd have protested. Any show of weakness on her part would bring in the vultures. Right now, she was pretty fucking weak. But she was just too emotionally and physically drained to protest without a good reason. It wasn't like she had a lot of choice. She was in no shape to do anything herself.

The next thing she knew, Tito was lifting her into his arms and carrying her outside. He gently set her in the passenger seat of Marge's Pinto and buckled her in. Marge slid in behind the wheel and started her baby up.

"Purrs like a kitten every time," she said, rubbing the dashboard like she might a favorite pet. "All thanks to you, sweet girl. Now you just relax. I'll get you home safe and sound."

Rosanna must have dozed off because the next thing she knew, Thorn was lifting her out of the car. He gathered her up in his arms and carried her inside. Mariana was beside him, a worried look on her face.

"You're OK, Rosanna," she said softly. You're going to be fine."

"Need to leave." Rosanna's voice was barely above a whisper, but she got out the words. "Just let me pack my shit."

"Later," Mariana said firmly but not unkindly. "Right now, you're going to rest. I'll sit with you and make sure nothing disturbs you."

"You don't have to do that. I swear I'll stay put until tomorrow, but then I'm outta here."

"That's fine," Mariana said. She opened the door to Rosanna's bedroom and Thorn carried her inside. He laid her on the bed and Rosanna looked at Mariana. The other woman gently smoothed a curl away from Rosanna's forehead. "If you still want to leave tomorrow, Thorn will make sure you have a safe place to go. Tonight, though, I want you to rest. I'll help you get a quick shower or a bath if you want. It will relax you so you sleep better."

Rosanna thought about that for a long moment. "Why are you being so nice to me? Red doesn't want me. He said I'm nothing but a stupid whore." She looked away. "Even told his son he could have at me if he wanted. Apparently, I can't satisfy Red or anyone else." Not exactly what he'd said, but close enough. The meaning had been abundantly clear.

Mariana sucked in a breath before calling Red all kinds of very unflattering names. Thorn laid his hand on his wife's shoulder. Mariana looked up at him. "Well, if you think you're changing my mind about him just because he's in your club, think again! Rosanna is wonderful, and Red doesn't deserve her!"

"Fully aware of that," Thorn said. "So's he."

"I just want to pack my shit," Rosanna said. "If you know a place where I can stay for a week or so, just until I can get on my feet, I'd appreciate it."

"I'm working on that," Thorn said. "El Diablo is supposed to call me. I think he'll agree to let you stay there as long as you want."

"El Diablo?" The very name gave her chills. No one could figure out which side he was on. Rosanna suspected he was on his own side. With his own agenda that might or might not involve Salvation's Bane or any other club. She hadn't met the man, but by all accounts, he made alliances to his benefit. "Do you trust him? Because I'm not sure I do."

Thorn gave her a thoughtful look. "Do I trust him with everything?" Thorn shook his head. "Not in the least. But he isn't cruel to women or children. Any who live in the Black Reign compound are taken care of. Spoiled, by all accounts. He won't abuse you or use you as any kind of leverage. At least, as long as you don't betray the club or anyone in it. As long as you take any problems you have with any member of Black Reign to him or his vice-president, you'll be fine."

"Didn't know Black Reign had a vice president," she said. "I'm not sure I've ever heard them mention him."

"He keeps on the down low," Thorn said. "His name is Samson. He seems like he keeps to himself, but he knows everything going on. Just remember that. Always tell the truth, no matter how painful. They'll never judge you unless you give them reason to. Lying or betraying one of them is really the only thing you could do to earn anyone's displeasure."

Rosanna couldn't well admit to being scared of going where Thorn told her to go. Besides, if she didn't, she risked being caught out on her own when Anthony brought whatever goons he commanded. In her experience, the police weren't always her friend. "If you think it's best," she managed.

"I wouldn't send you anywhere if I thought it wasn't safe, Rosanna. I hope you understand that."

The door to her room opened and Mae, Justice's ol' lady, entered. Of all the women at the clubhouse, Rosanna thought she might like Mae the most. She was spunky and good-hearted. If there was ever a problem the woman couldn't fix, Rosanna hadn't heard of it. Mae didn't talk, just quietly entered the room and moved beside Mariana. There was concern on her face, just like Mariana.

"Why?" Rosanna asked. Her whole world seemed to have fallen apart. Once again, she had no one. When she left Salvation's Bane, she'd be on her own again. The thought not only brought grief to her heart but exhausted her. She'd gotten used to relying on the club for safety, but also companionship and comfort. They had each other's backs, and she'd loved that part of their tight-knit group. Now, she was going to be an outsider again. She'd have to look out for herself.

Mariana and Mae looked at each other in confusion. "Why what?" Mae asked.

"Why would any of you care what happens to me when I leave? I won't be part of you anymore."

It was Justice who spoke. Rosanna had no idea when he'd slipped in, but suddenly her room seemed pretty crowded. "Rosanna, you'll always be one of us. We're not giving up on you just because you've given up on Red. Bastard probably deserves it."

"We know you'll be more comfortable getting away from the clubhouse and Red, so we'll do everything we can to make it happen," Thorn said.

"And just so you know," Justice added. "We'd never send you to Black Reign if we didn't know you'd be perfectly safe. El Diablo is certainly a wild card, but he's not evil. If he agrees to let you come to his compound, he and his club will protect you."

It took some moments for Rosanna to process this. Had she made more friends here than she realized? "I'm not even really a club girl," she muttered. "I help at the garage and steal cars, but I don't mingle with the other girls, or get on with the guys."

Mae reached out a hand and took Rosanna's, squeezing gently. "You do your part. Besides, Marge would be without her prized Pinto if not for you. If that happened, she might get angry enough to withhold the Marge Specials. If you did nothing else for the club, that right there is worth ten club whores to the single guys."

"And the married ones," Justice muttered. Mae slapped his stomach with the back of her hand, to the chuckles of both him and Thorn.

"Hey, a man's gotta eat."

"Go make yourself useful and call Rycks," Mae said. "If El Diablo isn't available, Rycks can speak for him in this matter. I don't want Rosanna to leave, but she shouldn't be uncomfortable one moment longer than she has to be."

"Fine," Justice said. "But I stand by my assessment. And if she does move to Black Reign permanently, I want it understood that Red is the only one cut off from the Marge Specials. You girls better back us on this."

For the first time since Red had shattered her world for the last time, Rosanna smiled. Maybe this bunch *was* a family to her. Unconventional, but family.

"Get some rest," Mariana said with a gentle smile. "I'll make sure no one disturbs you. When you wake, we'll let you know the arrangements. If it's approved for you to stay at Black Reign, Justice and Thorn will take you and get you safely settled in."

"OK," she agreed, suddenly more tired than she'd been in a long time. She'd probably break down again once she was alone, but this was it. The last time. Red would never get another piece of her heart ever again. Assuming they worked everything out and she got to stay with Black Reign, she'd never have to see Red again. Which was fine with her. As far as she was concerned, Rosanna never wanted to lay eyes on the fucking bastard ever again.

* * *

"Fuck!" Red sped down the highway on his bike, swearing at the top of his lungs. If everyone who saw him thought he was crazy, who gave a fuck? He had this one space of time to vent and grieve before he had to go to work. There was likely no way to fix this between him and Rosanna. He'd said what he had in order to keep Anthony and Joy off balance. It was the way he'd always dealt with them. Make it seem like she was nothing to him, and they'd back off. He didn't take into account Rosanna would believe his words, too. Which was worse than stupid on his part. What woman wouldn't believe what he'd said?

He should be the one protecting her, but Thorn let him know El Diablo had agreed to take her in at Black Reign, so that option was off the table. El Diablo would lock that place up so tight there was no way Red could get in unless Black Reign let him. Didn't mean it would keep him from trying. Red knew in his heart he'd never be able to stay away from Rosanna. He'd try, but he'd still be camped outside the Black Reign complex like a fucking stalker. She'd never be happy with someone else because Red would run off any man she tried to be with. It wasn't something he'd set out to do, but it would happen.

There might not be any way Red could fix his broken relationship with Rosanna, but he could damn well take his son out of the equation. If Joy fucked with him, he'd take her out as well. He was just waiting on a call from Wrath.

Two hours later, Red pulled back into his garage's empty parking lot. He wanted to punch something. *Needed* to pulverize someone until they begged for mercy. He was just about to start his Harley and head to a local fight club when his phone rang. Wrath.

"What did you find?"

"Lots of things. Some good. Some not." There was a small silence as Red heard the other man setting his phone down. "You're on speaker," Wrath confirmed. "El Diablo is with me."

"Not sure where to start with this one," El Diablo said. His usual easy-going, if sarcastic, English accent was all too serious now.

"Start with Rosanna," Red said, needing to know exactly what the danger to her was.

"No one is looking for your girl," Wrath answered immediately. "Her mother was confirmed killed in a house fire two months ago. Apparently, an accelerant was used, and the place burned extremely hot. Didn't burn her to ashes, but there wasn't much reason to do an autopsy. Place was a known crack house. Neighbors even swore they saw her mother just a couple of days before the place burned. Most likely, they heard the radio and assumed it was her inside the house talking to someone. Charlotte police looked at Rosanna briefly, but those same neighbors said they hadn't seen her in several months. Apparently, Rosanna was well liked in the neighborhood, especially by the kids. Helped out several of the older residents. When she stopped checking on them or coming around to visit, they missed her. As far as CPD is concerned, Rosanna left long before her mother's death."

Red gave a sigh of relief. "Well, at least that's something."

"Yeah," Wrath said. "That's the good news."

"The bad news is," El Diablo said, "your son is very connected in the DA's office. Too connected for his own good."

"Explain."

Wrath took up the narrative. "He knows what they do. He knows the DA, Harold Collins, has a thing for young boys. He also knows he's not always content to watch illegal porn. The man and a couple of his associates sometimes indulge in the real thing."

Red sucked in a breath, his stomach heaving for more than one reason. This might all be taken out of his hands if El Diablo thought Anthony or Joy were in any way linked with these kinds of scum.

"Collins and his associates party on a private yacht from time to time," El Diablo explained. "The owner tries to be shrouded in secrecy, but I've got him nailed down. He's being taken care of as we speak. Collins and two of his associates are going to take jobs elsewhere before disappearing for good. No one will be the wiser. That's a done deal."

"Are you going to disappear my son as well?

And was Joy involved?"

As he asked the question, Red had a moment when he saw a bright-eyed, strawberry-blond-haired boy of four, running to him and jumping into his arms with a glad cry. Red could remember holding the kid up in the air and swinging him around and around, laughing when Anthony laughed. He remembered pushing him on a swing at the park. Swimming in Lake Worth Lagoon together. The first time he'd put the kid in front of him on his Harley and rode around inside the Salvation's Bane compound. Anthony crawling up in his lap as they watched some stupid Disney movie Red had no interest in but enjoyed just the same. The clean scent of his son's hair as he fell asleep with his head on Red's shoulder…

The first time he saw Anthony after Joy had left and taken the boy with her. Anthony's twelfth birthday when he'd taken a serrated blade and tried to kill Red in his sleep. There was still a faint scar on Red's neck. All that love and happiness had turned to hate inside Anthony. Though Joy was very much to blame, Red knew he was just as guilty. He hadn't fought hard enough to be a part of Anthony's life. Even if the kid had hated him, if he'd remained a presence, Red might have stopped him going down whatever destructive path he now found himself on. He'd failed Anthony in that regard. But he couldn't let his son die without giving him a chance to fix the situation.

"We haven't decided," Wrath said. "And no. We don't think Joy is involved. I'd like to know your thoughts. He's your son. I'd say it depends on exactly how deep in he is. He's not hoarding child porn or bringing kids to Collins, but he knows about it all. He hasn't arranged any meets or been in any form involved in what they do, but he knows and has done nothing about it."

"What if he helps us?" Red asked.

"Helps us how?" Wrath asked. There was genuine curiosity in his voice.

"You're on the inside, Wrath. You can keep eyes on him."

"True."

"So, how about this…"

Chapter Nine

The very last thing Red wanted to be doing tonight was waiting inside his son's house so he could nab the guy and take him off to a secure location. Oh. And then there was the torture he'd planned. Justice, Lock, and Samson were with him to make sure things didn't go too far. As vice president of Black Reign, Samson was there to be sure his club's interests were protected. As far as Red was concerned, the bastard could go fuck himself. He'd do this his way or not at all.

Red kept trying to hold the images of Anthony's childhood in his mind, but he kept seeing the sneer on his son's face as he offered Rosanna his card. This was going to seriously try Red's patience. Also, if he were completely honest, he was anxious because, if it came down to it and he had to kill Anthony, Red wasn't altogether sure he could do it. The man was irredeemable in some respects, but he was still Red's son.

"You know this may not go like you want it to, right?" Justice's voice was soft through Red's earpiece. The men were spread out, watching the house from different angles so they had an accurate view of who approached the place.

"Fully aware," Red responded. He didn't want it to come to that, but there was a high probability his son would balk just to spite him. If he did, Red would have no choice but to kill him. The man was in too deep and was at the tipping point. If they let him go, he might think he'd dodged a bullet. If he was even in the least inclined to hurt children or see them hurt, then he'd be shoved off the cliff into that dark abyss by Red's inaction. "If it has to be done, I'll be the one to do it. I promised Joy."

"If you can pull that off, you've got bigger balls than me," Justice said.

"And ice around your heart," Lock added.

"No, he don't." The deep voice belonged to Samson. From what Red had observed, the man was silent most of the time. But he saw everything. Justice said the man could read people better than anyone he'd ever seen.

"Yeah?" If Red sounded defensive, it was because he'd only met Samson once. Thirty minutes before they'd left for this job.

"You're puttin' on a fuckin' show tonight, how this is about your kid turnin' a blind eye to scum-suckin' pedophiles. That's the reason El Diablo wants him out of the picture. Not why you do."

"Ain't that reason enough?"

"Sure, but that ain't your reason."

Red ground his teeth. "So, explain to me. You know. Since you know me so fuckin' well and all." Red couldn't keep the sarcastic sneer out of his voice.

"You want that fucker dead because he threatened your woman. You got a soft spot for Rosanna, and your son's a threat to her happiness if not her life."

"You might think you know me, Samson. But you don't. I won't deny you're right in this. I'll do whatever it takes to protect Rosanna."

"Even killing your own son?" Lock asked. "Seems pretty cold hearted to me."

"For some, maybe," Samson said. "For Red, it's more that he knows more about the man than he wants to. He knows Anthony would hurt Rosanna in unspeakable ways just to get back at Red. His heart isn't cold. Where Rosanna is concerned, it's white hot."

"Fucker," Red muttered. But he knew Samson was right. If a twelve-year-old kid could try to slit his father's throat, what was the man capable of? The same man who sat by and watched as his bosses tortured children and didn't lift a finger to help. Ironic since they all were supposed to be the ones prosecuting such crimes.

"He's here," Justice said. "Pullin' into the driveway."

"He's alone. I'll pull the SUV around back away from the lights." Samson was prepared for Anthony to fight, but, if Red did this right, Anthony would go eagerly, if not willingly. No. He wouldn't go willingly. But if he thought it was the only way he'd live through the night, he'd go.

"Should be entering the house. You ready?" Justice sounded concerned, but Red was more than ready. More than one thing ended tonight. Red tried to work up the dread about telling Joy what he'd done to their son, but couldn't. They would both reap what they'd sown.

Red stood leaning against the island in the kitchen, his arms spread before him, bracing himself lightly. Anthony walked in and straight to the fridge, pulling out a bottle of some kind of fancy-ass beer. Red was silent while Anthony opened the bottle and took a healthy pull. As he closed the fridge, the man caught sight of Red and started. As recognition replaced shock and fear, Anthony scowled.

"What the fuck are you doing here?"

"Came for you. You gonna come nicely or we gonna have to have a disagreement?"

Anthony took another pull of his beer, taking three healthy swallows. He set the bottle on the counter. "Mom said you'd be coming for me." He snorted. "Guess this the part where I'm supposed to beg for my life."

"You could, I suppose. Or you could just do what I fuckin' tell you." Red didn't raise his voice or move. He just stared at the young man who was his son.

"You know," Anthony said. "Mom always said you didn't give a fuck about me." He spread his arms wide. "I guess she was right. I don't mean anything to you. Do I?" It wasn't a question.

"Actually, Anthony, you do mean a lot to me. I remember the times before Joy took you away and you were my world, or, at least, the best part of it. What happened after she left is on her."

"If you'd just married her, she wouldn't have left."

"Yes, she would have. She was never suited to being a lifer in an MC, and it's the only life I know. She'd still have left. She'd have just made more people miserable along the way. Only difference might've been your take on the whole thing. If you'd been older when she left, you might've understood more."

"What's to fucking understand?" he yelled. "You didn't want either of us in your life! You drove her away!"

"I didn't." Red didn't raise his voice. "Other than her taking you, I didn't care if she stayed or left. Coming home to you was the highlight of my day. Joy left because she knew taking you away from me was the only way she could hurt me."

"So, you're saying my entire life, all the shit Mom told me about you, that she wanted me to hate you? It was all designed to hurt you?" He scoffed. "Seems a bit conceited to me, but whatever helps you sleep at night."

Red shrugged. "Believe what you will, but tell me how many teenage boys you know who try to cut their father's throat unless he's been abusin' them in some way. Joy knew I'd never retaliate against you, nor would I put you in a hospital. I did exactly what she wanted me to do, and it was probably the biggest mistake of my life."

"Oh, yeah? What was that?"

Red straightened and shrugged. "Absolutely nothing. I let you go back to her. Told her what you'd done, watched her try to suppress her smile, and I let the two of you go. Like it or not, boy, your mother made you into the man you are today. Not me. Which I take responsibility for."

That caught Anthony off guard. "How can you take responsibility for me when you say it wasn't your fault? Like I'm some kind of fucking monster. I'm a fucking lawyer, you ignorant fuck! Assistant District Attorney for the state of Florida! What the fuck are you? A mechanic in a biker gang? A car thief?"

"All of that and more," Red said. "You can add killer to the list as well. With all that, I'm still not the monster you are."

Anthony laughed. "I'm on the right side of the law, you motherfucker. How am I a bigger monster than you are?"

Red was silent for a long moment, meeting his son stare for angry stare. When he finally spoke, it was soft but deliberate. And very, very deadly. "Because when I know there are children being hurt, I fuckin' do somethin' about it."

The silence was deafening. Anthony went pale, then dropped his beer bottle on the floor, where it shattered on the expensive tile. The look on Anthony's face said he knew death was coming, and there was nothing he could do to prevent it. "How did you know?"

"Doesn't matter. What does matter is that you have one chance to get out of this mess. If you want it, you'll come with me now. No lip. If not?" He shrugged. "I promised your mother I'd make it quick."

Anthony's head snapped up, his gaze finding Red's. "You'd do it yourself? You say it so casually."

"You're my son. My responsibility. If it has to be done, it will be me who does it. I won't leave it to anyone else. Not even the court system."

"Well, bully for you, Ian. Glad you're finally taking responsibility for something." He'd gotten some of his bravado back, but he was still pale and had broken out in a sweat. Red could see his pulse racing at his neck. "So? What're you gonna do to me?"

"Like I said. You're gonna come with me, and we're gonna have a little chat."

"We can do that here."

"True. But that chat don't go the way I want it to go... well. Being in a crowded neighborhood isn't the ideal place for this conversation."

"You're a real bastard, Ian."

"Never claimed to be anything different. You coming quietly?"

"Do I have a choice?"

"Yep. Don't mean the outcome will be any different. Just more painful."

Anthony grabbed another beer from the fridge, popped the top, and chugged it. "Guess it's gonna be a long night."

"I suppose so." Red let him finish his beer, then led him out to the black SUV behind his house. Justice opened the back door to allow Anthony to climb in. Justice then trotted around to the other side and climbed in, leaving Red to slide in beside Anthony so the younger man was sandwiched between the two of them. Samson drove in silence.

It took them roughly an hour to get to their destination, a rough cabin in the swamp. Once inside, Red shoved Anthony into a chair in the middle of the room. "You get one shot at this, boy," Red said. "You fuck up, you die. That simple."

"Looks like I don't have much choice. What do you want from me?"

"There's an investigation inside the DA's office. It's broad and sweeping. Everyone is being looked into by, shall we say, people who don't much care for the kind of law they practice."

Justice snorted at that but kept quiet.

Red continued. "We want you to give us as much information as you can on every single person in that office. Personal or professional. I'm talking clerks, secretaries, even the fuckin' janitors. But most especially, the lawyers and cops working with them. You can start with who knew about the sex-trafficking ring on the bigshot billionaire's yacht."

"How did you find out about him? He thought he was completely hidden."

"Not your fuckin' business. Just know that I know. And so do my friends. My advice would be not to try to pretend you know nothing. Because we can link you to several things. The only reason you're still alive and being given this chance is because we haven't linked you to that ship or the man who owns it. We do, and you're dead within the hour."

"Then I'll be fine," he said. "Fucker gave me the creeps the only time I ever met him. He was coming in as I was leaving. They invited me, but I declined."

"That's not all we need you to do for us. We

know they're rigging the system against their enemies. You're going to find out who's behind it all. And, yes, we have people on the inside who are keeping an eye on you. You won't know who they are, but they may test you from time to time. You don't report something, we'll know. That makes you untrustworthy. Which makes you useless to us. Which makes you dead."

"This is a nightmare." Anthony shook his head, scrubbing his hands over his face afterward.

"You think so? What do you think it's like for those kids on that fuckin' boat? Or the people wrongfully convicted because of prosecutorial misconduct? You're having to spy on your coworkers. They've lost their lives as they knew them."

"And if I get caught, they'll kill me same as you. Only they won't go as easy on me." Anthony blotted his face with his shirtsleeve several times. "Look, I'll just lay it out for you, Ian. The DA's office is fucking *packed* in shit, it's so dirty. I knew it was happening when I interned, but I had no idea how far it all went until I got into casework. I have no idea who they actually answer to, but they're either scared as shit or paid too well to protest. Likely both. It's how Collins got invited to that ship. Part of his payment for doing whatever his handlers tell him to do."

Red thought about that for a moment, exchanging a long look with Justice. "Do you know what their ultimate goal is?"

"No clue. But it's big. At first, I thought they just wanted a monopoly on… I don't know, *something* in the city. Everything, maybe? They want Palm Beach to be their own personal empire. With all the goods and money flowing in and out of it to be theirs. Sounds impossible, but I'm telling you, that's what it feels like to me."

"Kid might be closer to the truth than he knows," Samson said into Red's earpiece. He hadn't gone inside, preferring not to be identified.

"You." Anthony indicated Justice. "You gonna be in there?"

"Me?" Justice looked horrified. "Oh, hell no! I'll be dead before I ever set foot in that place again. I'm here to support Red and to make sure you behave."

"You'd be better at this than me," Anthony said, looking pleadingly at Justice. "If the rumors are correct, you were a better lawyer than I could ever imagine being. You'd be perfect for this."

"Look, kid. First of all, I got disbarred. Not because the DA snowballed me, but because I threatened to kill a guy I prosecuted. He later died. I didn't do it, but I deserved what I got. So, there is no way I could possibly do this. Second, I'd just as soon kill every single motherfucker in there than try to help that pisshole out. There are a few good people there, mostly low-level staff, but if they know what's going on, they can get another job. Jobs open all over the fucking city. I ain't got no desire to look at those fuckers every fuckin' day. This is your penance. You can damned well pay it."

"So," Red continued. "Just so we're clear. You're going to make a report to me every week on anyone who has access to trial information of the police investigation. If you fail to turn up information, or if you tell anyone about the internal investigation, you're dead, and there will be nothing I can do to stop it. You're only here now because I went to bat for you, thinkin' you might be of use."

"What if I can't find anything? I can't manufacture shit out of thin air."

Red shrugged. "My advice is to dig hard. You know who's dirty and who's just tryin' to get by. You can start there. Detail what you know for sure and who you know it on. Also," he took a menacing step toward Anthony until he towered over him, "I suspect this will take up all your free time. You'll have no time to investigate Rosanna or me. In fact, I'd think it was in your very best interest to simply forget you ever met Rosanna."

Anthony sneered. "Hard to forget a little beauty like that. She --" Before he could finish his sentence, Red backhanded him so hard it knocked his chair over with him in it. Anthony smacked the side of his head on the floor. When he tried to get up, Red was on him, slamming his head back against the floor, one big fist wrapped around Anthony's neck.

"You'll fuckin' forget you ever fuckin' met her! You don't, that quick death I promised your mama will be nothing but a fuckin' pipe dream! I'll pull out your insides and feed them to you while you die slowly."

For the first time since Anthony had tried to slit Red's throat when he was twelve, the boy looked afraid. Very afraid. Red guessed there must have been something in his eyes that told Anthony he was deadly serious. Because he was.

Anthony grabbed Red's wrist, trying to lessen the grip Red had on him. but Red held fast. He wanted the kid to feel like Red had his life in his hands. Because he literally did. "You will do what I've told you. Yes?" Red sounded more in control now than he had only moments before.

"Yes," Anthony gasped out, the word strangled and husky.

Red gave him a hard shove as he let him go. Anthony crumpled to the floor. "Get him up," Red said to Justice. "Take him someplace and drop him off, then come back for me."

"I hear you, brother," Justice said, hauling Anthony to his feet. "Come on, Peewee. Let's get you outta here before Red changes his mind."

"He was going to kill me."

"Still might," Justice said matter-of-factly. "Only reason you're still alive is because he's under orders not to kill you without good reason. Personally, if he'd strangled you to death, I'd have sworn you had it comin'."

Anthony looked back at Red. "I was just trying to figure out how to get out without getting my license pulled. If I rat them out or leave, they'll pin something on me, and I'll either be disbarred or spend the rest of my life in jail. Probably both. Like him." He indicated Justice. "You understand. Right?"

Justice shook his head. "I took my punishment like a man. Pled guilty to keep my brothers out of it. You're cryin' to the wrong damned person."

"To paraphrase a favorite movie, Anthony, anyone who knows someone is sexually abusing children takes his leaving a little too slow. You crossed the line, Anthony. Now you gotta pay the price."

Anthony went with Justice without another word. Defeated. But alive. Red wasn't sure how he felt about it, but he knew he'd given the kid every opportunity to earn his reprieve. Anthony might still die later, but he'd at least do this.

After it was over, Red would reevaluate the situation. Deep down, Red knew this wouldn't last. He knew his son was already dead. Maybe he'd bought the kid some time to straighten out his life. That slim possibility was the only thing that might save him.

* * *

It was late when Samson brought Red and Justice back to the Black Reign compound. Late, but not too late for partying. From what it looked like, the whole place was there. Club girls everywhere, and not a stitch of clothing in sight. Normally it was a scene Red would have happily partaken in to forget Rosanna. Not that it was even remotely possible. The girl would forever haunt him. He'd always wonder what he could have had if he'd handled his son and Joy differently. But old habits die hard. He'd learned his lesson, but it was way too late for it to matter.

"Red!" El Diablo greeted him as he approached the bar. Red nursed a beer while he waited. "I'm so happy things worked out the way they did. Please know that I understand the position you were in and never took the situation lightly." The man gave him a friendly smile and looked as if he sincerely meant what he said.

"Let's get this over with," Red muttered.

"So anxious to hurt your woman again?" El Diablo didn't scowl... exactly. But it was a clear reprimand.

"I didn't do it on purpose," Red said on a growl. "It's just how I dealt with Joy and Anthony. That was just one mistake in a long string of them."

"Ah, I see," El Diablo said. "I take it you'll never make that mistake again?"

"Ain't a fuckin' moron."

"Considering you hurt her multiple times, I'll have to disagree with that assessment, but I'm willing to let you try once more with her."

"Since when do I need permission from you? Ain't part of your club." The fucking nerve of the guy!

"You're not. Dearest Rosanna, however, is. At least, she's under my protection until she says

- 136 -

otherwise."

Red started, actually jerking back like he'd been slapped. "What?"

"Oh, yes, Red. Thorn and Justice brought her to me. I gave my permission for her to stay here, which makes her part of the family I protect ruthlessly. Which means, you make her cry again, you die. Slowly." The man had the audacity to smile at Red like nothing was wrong.

"Ain't got no intention of making her cry," Red said. "I just... I need her back."

"Ahhh. I see. Well. You've got your work cut out for you. I'll give you one chance." El Diablo accepted a drink from the bartender. Looked like a Scotch on the rocks. "After that, she'll have to be the one to go to you. I won't have you or anyone else harassing her. Besides, what makes you think you deserve another chance with her?"

"I don't."

"But you're taking it anyway? What if she's moved on? Found her someone more worthy of her dedication and loyalty? Would you risk her happiness for your selfish notions?"

Red winced but didn't back down. "Doesn't matter how I answer that question. I'm fucked either way. If she tells me to leave her alone, I will. But I've got to have the chance to explain myself." Red clenched his teeth, trying not to admit how truly hooked he was on Rosanna. "I... need her. She's the only good thing in my life, and I can't leave her with things the way they are right now."

El Diablo studied him as he sipped his Scotch. "Fine. She's upstairs settling in. Probably knows you're here, because the club girls here like to keep everyone informed when fresh fish come into the compound.

They probably had your name, rank, and serial number the second you rolled through the gate with Samson."

"If she knows I'm here, then it's just a matter of time," Red said softly. "If there's a chance I can fix things, she'll come to bust my balls. If she's done with me, she won't give a damn if I'm here or not."

"Precisely," El Diablo said with a bright smile. "So we'll know without you having to make a scene."

"Don't mean I won't try to get her to talk to me," Red said under his breath.

As if on cue, Rosanna came stomping down the stairs, angrier than Red had ever seen a woman. If he hadn't been so relieved she'd come down at all, he might have been a little unnerved. She spotted him, and her expression grew even more fierce. Her face flushed from the neck up, and Red swore he could see steam coming from her ears she was so angry.

"You cocksucking son of a bitch motherfucker!" Rosanna yelled as she advanced on him. Most of the activity in the common room had stopped to watch the unfolding drama. As she beelined toward Red, she snagged a pool stick from someone and brandished it like a weapon, swinging at Red as soon as she got close enough. "I'll take your motherfucking head off!"

"Better watch it, Red," someone called.

"Ohh!" Several of the brothers exclaimed as they laughed when Rosanna broke the fucking cue stick over his back. It was a hefty blow, no doubt. Red actually went to his knees. He barely managed to block the jagged end of the stick when Rosanna tried to stab him in the side of the neck with it. Several of the bastards pulled up chairs and grabbed beers like they were at a prize fight.

"Fucking asshole!"

"Rosanna, calm down." He knew it was the exact wrong thing to say, but he couldn't help it. It just slipped out.

"Calm d -- *Calm down*?"

"You seem a little... aggressive. We can talk about this like reasonable adults." He winced. Yeah. Another wrong thing to say.

"*Reasonable*? I'll show you fucking reasonable!" She yelled like a banshee and launched herself at Red. He caught her in midair, but she wrapped her legs around him and punched and slapped at him about the head and neck. Red was surprised she wasn't biting. Had she intended to draw blood, she could have at any time.

The boys continued to cheer her on at Red's expense, offering instructions. Some of which she took. Needless to say, Red was going to be black and blue by the time this was over. Out of the corner of his eye, Red saw El Diablo sitting at the bar passively sipping his Scotch as he watched intently.

"You think I'm a dimwitted whore? Giving your fucking son permission to take me because I'd never satisfy him? I seem to remember making you scream at the top of your fucking lungs many times over, you fucking prick!" Finally, she wiggled out of his arms and kicked out at his shin, retreating a few steps away from him. She was breathing hard, but there were tears in her eyes she refused to shed. "I was nothing but good for you. We were a dynamic team. And you just threw me out like so much fucking garbage!"

Red grunted, straightening before stomping over to Justice, who handed him a vest. He marched to Rosanna and turned it so she and everyone else could read the back. It had the Salvation's Bane skull emblem on the back as well as a top and bottom rocker. They said: "Property of" and "Red."

"There's no way I'd let some dimwitted whore know my business, Rosanna. You know everything because you're highly intelligent and the sweetest, most giving soul I've ever known," he said, his gaze boring into Rosanna's as he spoke. "You're sleeping with me, but there has been no one else in this club you've had sex with. My brothers ain't shy about that. They'd tell me if they'd had you. Second, Anthony is welcome to *try* to take you. Because I will kill my own spawn before I'll allow the fucker to harm one single hair on your head. He knows that now. And lastly, there is no way you could satisfy Anthony, because there will never be an occasion for you to try. You get me?"

Rosanna looked hard at the vest for several seconds. Red was actually afraid she might not take it, or worse, throw it back in his face. Then she snorted and snatched the thing from his hands. She put it on with snappish movements, all the while shooting him killing looks. She pointed a finger in his face. "If you ever pull a fucking stunt like this again, I will fucking kill you!"

"Well, what do you know?" Rosanna said, looking down at herself, fingering the vest before twirling around to show Joy the back, then facing the other woman again. "It does say 'Property of Red' on the back, don't it?" She gave Joy her best smirk when she really wanted to claw the woman's eyes out. "Guess that means you ain't shit, much less Red's ol' lady."

"Little whore stole that!"

"Try again," Rosanna said. "Everyone here just witnessed Red giving it to me." She turned to Red then, a thought occurring to her. "If you made this for her years ago, you won't have to worry about knocking me up. I'll cut out your balls."

Red raised his hands in defense almost instantly. "Swear to God, Rosanna. I had it made about a month after you moved to Salvation's Bane. I just wasn't sure I could give it to you."

She narrowed her eyes at him. "Why the fuck not?"

"Woman, you're younger than my son. I felt like a fuckin' pervert."

OK, she could see that. Didn't mean she was letting him off the hook. "So you feel like less of a perv now?"

"Not really," he muttered, then snapped his gaze back to her. "Don't mean I'm fuckin' givin' you up, Rosie. You're mine."

"Then, what about Joy?" Rosanna crossed her arms over her chest, looking from Red to the *MILF* standing in front of them.

"Joy ain't got nothing to do with us."

"She's here, ain't she?"

"Don't mean I wanted her here. She knows the score."

Chapter Ten

Rosanna never expected the day to end like it had. Red had given her his property patch in front of everyone, claiming her in the most permanent way a biker could. Their fight had been great entertainment for everyone. The more violence the better and, really, she had hardly scratched him. OK, so the attempt at stabbing him might have been a little much, but if he couldn't fend her off then he really *was* too old for her anyway.

Now she stood there facing Red. She wore his vest proudly, daring any of the club girls around them to challenge her. More than one of them looked like they wanted to, but just shot her killing looks before backing away to find their own man for the night. She was just about ready to completely forgive Red when the door opened.

Dressed in leather shorts and a halter top that did little to conceal her ample breasts, Joy waltzed into the place. Immediately, the great room went quiet.

"Motherfuck," Red muttered. Samson glanced at Red, then at El Diablo. The president shook his head and nodded to Rycks. Apparently, El Diablo wasn't going to give Joy status by greeting her himself.

"Don't seem to recall inviting another club to this party," Rycks said. Lyric, his woman, stood close by but let her man do his job without complaining. "How'd you get in?"

"I'm Red's ol' lady," she said, lifting her chin and sounding as confident as the day was long. "If he's here, I'm here."

"Red?" Rycks looked back at Red and Rosanna.

"Don't look at me," he said, nodding at Rosanna. "She's the one wearin' my vest."

Rosanna scoffed. "Might want to explain it to her again, because it don't look like she got the fucking message."

"I'm standing right here," Joy said in a huff. "Don't talk about me like I can't hear you."

"I could give two shits if you hear or not," Rosanna said, turning to her. "I happen to think you're a fucking bitch, and I'm just looking for a reason to mess up all that makeup you cake on your face."

"Little girl, I spent most of my life in an MC. I can fight with the best of --"

Rosanna attacked, driving the heel of her hand into Joy's chin. The other woman's head snapped back, and she staggered backward in her ridiculously high heels. Lucky for her she backed into a pool table before she completely lost her balance. Rosanna followed, continuing to rain blows on the other woman. They weren't well placed or even well aimed -- she just wanted to get her message across. Red was hers. Joy could keep her paws off, or Rosanna would beat the shit out of the skanky bitch.

"Think you can fight me? I'm just fucking crazy enough not to fucking care!" Rosanna screamed while she pummeled Red's ex. "That's for belittling him in his own garage because you knew he wouldn't defend himself. And that's for making his life hell. And this?" She slapped Joy across the face three times in rapid succession. "That one's for just being the fucking bitch you are!"

Joy whimpered and screamed with every blow Rosanna landed. She tried to fight Rosanna off, but the girl stuck to her like glue.

Finally, someone grabbed Rosanna around the waist and pulled her off. Rosanna just threw herself back in the general direction of the older woman. If anyone wanted Red bad enough to fight for him, Rosanna was game. Because she definitely wanted him that bad.

"Easy there, little wildcat," Red said in her ear as he lifted her up off the floor. Must have been him the first time, but she didn't know. "I think she got the message."

"You just made a mistake," Joy hissed, breathing hard. Her lip was split in two different places, and she blotted it against her arm. "I'll have you arrested."

"The only mistake I made was not fighting you for him the first fucking time I met your skank ass. Go on. File a report with whatever police department you think will listen. I'm half your size. I look like a kid and can act like one if I need to. I'll have the cops eating out of my hand, and you'll look like an idiot."

Joy blinked, then looked at Red. "She's not the mousy little grease monkey from your garage."

Red chuckled. "Nope. She's my woman."

Joy snorted wistfully. "You were never that proud to have me on your bike."

"You were never meant to be mine. You knew it. I knew it."

"Well, I hope the fuck she knows it. I hope she's worth it, Red. You tossing out our history like this."

"The only history we had was Anthony, and you turned him so completely against me I'll never get him back."

"At least he's still here," she said softly, then glanced at Rosanna. "Well. I'm always here. When she decides to trade you in for a younger model, give me a call. We can work things out."

"That's it," Rosanna said, snagging one half of the cue stick she'd broken over Red's back. "I've had enough of this bitch."

Rycks stepped between Joy and Rosanna. "All right, all right. You've made your point, Rosanna. Go home with your man. Take it out on him. Much as I understand why you want to do it, I can't let you kill her here. She walks into Salvation's Bane, though. Well. That will be Thorn's mess to deal with."

"You." He pointed at Joy. "You're not welcome."

"How'd she get in in the first fuckin' place," Red groused.

El Diablo spoke for the first time. "I let her in. I needed to see for myself if my dearest Rosanna still wanted you. Had I known you'd brought your property patch, I'd have let it go at that."

"Bastard," Red grumbled.

"Now, now. None of that. Take your woman and go home. I imagine you have some things to, shall we say, discuss." His smile wasn't unkind when he looked at Rosanna next. "You, my dear. Take care. If that old dog treats you badly, you know where to find me. You'll always be welcomed at Black Reign."

"Thanks," she said. "I appreciate you taking me in on such short notice." She hiked a thumb over her shoulder in the general direction of Joy. "Sorry about the altercation."

"Rubbish," El Diablo said with a grin. "The boys are always up for a good cat fight. Just don't make a habit of it."

The smile on Rosanna's face was worth the beating she'd given Red. "No promises."

"Go, then. Get out before I decide to keep you myself."

Rosanna turned and marched out, throwing over her shoulder, "Coming, Red?"

"At your service, ma'am," he responded.

* * *

Red followed her out to the parking lot. She knew exactly where his bike was parked. Probably had watched as he, Justice, and Samson rode in. Thank God, Samson had let them stop by the Bane clubhouse and get their bikes. Red wasn't sure he could stand having to hitch a ride back to Bane, but he'd have done it to get his woman alone and finish working shit out.

"Don't think you're off the hook, Red. You're not," Rosanna said in a snippy tone.

"I know. But you're coming home with me. Right?" He hated having to ask, but he wasn't taking her for granted.

"For now," she replied. "Whether or not I stay there depends on you."

"Copy that."

Red started up his Harley, revving it several times until Rosanna's slim arms wrapped around his waist and she pressed her cheek against his back. When he felt her small sigh, he put the bike in gear and took off.

Instead of going straight back to the garage, Red rode for a while. It gave them both time to think about what they needed to say and, more importantly, gave Red a precious hour with Rosanna wrapped around him. Her small breasts were mashed against his back, and he swore he could feel the heat of her pussy against his ass. By the time they pulled into the garage, Red was hard as steel, knowing she had to be the one to make the first move in that department.

Surprisingly, Rosanna didn't move right away. Instead, her arms tightened around him, and she clung for long moments after he'd parked the bike. Red put his hands over hers, rubbing gently.

"Come on, little wildcat. Let's go talk this out."

"You hurt me, Red. Really bad." She sounded

heartbroken, like she had nothing left to give. Panic set into Red like he'd never experienced.

"I know, baby. Did you hear me when I explained everything I'd said? It was the fuckin' truth. Every Goddamned word. And I swear to you, by God and sunny Jesus, I will never back off from Joy or Anthony ever again."

"They made your life miserable," she said, sniffing once. It wasn't a question.

"Every single person in my life they thought I cared about, they made a target. Most of it was verbal, but there were times it got aggressive. Not with them, you understand. But they are both just as connected as I am in that department. That was for any club girl who hung around too long. As you probably know, most club girls don't back down easily. A surprise beatin' or two generally made them back off."

"Was it only the girls, or did they target your club brothers?"

"No. Joy knew better. Yes, we protect the club girls, but some of them tend to get themselves in jams of their own making. Joy knew that. So she'd orchestrate it. But there was never a woman I cared enough about for her to have to use any real muscle. She would have with you, though."

"What about Anthony?"

Red sighed. "Anthony is another story altogether. He let his mother take care of any women in my life, but he tried on several occasions to go after my brothers through legal channels. Probably why Justice ended up in prison, though Anthony was just starting college. He already had his foot in the door through some contacts Joy made to keep her up financially in addition to the money I gave her. I think that might have been the first real taste of revenge the boy got against me."

"So, why would you expect anything to have changed now? Anthony and Joy both still hate you, though why Joy put on that little show tonight is beyond me."

Red snorted. "Glad you didn't let her get away with it."

"I'm done backing down from either of them, Red. I stayed quiet for the most part because I felt like that was your business. Not anymore. Not if we're going to try to make this work between us."

"Anthony won't be a problem. He's riding a fine line between life and death right now. One toe out of line and I'll end him without a second thought."

She started, her arms jerking from around his waist. He looked back at her, meeting her shocked expression with his steady gaze. He wanted her to see how serious he was about this.

"But he's your son! Don't you want to protect him?"

"I do," he said. "But he crossed a line he should never have crossed. I'll tell you if you really want to know, but it's all club business. The reason we let him live. The reason he needs to die."

"Tell me," she whispered.

So he did. Detailing the ties to sexual offenses against minors by people Anthony worked with in the DA's office and how Anthony did nothing to stop or prevent it. About how his son was tasked with reporting back to Red and how they had Wrath embedded in the DA's office to keep an eye on everyone.

"We think the whole office has been packed with people loyal to a sect of organized crime far above anything we've ever encountered. Palm Springs is just a small part of what they have going on. Like a *really* small part. The best anyone can figure is it has something to do with the planned construction on the shipping port. It will allow more and larger ships to dock and unload." He waved a dismissive hand. "That's all El Diablo's shit. He's the one who seems to know what's going on, not to mention how to stop them. The only reason I know about it is because of Anthony."

"You'd really kill him?"

"I don't want to," he said, looking away. "I remember the boy he was. The way he loved me and I loved him. I'd do anything for that boy, but not if he hurts children."

"You said he didn't."

"But he knew it was happening and allowed it. He never took part in anything to do with it, but he knew. If Thorn hadn't said to follow El Diablo's lead in this, he'd have taken his last breath last night. Several times I thought I might have to kill him."

"For what it's worth, I'm glad you didn't."

"Might still have to."

"If it comes to it, get Thorn to do it. Or to at least put someone else on the job."

"No. I promised Joy it would be me who did it, if it came to that."

She scowled. "Joy." She spat. "She's as bad as he is. Maybe not in the hurting kids department, but how do you think he got that way? It certainly wasn't you. Joy saw to it you had very little contact with him."

"She did."

"Then she doesn't deserve a say in this. If he has to be… eliminated, I don't want it to be you."

"Can't do that for you, Rosanna. Anything else and I'm your man, but this is something I have to be in charge of."

"Red?" The voice was decidedly female and grossly familiar.

"Motherfuck," Rosanna said. "That's it. This bitch is getting ready to die."

"Wait!" Joy said, her hands up in surrender. "I'm not here to cause trouble. I swear. Red's your man, Rosanna."

"Damned straight he is. What do you want?"

"To apologize," she said softly. "To both of you."

Rosanna glanced at Red and raised an eyebrow. "This should be good."

"Look. I was wrong," Joy said, diving right in. "About a lot of things. Mostly about keeping Anthony out of your life, Red. But also about you, Rosanna. That whole thing tonight was to prove to you how much you wanted Red in your life."

"I already knew that, you bitch," Rosanna said, her anger rising with every second. "I didn't need to beat your ass to know that! I already knew it!"

"Just calm down," Joy said, backing away. "El Diablo thought you might need a bit of a reminder and that everyone else might benefit from it, too. He was under the impression you might have a bit of a temper on you." She shrugged. "So I took one for Red. Guess it's the least I could after all I've put him through."

Fuck. Joy actually sounded like she regretted their past. Rosanna wasn't a bitch, but she wanted to pound on the woman some more. If she kept being mean, she'd be no better than Joy.

"Not sure it makes up for taking away his son, or anything else you did, but whatever helps you sleep at night."

Joy looked away, blinking. When she spoke, she didn't meet Red's gaze. "Is Anthony alive?"

"For now. Whether he remains that way is mostly up to him. The only promise I can make is the one I already have. If it has to be done, I'll be the one to do it."

"Red --" He put a hand on Rosanna's shoulder to keep her quiet.

"You'll make it painless."

This time, Red hesitated. "If I can. He's done some pretty bad things, Joy. Stuff I'd normally make a man suffer for."

Rosanna thought the woman would dissolve into tears or beg for her son's life or both. Instead, Joy just shut her eyes and took a steadying breath. "I understand. Just promise you'll do what you can."

"That I can promise," Red said gently. "Now, you need to leave. My advice is to not contact Anthony for a while. He needs time to figure out how he's gonna handle this."

"And I've already fucked up his life enough," she said softly.

"I wish I could say different, Joy," Red said with a shake of his head. "But you let your hatred of me blind you to what you were doing to that boy. Now, you've both got to live with the man he's become. I share in that responsibility because I should have fought you for him and didn't. Which is why I'm willing to be the one to put him down if it comes to that."

Joy looked at him as if he'd just gutted her. "You're a cold-hearted bastard, Red," she whispered.

"Never claimed to be anything else."

"Would you do it to her son? Your precious Rosanna's son?" she scoffed bitterly.

"I'd do it to any man who crosses that moral line Anthony has. Like I said, he's only alive because he's useful at the moment."

"Remember this, girl," Joy said, looking at Rosanna. "You think he's a good man, but he's not."

"I don't think he's a good man," Rosanna countered. "I *know* he's a good man. He's willing to do what has to be done, no matter the cost to himself. Sure, he could leave it to the authorities, but it sounds like the authorities are part of the problem. If he waits for justice that way, it may never come. And more children will be at risk. This isn't Red's fault. No matter how you want to spin it."

"Fine," Joy said, softly. "I didn't expect to change your mind, Red. Never was able to. But I had to try."

Red just nodded. Then Joy left.

"She gonna go to the cops?"

"No," Red said.

"You seem pretty sure."

He turned to Rosanna with a raised eyebrow. "El Diablo and Thorn both have eyes on her. She even hints at going to the cops, and they'll take her out. She was a club girl and lived at Salvation's Bane for years. She knows the score. She might never see the men on her, but she knows they're there."

They'd come to the part Rosanna had been dreading. "You still have feelings for her?"

Red sighed. "Let's get ready for bed. I have plenty to tell you about all that, but I'm doin' it with you naked in my arms. After that, we'll see what happens."

"You think I'm getting naked with you?"

"If you want this story, you will."

She heaved out a big sigh. "Fine. Get me naked."

He led her up to his office and the adjoining room. "I've never brought a woman here, Rosie. Not Joy. Not anyone. Only you."

"This your home?"

"As much of one as I have."

The place wasn't more than a bedroom and bathroom. But he didn't really need anything else. The break room in the garage had a full kitchen, not that any of them used it. There was also a TV if he wanted to watch something. His room just felt... cozy. Like it was a hideaway from everyone. In a sense, Rosanna supposed it was.

"I know it ain't much, but it kind of reflects my life, I guess. The garage is the important part. This is a place to sleep."

"I was just thinking it suited you."

"You know, I can build you a home, Rosanna," he said, looking at her with so much feeling Rosanna felt her heart soften when she needed to keep it hard. At least for a while. "I just never built me one 'cause I never thought I'd have a woman of my own."

"Except for Joy."

Red sighed, sinking down on the bed tiredly. He scrubbed a hand through his hair. "Yeah. Joy." He gave a derisive snort then looked up at her. "Get naked. You want me to tell you this, I want you naked."

Rosanna nodded, then stripped before Red's avid gaze. The second she stepped out of her panties, Red reached for her, pulling her onto his lap to straddle him. He wrapped his strong arms around her and just held her there for long moments, his face resting against her chest.

After a while, he took a deep breath in, then let it out before taking one nipple into his mouth and sucking gently.

"If I live to be a hundred, I doubt I'll ever get my fill of you, Rosie."

"I hope not," she said, cradling his head to her breast. "I hope I always make you want me."

"You do, baby. You will." He turned his head and latched on to the other nipple. "Mmm," he growled. "Sweet as a ripe berry."

"Red," she said, trying to sound stern. "More talk. Sex later."

He looked up at her, disappointment on his face, then sighed. "Fine."

"Good. Now take off your shirt." Instead of waiting for him to do it, Rosanna helped him strip off the tight tee. "It always amazes me how sexy your body is," she murmured. "You're big and strong. I love the way it feels when you wrap me up in your arms." She ran her hand lightly over his shoulders and his arms. He was a beautiful specimen of a man. Yes, he had scars, and there were more than a few gray hairs on his head and chest. But there had never been a man who compared to him in her eyes. "You're everything I could ever want, Red." Her whisper was husky and full of emotion.

"You told me you loved me once," Red said. "Do you still? Because I've never loved or been in love with a woman before, Rosie. You? Yeah. I love you. And I'm so in love with you it fuckin' hurts."

She smiled down at him. "As long as I've waited to hear those words, Red, you're avoiding the subject. I'm not continuing with that until you tell me about you and Joy. It has to be done, and I want it out of the way so we can get to us."

Red slid his arms back around Rosanna. One arm was securely around her back, the other cupping one cheek of her ass and kneading. "I met her when I was young, dumb, and full of cum, as the saying goes. She was sexy as all get out and great in bed. Even though she was at Salvation's Bane and claimed to be a club girl, she wasn't. Not really. She had too much of the old man's money in her attitude to really fit in there.

"I'm not sure why she set her sights on me. I had no aspirations to be president or any officer in Bane. I had my talents in the garage, and I used them for the club. That's all I wanted to do. But she focused on me. I let her because I had nothing better lined up." Again, he lapped at one of her nipples. Good as it felt, Rosanna was determined to get through this.

"So she decided you were hers. But you didn't reciprocate?"

"No. She told everyone she was my ol' lady, but I never put a property vest on her or in any way indicated we were exclusive. I had my club girls at parties. She fucked every brother she could get to do her." He shrugged. "It wasn't much of anything other than us being fuck buddies. At least, until she got pregnant."

"Why not use protection?"

"Oh, believe me. I did. Unlike with you, I was the one insisting on condoms. She told me she had an IUD, but I still didn't take any chances. So, she got me drunk. Not that I cared. The only thing I got pissed about was that we hadn't used a condom. I told her if she got knocked up, it was on her. I was angry, and you know my temper."

"So she got pregnant?"

"Yeah. Looking back, she must have been keeping track of when she was ovulating or some shit."

"But why get pregnant? She had no expectation you'd marry her."

"Probably why she got pregnant. Like I said. I have no idea why she fixated on me. Probably because I didn't pay enough attention to her, and she couldn't accept that I didn't want her. She's still a beautiful woman, but nothing like she was twenty-five years ago. It was just the princess attitude she had. She wanted something she couldn't have, so she figured out a way she could get it. Get knocked up, nab the biker."

"OK, so obviously that didn't work out like she thought."

"No. I mean, I bought a little house for us. I was with her through the pregnancy and birth. I helped raise Anthony and loved every second of my time with him. But I never loved her. Never pretended to be faithful to her, and I never intended to be. She knew that and still accepted what I offered. A presence in her and Anthony's lives. I gave her whatever she needed financially, but it wasn't enough."

"Do you think she loved you?"

"Na. She just didn't like losing. Just like tonight. She knew I wanted you. If she'd thought for a moment that I'd actually go through with givin' you a property vest, she'd never have agreed to El Diablo's little stunt. She thought if she made an appearance looking like a badass club girl, I'd rethink my commitment to you and prove everyone wrong. I was still a horny biker, willing to fuck anything that moved." Red undid his jeans with Rosanna still straddling him. He managed to slide them down his legs and kick them off. Then he moved closer to the center of the bed and lay down, bringing Rosanna to rest on top of him.

"So, why did she leave with Anthony?" Rosanna still wanted to hear what he had to say, but she was rapidly losing focus. His dick was throbbing against her bare mound, and she was sure she felt precum leaking from the tip between them.

"Attention. I loved Anthony with all my heart.

That boy had me wrapped around his little finger from the second he was born. When Joy realized I'd never love her the way I loved him, she did the only thing she could think of to get back at me."

"Take your son away."

"Yeah. But that wasn't all she did. From the time they left, she poisoned him against me. I have no idea what she said to him, but Anthony hated me so much that, when he was twelve, he tried to slit my throat in my sleep." He lifted his chin and moved his beard out of the way so she could see the scar running down his neck.

"Oh, my God!" The shock was horrible. Rosanna could only imagine how Red felt. "What happened?"

He shrugged. "Nothing. I called Joy and she picked him up. He didn't yell and scream. He just sat on the couch looking at me like he was just waiting for his moment to finish what he'd started. There was pure evil and hatred on his face. That was the moment I realized I'd lost my son."

"She comes back to this garage, Red, I'll kill her myself."

He smiled. "I believe you, little wildcat. But as much as she did to make him hate me, I didn't do anything to make him *not* hate me."

"You got him scholarships and grants to the schools he wanted. You paid for what was left. You kept up Joy's lifestyle."

"Yes. But I didn't make a big deal out of it. I just did it. It was the only thing I knew to do. I think, maybe, I thought Joy would tell him I'd been the one to help, but that was a foolish thing to expect. What I should have done was fight for full custody of him. Not just joint custody. Probably wouldn't have happened, but if I'd made a big deal out of it, maybe he'd have seen that I wanted him in my life."

"She'd have just figured out an explanation and twisted it to suit her needs. Told Anthony you were trying to keep him from her out of spite when it was exactly the opposite. I'm not really sure what else you could have done, Red."

"I don't either. Still doesn't mean I don't look back and wonder."

"He's not lost yet, is he?"

Red shook his head. "Don't know. I'm pretty sure that, if I hadn't come up with a way for him to help in this fucked-up mess at the DA's office, El Diablo would have ordered him killed. Thorn would have taken my side against Black Reign, but, honestly, given what I know he was privy to and did nothing to stop, I'm not sure I'd have protested much. What kind of person does that make me, Rosie? That I'd kill my own son?"

"It makes you a selfless person, Red. I can't imagine how you feel, but knowing that you're willing to pass judgement on Anthony in this kind of situation doesn't make you less in my eyes. It makes you more." She cupped his face in one of her hands. "So, yeah. I love you, Red. That's not changed. And it won't. But I'm done with you being indifferent to me. I'm done with you letting those two assholes talk shit about me, even if it's in an effort for you to keep how you feel about me from them. I get what you were trying to do, but it hurt, Red. I didn't like it."

"Never again, Rosanna. I'll defend you with my last breath. No one will ever talk to or about you like that ever again. No matter who it is or what the agenda is."

She smiled brightly at him. "Good. Now. Tell me you love me, then fuck me until I forgive you."

He chuckled as he rolled them over so he was on top of her. Then he thrust inside her, and Rosanna gasped out his name.

"Rosanna Creamer, I absolutely love the everlasting fuck outta you."

"Aww, you say the sweetest things."

Several hours and many screams later, Rosanna did, indeed, forgive him.

Demon's Little Lamb (Shadow Demons 2)
Marteeka Karland

Ivanovich knows the new intern he's hired at Argent Tech comes with a price tag. It's possible the young, sexy college grad is in bed with the people trying to stage a takeover of the company he and his brothers built as a cover for their underground activities. With the help of a former member of one of the most dangerous and influential shady organizations in the world, Azriel and the Shadow Demons are about to stage a takeover of their own. Of the permanent kind.

All Lamb Newsome wants to do is start an exciting, promising life after graduation. The break she takes in the Florida Keys before starting her new internship started things off smashingly. There she meets a wealthy man who is familiar with Argent Tech and they hit it off from the start. Both in bed and out of it. When she finds out he's married, things unravel quickly. The mess that follows isn't what she expected, however. Instead of a jealous wife, she has one of the owners of the company after her. In retrospect, she realizes she really shouldn't have fallen for the guy, but the sex is just that good.

Had she known the stakes, Lamb wouldn't have bet her heart. Now all she can do is believe in her Shadow Demon -- even if she doesn't know how he lives in the shadows. Now, she has to survive. But how is she supposed to do that on her own? And how can she ever trust her heart again when all it wants is the Shadow Demon she can never have?

Chapter One

"I got it! I got it!" Lamb Newsome thought her heart was going to beat through her chest. Her university advisor had gotten her an invite to apply for an internship at Argent Tech in Rockwell, Indiana just over a month ago. The invite alone was a monumental accomplishment, but to actually have been accepted? Yeah. She was on cloud nine.

"Shut up! You lie!" Karen, her best friend and roommate, looked at her with wide, round eyes, a huge smile splitting her face.

"Swear to God! Look!" She thrust the certified letter at Karen, who took it and read, her grin growing ever wider as she skimmed the important parts. "It's signed by fucking Azriel Ivanovich himself!"

"I know, right?" Lamb stopped, then snatched the letter back, frowning as she examined it, holding it up to the light and everything. "You think he actually signed it? Might be a stamped signature."

"Girl! That letter is on the fanciest paper stock I've ever seen. Of course he fucking signed it!" They both let out a squeal of delight. "When do you start? Will you still be able to go to Key West with us?"

"Yes. With about eight days to spare. Just enough time to recover from any hangovers and sunburn I bring home with me."

"I can't believe you're going to be interning at Argent! I'm so jealous!" Karen didn't look jealous. She looked as happy as Lamb was. They'd both worked so hard for the best jobs after grad school. Sure, they'd competed for every honor earned, but neither woman had taken their rivalry seriously.

An internship wasn't permanent work, but it helped get her foot in the door and would give her valuable knowledge she'd have going into the next phase of her life. If she did well enough, and there was a spot available, she might even get to stay at Argent. That was a just a fleeting thought, though. Not an expectation. Argent rarely took on interns and never kept them longer than two years. But every single one had gone on to be one of the top minds in their given fields. She and Karen had competed for the Argent internship as well. Lamb figured it could have gone either way. She just got lucky.

"I can't believe it either. But I'll take it."

Karen didn't ask about the pay, and Lamb had no idea what it would be. Didn't care. She doubted anyone who'd been offered a spot had truly cared about the income. They'd pay her what she was worth to them. Had they not thought she had potential, they wouldn't have offered her a spot to begin with.

"You still ready to leave in the morning?" Karen gave her a grin as she took a pull from her beer.

"I'll have to make a quick stop by campus to meet with the contact from Argent, so I'll be a couple hours behind you guys, but yes. I'm still leaving tomorrow morning."

"Awesome! We'll save you a seat and have a mimosa ready for you when you get there."

"Sounds perfect."

They spent the rest of the evening drinking and celebrating. By the time Karen and the other three women in the group had stuffed their suitcases in the trunk of Karen's little BMW, Lamb was in her car headed back to campus. The Ford Focus Lamb drove wasn't fancy, but it would get her to the Keys and back.

The meeting on campus took less than an hour. By the end of it, Lamb was ready to cancel her vacation and start work immediately, but the man who'd spoken with her had insisted she take this time to relax. He promised she'd get little enough of it once she started work for them. Lamb had shaken his hand, unable to keep the huge grin off her face, then left.

* * *

Day two on the beach was like a dream come true for Lamb. The sun was hot, the waves relaxing, and the drinks plentiful. She'd say the guys were hot, except most were three times her age and interested mostly in golf. Which was fine. The few men she'd met who'd offered to buy her a drink were interesting to talk to. She'd also made it clear she wasn't there to hook up with a rich guy, but she was definitely up for a lively debate or a stimulating round of chess. Most laughed and declined her offer, but a couple took her up on it. One gentleman scratched his head after she'd beaten him soundly in three rounds of speed chess before laughing loudly and shaking his head in disbelief.

"You've got beauty and brains, young lady. Don't ever let anyone tell you differently. Not sure what you're doing with your life, but you'd better make it count."

"Yes, sir," she responded, taking his hand when he'd offered it to her.

"Don't let these old fools here have the satisfaction of buying your affections. Keep your head in the game, and you'll get very far on your own merits."

"Sound advice, sir," she said with a grin. "I'll make sure to follow it to the letter."

That was the evening of her second night. She went to bed with a smile on her face and joy in her heart. The future was so bright, it was almost inevitable she'd find the dark somehow.

"You played a fine game."

She was sitting on the beach the next morning playing chess with another older man when they were approached by a bystander. The compliment came from a distinguished-looking gentleman dressed in khaki shorts and a hula shirt... and with the sexiest British accent. It wasn't a thick accent, just enough to be a turn-on for Lamb. This was a man she could sit and listen to all day long. How he managed to look distinguished in that getup was amazing, but somehow he pulled it off. He had a full head of dark chestnut hair with silver at his temples. He was fit, but not overly muscled. It was the kind of body that would look good in a suit and could still show muscle in clothing like he was currently wearing. Lamb bet he had a fine washboard abdomen and defined arms under the short sleeves.

"Thank you. Chess is a hobby of mine. Helps me relax sometimes."

"Everyone needs something to settle their mind."

"I suppose that's true." Lamb smiled at him. He was handsome in a conventional way. Nothing overt or over the top. Nothing overblown or obviously fake, though she suspected he'd had some kind of plastic surgery done to his nose. There was just something about it that didn't quite fit the rest of his face. There wasn't a laugh line to be seen at his eyes or mouth. He was almost too perfect.

He held out his hand. "I'm James Luxemberry."

"Lamb Newsome," she answered. "Are you here for the sand and the sun?"

"Most assuredly. And the sea. I've not spent nearly enough time on my yacht as I'd intended."

"Wow. That sounds like fun."

"It can be." He gave a little secretive smile. "What are you drinking, my dear?"

"Captain and Coke."

"Ah. Rum. Perfect choice."

And they hit it off from there, talking well into the night. Lamb was fascinated by James. He said he'd been the CEO of a large tech company on the East coast. Rush Developments was a weapons manufacturer, one James had had a hand in running for the better part of seven years until his retirement six months prior.

"It's a heady feeling," he said when she asked him what it was like at the corporate level. "Not sure it's as exciting as being on the developmental end. That's where I started, you know. Research and development."

"And you worked your way up. Very inspirational." She meant it, too. Though she had no aspirations of being in upper management, his life had to have been fascinating, and she respected him for his achievements. He had a magnetic personality she was aware she was getting sucked into. Though why he'd chosen her to flirt with was beyond her reckoning. Lamb was rather mousy and was comfortable with that description.

James shrugged. "Everyone has to start somewhere. You, for example." He sat back in his chair and waved at her. "You're obviously a very bright young woman. What are your plans after university?"

She grinned. This was the first time she'd had a chance to tell anyone of her big score other than Karen and her friends. "I've got an internship. In eleven days, I start working at Argent Tech."

James's brows went up, and he sat up straighter. "Argent?" He gave her a million-dollar smile. *Sigh.*

"You really must be something. That's the best possible internship you could have hoped for."

"I know. I'm just lucky, though. My best friend was also accepted as a candidate. She's just as qualified as I am and actually more suited to the job. They're taking a chance on me, and I know it. I won't let them down."

"Nonsense." He waved away her concern. "If you were chosen for the one internship they offer every two or three years, then you more than deserve it. I don't know the man personally, but I'm told Azriel Ivanovich vets every single candidate for that spot himself. If that's true, I can guarantee you got the job because you were the absolute best applicant. Congratulations."

"Thank you."

Yeah. The man's charisma was off the charts.

"Another drink to celebrate." He waved the bartender over and they both refilled, each taking a sip. Lamb wasn't drunk by any means. Just pleasantly buzzed. She could tell by his grin he thought she was further along than she really was. Lamb thought about telling him not to bother. If she decided to sleep with him, she didn't need alcohol. She also wasn't stupid enough to get drunk with a strange man, no matter how suave he was.

Finally, around three in the morning, she called it a night. He'd tried to keep giving her alcohol, but she'd stopped drinking a couple hours before, choosing instead to nibble on various appetizers she'd procured from the bar's restaurant.

"You know, you're a very beautiful woman, Lamb." James took her hand and kissed the back. "Beauty and brains. That's a deadly combination to a man like me."

"I'm sure you've got any number of women falling all over themselves to be with you. I'm sure it's a hazard of your station in life. And your charisma. You could charm the pants off a nun."

They both laughed.

"I've never been interested in religion," he said softly, meeting her gaze boldly and with a wealth of meaning.

"Can't say I have either." Lamb's breath was a little bit ragged. Yeah, she was turned on. The man was intriguing to say the least. Had she met him under other circumstances, she'd probably have assumed he was married and not bothered. He was pleasing enough to look at, but way too sophisticated for her. Just to ease her conscience she said, "You know I have to ask if you're married. I'm many things, but I don't fool around with another woman's man. Not even casually."

"I'm sure you've guessed, I'm not exactly hurting for money. Suffice it to say, a man in my position can't afford affairs if he wishes to stay in that position financially."

"Can't argue with that." Though she knew it was a non-answer. She glanced at his left hand. No ring. No tan line. No mark as if he'd worn a wedding band and simply taken it off. Sure, he could just not wear one, but he'd been with her for hours. No one had called him. No one had come to get him. He appeared to be exactly what he was: a bachelor enjoying his freedom.

Deciding to just go with it, Lamb accepted his offer to show her his yacht. Which she was sure would lead to more than simply touring the place. Especially at three in the morning.

Sure enough, half an hour later, she found herself in the master suite of the most luxurious boat she'd ever imagined. If she'd been paying attention, she was sure she'd have enjoyed all the things he'd shown her, but all she had eyes for was the man currently undressing her. He might be too perfect and know how to keep her distracted, but Lamb didn't care. She wanted the experience. Given the fact that she'd just graduated with her masters in four years, there had been little time for a personal life. Sex had been non-existent since that one time on prom night. She knew she wasn't the best judge of things, but she liked the way he made her feel. As long as she was careful and protected herself while she was with him, everything else would work itself out.

James kissed her body reverently, expertly. Lamb sighed and threaded her fingers through his hair. He chuckled when she gave a little squeal as he nibbled at the delicate skin of her neck. Lamb couldn't help her own giggle. It soon turned into a little moan of pleasure as he made his way to her breasts.

Each peak received a little suck and flick of his tongue. Lamb liked what he was doing but found herself wishing he'd be a little rougher. That he'd pull at her nipple harder with his mouth. Still, she arched into him, needing him to keep going. Sadly, he slid farther down her body to kiss her navel and twirl his tongue inside it.

She thought he was going to go farther, but he didn't. Instead, James sat up, pulling her to him with leverage on her thighs. Lamb lay open to him, her legs draped over his, his cock hard and aggressive as it pointed to her wet pussy. He guided himself to her entrance and Lamb realized he wasn't going to put on a condom.

"Wait," she said, pushing at him with one small hand. "Use something."

He grinned, but Lamb thought it looked strained. Perhaps he was just that into it. "Would be much better without. Are you sure?"

She smiled to take the sting out of her request. "Please. It's only responsible since we hardly know each other."

Something in the way he hesitated made Lamb's alarm go off. If he refused, she realized she was in a bad position to deny him. She tried to keep her features relaxed, not wanting to rock the boat, so to speak. It was her body. Lamb had no idea why she felt bad about knowing she'd force the issue or leave, but she did. Probably her innate need to please people. Had they been in even a semi-committed relationship, she'd have let him have her without a condom. But she'd just met him a few hours ago. Even having sex with him wasn't the smartest thing she'd ever done, but doing it unprotected was just idiotic.

Finally, he gave her a smile and a slight nod. He lay on top of her and reached toward the bedside table for the drawer. Inside, he fished around until he found a condom packet and handed it to her. Sitting back, he nodded at her. "You want it? You put it on." His expression wasn't unkind. In fact, that million-watt smile was firmly back in place. But Lamb wasn't buying it. He was angry he'd had to do this one small thing. Why, she had no clue. But he'd definitely not planned on her insisting on protection.

Obediently, she ripped open the pack and sheathed him in it, taking extra care to stroke him as she did. No need to make him think she was having second thoughts. She was, but realized it was far too late to stop this now. Not without a good reason. And, honestly, she still wanted the experience. She wanted to have sex with a man who knew what he was doing and could make it good for her. There had to be one out there. Right?

This time, when James pressed against her opening, Lamb braced her feet on his calves and lifted herself, forcing him deep. He groaned and let his head fall back, his cock pulsing inside her.

"Ah! So tight!"

"Feels good," she sighed. It did. She felt full and stretched, but deliciously so. When he leaned over her to find her lips, Lamb met his kiss with one of her own, opening her mouth to accept the thrust of his tongue.

He rocked into her, the pleasure increasing with each movement. The orgasm was still out of her reach, but Lamb could feel it rising with each surge of James's body inside hers. She moved with him, quickly learning the way he needed her to move. He grunted with each surge forward, tightening his grip on one of her thighs as he moved. Over and over, he slid in, then out. Lamb stayed on the edge of a precipice she couldn't quite fall off of. No matter what she did, she couldn't seem to get that little bit extra she needed.

But it still felt wonderful. His skin slapped hard against hers, echoing in the spacious cabin. The sea breeze wafted through the room, kissing their skin and creating just one more measure of sensation to push her where she wanted to be. To no avail.

Finally, James cried out, his cock pulsing inside her as he reached his peak. Lamb was frustrated, but didn't want to admit she hadn't come. She knew he'd ask once he'd finished. Didn't all men ask? If she lied, it wouldn't help anything, but she was adult enough to know that men who picked up women like James had done weren't exactly in it for the woman's pleasure.

She had two choices. Lie. Or tell the truth. No, she hadn't come, but she'd been damned close. Just a little more… something. Friction on her clit. Another deep, sensuous kiss. A little dirty talk. *Something*. Would get her off. She knew it.

"God, that was good," James gasped. "Your little pussy's so tight around me I can barely think. Did you come?"

"Yes," she said, unsure of what she was going to say until she said it. Fuck. She'd figure it out. She hated lying, but she'd probably never see James again after tonight. If she did, it was only a temporary thing. If nothing else, she had to leave in a couple more days. "So good…"

He grinned at her, kissing her lips tenderly. "You know, you could stay with me. I'm here until the end of the month. When do you have to be at Argent?"

"I'm supposed to leave in two days, but I don't have to report to the campus until the eighteenth. I was supposed to have that time to recoup."

"Stay with me." He said in no uncertain terms. "Stay with me, and I'll help you celebrate."

"I wouldn't want to intrude."

"You're not. I'm here all by myself. It would be nice to have some company for a change."

"I'm sure you're not hurting for companionship." She smiled, reaching up to caress his smooth jaw. Just one other aspect about him that was picture-perfect.

"I could have another woman if I wanted, I'm sure. But you fascinate me in a way no other woman ever has. I'd very much like to spend the rest of your time here with you. Please."

Lamb smiled. Why not. "OK."

* * *

The remaining five days of her vacation, Lamb spent with James. Her friends had gone on home and she promised to text or call often, which she did. James showed her a wonderful time. Fine dining and entertainment, along with all the comforts money could buy, were on the menu every day. At night, they had lots of sex. Though James wasn't very inventive, he seemed to enjoy her body as much as she did his. More even. And Lamb did enjoy him. She managed to have more than one orgasm, but nothing life altering. Which led her to believe she just wasn't a sexual person. Sad, but there it was.

Always, James tried to forgo the condom, but the more he did, the more she insisted, using the excuse that she wasn't on the pill and couldn't afford to get pregnant at this time in her life. It seemed to upset him, especially their last night together, but Lamb was firm. He abided by her wishes, but she got the feeling he was angry about it.

She could have confronted him -- and probably should have -- but it wasn't worth it to her. As long as he did as she asked, there was no reason to get into his reasoning for not wanting to use a condom. Which baffled her to no end. He was, by all appearances, a very wealthy man. Wouldn't knocking up a complete stranger be bad for him? She'd never try to take him to the cleaners, but most women she knew would. He didn't know her, and he wasn't stupid. So why was he so insistent?

In the back of her mind, it was a warning. A red flag she shouldn't ignore. But she did. She settled for the experience she wanted and didn't ask him anything. When they parted ways, she intended to get his number so they could get together again, but every time she intended to, something would distract her. By the time she was in her little Focus headed back to Indiana, she realized she'd never gotten his number.

And he hadn't gotten hers.

Oh well. She was moving on to the next phase of her life. A man in the mix would just complicate things. She needed to focus her entire attention on learning as much as she could at Argent Tech in the little time she had there. With that thought firmly in mind, she turned up the radio, put the windows down and sang at the top of her lungs until she reached cooler weather farther north. Lamb Newsome was taking her life by the horns. She was in control of her own destiny. Time to make the most of it.

Chapter Two

"Everyone's in play," Geovanni's voice said through Azriel's earpiece. "The girl just entered the building and is headed for the ballroom."

"Good. Let the appropriate staff know when she gets deeper into the area. They need to subtly push her in Luxemberry's direction. I want them running into each other sooner rather than later."

Azriel Ivanovich was nothing if not a cold-hearted bastard. What he was doing was cruel, but, then, he'd never been nice to his enemies. He was fairly certain the only partially innocent person in this whole endeavor was Rachel Luxemberry, and she was questionable. She might not be involved in the conspiracy to take over Argent Tech, but she was guilty of many other things. As far as he was concerned, her husband, James, and the little tart they'd placed in an internship at Argent deserved whatever happened next.

He'd been more upset at himself for getting sucked in by Lamb Newsome's intellect and innocence. He'd watched the interview with rapt attention. She'd seemed nervous, but excited. Passionate about the work she did at the university. It was that passion and enthusiasm that had won him over. She was intelligent and proficient enough in her field of study to be able to pick up easily what they had to teach her at Argent. She'd soak up that knowledge like a sponge and, if they were lucky, would agree to stay on after her internship was done.

All in all, Azriel had expected Lamb Newsome to be a tremendous asset in the future. To top it all off, she was absolutely stunning. Pale, creamy skin, silky black locks that fell in a cascade down her back to well past her hips -- she was exotic. Her eyes were a clear blue, making him think she had to have some kind of contact enhancement. A quick look at her file told him she didn't. Her vision was perfect, according to her eye exam. No. Lamb was a natural beauty. Slight, sensual curves softened her figure. Azriel longed to shape those curves with his big hands, then wrap his body around hers until she was as tangible as he wanted her to be instead of some nymph sent to torment his dreams.

Then he'd learned of her treachery. Or, at least, her complicity in it. He was about to get at least a modicum of revenge because he was fairly certain the little spy had no idea the man she was reporting to was married.

"She's on the move. Looking for someone." Giovanni Romano was the best computer intelligence person Azriel had ever met. He'd been bested once by Alexei's wife, Merrily, and by Suzie, a bright young woman with a very large, very protective man at Bones MC in Somerset, twice. Other than those two women, Azriel didn't know of anyone else who'd gotten past Giovanni's cyber security.

"Probably our James Luxemberry." Azriel would bet his fortune on it.

"Probably, but I'm not so sure." There was something in Giovanni's tone that brought Azriel to high alert.

"Explain," he snapped.

"She's greeted several of her coworkers with warm hugs. She's not self-conscious at all. There was an invitation that went out at Miss Newsome's request to one of the candidates we didn't pick." There was a brief pause while Giovanni looked for the name of the person he was referring to. "One Karen Leigh.

According to her cell phone records, she and Miss Newsome are close friends."

"So, you think Lamb is looking for Miss Leigh?"

"Possibly. She doesn't act like she's looking for a lover or a male companion of any kind."

"Hmm." He rubbed his chin thoughtfully. "Is Miss Leigh in attendance?"

"Not yet. She R.S.V.P.'d, but if she's coming, she'd be more than an hour late."

"Let it play out. If things don't unfold as badly as I think they will, at least she won't leave right away."

Azriel watched the deceitful little vixen wander through the crowd. With each passing second, she looked less and less excited. Up to this point, she'd been all smiles. Giovanni had been right in that she'd not looked like she'd been waiting for a lover. Not once had she looked for anyone during dinner. Instead, she'd happily chatted with her new colleagues, even making new acquaintances. Everyone she met seemed charmed by Lamb. Her grace and beauty were obviously more than skin deep. It made Azriel rethink the plan. If she were innocent, if James Luxemberry had been playing her, Azriel would hurt her even more. For some reason, that made his chest ache and his gut clench.

As he continued to watch, Lamb was skillfully nudged in the direction he'd wanted her to go. His staff was both efficient and skillful at carrying out his instructions. The smirk tugging at his expression couldn't be helped. Cain from Bones often scoffed at him and Alex referring to themselves as president and vice president of the Shadow Demons. They might not ride a fucking Harley, but it wasn't because neither of them could. They simply preferred the faster Suzuki Hayabusa or a Dodge Tomahawk, two of the fastest bikes in the world. Though both Bones and Salvation's Bane would probably scoff at the Shadow Demons, most of the time Azriel preferred speed to muscle. At least, in his choice of bikes. And if the Tomahawk wasn't street legal in the U.S., Azriel was rich enough to either simply pay the fucking fine or buy his way out of it. Whichever suited him in the moment.

He wondered which little Lamb would prefer? The noisy, rattling Harley, or the raw speed and power of a Ninja? It'd be fun to find out, especially if she were an adrenaline junky like him. She'd be so wet by the time he got her home, the sex would be out of this world.

Yeah. Not happening.

Three of his staff serving drinks slid gracefully out of her way and little Lamb came face to face with James Luxemberry. This first look at each other would tell Azriel most of what he needed to know. Namely, were the two in cahoots together or simply lovers who just happened to meet at a bar by a sandy beach? He held his breath.

"Here they go." Giovanni's voice came softly from the earpiece Azriel wore. He, Alexei and Giovanni often worked the ballroom like this. Always Giovanni was at his bank of computer screens with an eye on every corner of the room. Now was no exception.

Lamb was right next to James but her back was to James's side. When the server called out softly to her, offering Lamb another drink, Lamb turned so that she was almost facing James. She declined another drink, but set her empty champagne flute on the tray with a smile and a kind "Thank you." Then she noticed James. Did a double take.

"James?"

The man turned to her, a grin on his face. Until he got a good look at her. Then he froze.

"Ohmigod! James!" Lamb nearly squealed in excitement, throwing herself into his arms.

And Azriel… *saw red.*

* * *

The last person in the world Lamb expected to see tonight was James. She was so surprised and genuinely glad to see him, she forgot where she was or that there were people around them. She hugged him fiercely. "I'm so glad to see you!" Letting him go and pulling back to smile up at him, Lamb continued in a rush. "I thought I'd never see you again! When I left, I forgot to get your number or even an email address." Then she noticed the woman standing next to him who'd sidled closer, slipping her hand around his upper arm.

And her stomach dropped.

She looked from one of them to the other, realizing she'd fucked up royally. Stupid mistake. She should have gotten a feel for the atmosphere before she threw herself at James. Hell, this was a formal party. Throwing oneself at anyone wasn't the proper way to behave in this setting.

"I'm so sorry," Lamb said, backing off and looking down at the floor in embarrassment. "I hope neither of you will be offended. I was just happy to see James and didn't consider he'd be with someone else." She looked at the woman next to him when she spoke. "Please forgive my forwardness."

"You must be an old friend of Robert's," the woman answered. She didn't sound unkind or even angry. Just… cold. Stiff. Almost resigned. As if she'd been through all this before and didn't like it any more now than she had in the past.

"Uh, yes." Lamb shook her head, flustered. "No. Not exactly. We met a few months ago in Key West." She met the woman's gaze, hoping to convey her acceptance that Robert was with another woman. "I apologize for intruding."

"Key West?" She turned sharply to Robert. "You met her in Key West?"

"Miss Newsome was on a holiday she'd rescheduled from spring break. We talked in a bar for a brief period, my love."

The "my love" part made Lamb inhale sharply, something the woman didn't miss. Lamb also was acutely aware he'd reduced their week together to a mere few minutes in a bar.

"Well, Miss Newsome. It's lovely to have met you. I'm Mrs. Rachel Luxemberry. James's wife of ten years."

Lamb wished the floor could open up and swallow her whole. She'd slept with a married man. Not once, but many times over those days in paradise. No wonder he hadn't contacted her. Or given her a way to contact him. At the time, she'd kicked herself for not asking for a way to call him, to keep in touch. Looking back, she realized he'd distracted her every time she'd intended to. As if he'd known what she'd want and had long experience avoiding it.

"I'm so sorry, Mrs. Luxemberry." Finally, Lamb pulled herself together. "I wish I could say I'd heard so much about you, but was unaware James… that is, Mr. Luxemberry, was married. Please accept my sincerest apologies." Without another word, Lamb ducked her head again and retreated. Unsure where exactly she was going, she made it her goal to get out of the ballroom and someplace private where she could regain her composure. Once she was sure she could keep it together, she'd touch base with a few more of her coworkers and her boss, then get the hell out of Dodge.

The next half hour passed in a blur. Lamb made it to the ladies' room quickly and had her breakdown. Ten minutes later, eyes slightly puffy but nothing she couldn't explain away as a pet allergy, she was back out on the floor mingling. Every so often, she'd catch a glimpse of James. Every single time he caught her gaze and held it. The stress was starting to get to her.

Finally, she couldn't take it anymore. Lamb wasn't sure if she'd seen everyone she needed to or done everything she was supposed to, but she absolutely could not take another second. She was making her way out when James intercepted her, gripping her upper arm and bending close to her to whisper at her ear.

"Come with me, honey. We need to talk, and I need to explain things to you."

"I think things are perfectly clear. No need to talk or explain."

"Yes, honey, there is." He pulled her just outside the ballroom into what looked like a small conference room.

"Don't call me *honey*," she snapped. "How could you, James?" Lamb knew she sounded more hurt than angry. She might not love the cheating bastard, but she had developed feelings for him. How could she not? He was her first true lover. The first man she'd had sex with more than a couple of times. It hadn't been fabulous, but it had been fun. "How could you do this to your wife?"

"That's what we need to talk about, baby. Rachel and I have an… understanding. We both take lovers when we need to, but agree to always return to each other." He looked away, the muscles in his jaw clenching and unclenching. "It's an arrangement I've come to question since I met you."

Lamb couldn't believe the nerve of this guy. "Look. I understand that, for whatever reason, you don't feel you did anything wrong. I respect that. This is an arrangement you have with your wife, an arrangement I'm not really sure she believes in, but it's not the same for me. Marriage is sacred. And I hate to be misled."

"Would you have slept with me if I'd told you the truth?"

"No! How could you ever ask me that?"

"Because I wanted you from about five minutes into our conversation. You're bright, funny, and incredibly lovely. You matched me wit for wit. Do you realize how long it's been since I've had a woman keep up with me?"

"Wow. That didn't sound insulting or anything," she muttered. "Look. I can appreciate that men like you and women like your wife are in a situation where it benefits you to be together without really loving each other. Again, I get it. But I'm not like that. I'm not so judgmental as to think I'll never be like that, but I can tell you that I'm not there yet."

"When there is money involved, my lovely little darling, it goes with the territory."

"And I'm not that wealthy. In fact, my net worth is in the negative with all my student loans. I could sell every single thing I own, including my dog, and still not come out ahead. I like you. I enjoyed my time with you. But I will not continue a sexual relationship with you now that I know you're married."

James gave her a conspiratorial look, obviously about to change tactics. "You know, I can help you.

Here. At Argent."

She blinked. Of all the things Lamb was expecting, having James slide into her professional life wasn't even in the ballpark. "I thought you'd retired."

"A man in my position never really retires, Lamb. I still have connections. Even here at Argent. Rush Developments had several contracts with Argent that I personally negotiated. I could put in a good word for you. See to it you have a secure position here after your internship. We could work together to better both companies."

"If I get a job at Argent after my internship, I'll get there on my own merit, Mr. Luxemberry."

"Come on, Lamb. We're too close for you to call me by my last name." The bastard even managed to look hurt.

"I even asked you point blank if you were married! I'm fully aware you never denied it, but you led me to believe you weren't." She shoved her way past him, putting herself between him and the door.

"I'm so sorry, honey," he said, switching back to sweet and sincere mode. "I know it was wrong of me, but I was so taken with you I had to secure you for my own."

"You just said you always came back to your wife! That's your arrangement with her!" God, she wanted to pull her hair out. That was the problem with lies. One tended to forget them. Especially when thinking on the fly. Not to worry, though. He quickly recovered. Lamb wanted to snort in derision.

"I also said I was rethinking that arrangement." He stepped closer to her, prompting Lamb to take a step back. "The two of us could make an unstoppable team. I'd actually come here tonight in the hopes I'd see you." He smiled. "I'd just thought I'd have a chance to explain about Rachel before I saw you."

"It wouldn't have mattered," Lamb said softly, raising her chin. She just kept from wrapping her arms around herself for comfort. That would be a sign of weakness, and she absolutely would not look weak in front of this man. "You're married, Mr. Luxemberry. Any arrangement we might have had would be strictly platonic. Given we've already had sex, that scenario is simply impossible."

Before he could tell her he'd settle for that if it meant having her with him -- nudge-nudge wink-wink -- she raised her hand and continued. "You might be able to get over it, but I can't. Did I expect to ever see you again? No. Did I fall in love with you? Not at all. But I did care for you. I had these fond memories that all came swamping back when I saw you in that ballroom."

Oh, God. She could feel the tears pooling in her eyes. "I know it makes me a fool, but I was actually glad when I saw you in there. I'm sorry I made a scene in front of your wife, but if I'd been prepared, it never would have happened. None of it. And she wouldn't be embarrassed." Lamb knew she was rambling but couldn't help it. She was about to lose her composure and wasn't about to do it in front of this... this... *asshole*! "Now. If you'll excuse me. I've done my duty by my coworkers. I'm leaving."

"Let me at least see you get home, honey." James was actually still acting concerned. Did he think she was going to change her mind?

"I made it all the way from the Keys on my own. I can make it across town." She gave him a cheerful smile she knew didn't make it to her eyes. "It's been lovely, Mr. Luxemberry. I'll do my best to stay out of your way from here on out."

"Don't bet on it, honey. You're the one woman I need more than anyone. I'll change your mind."

Deciding to throw his own words back at him, Lamb gave him a hard glare. "Don't bet on it."

Chapter Three

"She's leaving the conference room," Giovanni said. Azriel adjusted his earpiece once more before rounding the corner. Perfect timing. Lamb hurried out of the room and nearly ran into him. James wasn't far behind her.

"Woah, there," he said as he reached out to steady her. She'd seen him in time to back up with a start, but had trouble keeping her balance in her heels. The dress she wore was a classic black. Simple, but elegant. Her arms were bare, and the contact with her skin nearly made Azriel sink to his knees. "Everything all right here?" Azriel looked up at James and subtly pulled Lamb closer, inhaling deeply of her clean, fresh scent. She let him.

He almost smirked. He doubted she knew who he was. If she did, she'd likely have shown some kind of reaction to him. He was, after all, one of the owners of a trillion-dollar company. Not likely she'd just waltz into his arms with no reaction whatsoever. Which meant the lover's spat he'd set up with Luxemberry had worked. She was moving closer to a man she didn't know instead of going to him for protection or support. It was a win either way. Either way, she was still in his arms, her soft body pressed intimately against his hard one.

"Everything's fine, Mr., er, Azriel." And there was James's attempt to pretend they were good friends. "Lamb and I were just discussing how she loves working here. I'm trying to convince her to come work for Rush when she's finished her internship, but I'm not sure I've managed."

"Given she's running away from you, I'd say you haven't." Azriel let his voice stay light, but inside something ugly was clawing to get free. Something that said no one scared this woman enough that she sought protection from a stranger. When James had said his name, she'd stiffened, and put her hands on his chest, pushing slightly. Azriel didn't let her go, though. In fact, he'd tightened his arms around her just that little bit so she knew he wasn't giving her up so easily.

James shrugged. "I'm afraid I did corner her. But, you have to admit, she's a very intelligent woman and damned good at her job."

Azriel's eyes narrowed just that little bit. "You know what she does here?"

"Here? No. But I know she's very technically minded. One of the brightest engineers in her class. Having looked at recommendations from her professors and the projects she worked on in grad school? Well. Anyone with any sense can see she's going to be a great asset wherever she ends up."

"Of that I have no doubt." He looked down at Lamb. The girl was playing her part well, ducking her head and avoiding eye contact with James like she wanted to be anywhere else, trying to make both men forget she was there. As if that could ever happen. "Are you considering an offer Rush Developments has put on the table, Miss Newsome? One of the agreements you made when you took the internship was that you gave Argent the first contract. If we want you, you have to stay here."

She glanced up sharply at James, her expressive features angry. "I am not. I don't deal with people who lie to me." She shrugged subtly out of Azriel's arms before acknowledging both men. "If you'll excuse me, gentlemen. I have an important meeting tonight."

"But you've not been here very long, Miss

Newsome. Won't you stay and dance? The staff here puts on a fabulous feast for these events." Azriel didn't want her to leave. He knew he needed to let her go, but, Goddammit, he wanted her in his arms! If she stayed, he could romance her. Show her how a woman of his would be treated. Fuck!

"I'm sure they do, Mr. Ivanovich. The hospitality and the food have been wonderful thus far. I appreciate the invitation, but I must decline." As she turned away, Azriel saw the sheen of tears in her eyes. For some reason, those tears were like daggers to his chest.

Azriel wasn't the only one watching her leave. Luxemberry looked like he might try to follow her. Like he wanted to take her away from Azriel's house with *him*. "Not happening," he muttered. "I suggest you either return to the party with your wife or take your leave. Either way, you will not approach Miss Newsome on Argent properties again."

"She's a grown woman, Azriel. She can decide for herself if she wants me or not."

"She already has."

"In any event, she's not your woman."

"Perhaps not, but she's my employee. At Argent, employees are family."

Luxemberry looked like he might argue the point, but, with one last glance at Lamb's retreating form, he shot Azriel an angry look and headed back into the ballroom.

Giovanni didn't need to give instructions to keep anyone in the area from getting too close to Azriel. His staff subtly moved everyone away from them without the guests realizing they were being herded. If people couldn't be maneuvered away and back into the main part of the ballroom, security let know they were too close to an off-limits area. This was Azriel's one shot at a good impression. He had to gain Lamb's trust in this brief window if he intended to turn her into a double agent.

She stood at the end of the driveway. Azriel knew she'd called a cab. He also knew Giovanni had canceled it the second she'd hung up. As he approached her, he noticed she was hugging herself. Also, that her slim shoulders were shaking. Crying?

"Miss Newsome," he said as he approached her from behind. "Is everything all right?"

She sniffed and hastily wiped her eyes with the back of her hand. "You asked that before."

"You didn't answer. When I ask a question, I require an answer. Little Lamb."

Her eyes narrowed, but she was still visibly trying to get herself together. "Yes. Everything's fine."

"Hmmm," he said, drawing out the word. "I'm a bachelor, so I admit I could be wrong, but from my observation of women, when they say everything is 'fine,' it usually means things are in no way 'fine.'" That got a twitch of her lips, but nothing else. "If you talk to me, I promise if I can't make it all better, I can at least shoot someone. Might not right a wrong, but it can be greatly satisfying." That got him a surprised laugh, though he had actually been serious.

"Really. Any problems I have are of my own making. I'd prefer you not shoot me."

"Now, that I can promise." He held out his hand for her. "Let me take you home. I don't want you leaving by yourself when you're upset."

Lamb gave him a startled glance before her gaze skittered away. "I appreciate the offer, but I've already called a cab."

"Nonsense. Cabs can take forever, even in this

neighborhood."

"I won't impose on you, Mr. Ivanovich. I'm a big girl. I can take care of myself."

He nodded his head. "I wouldn't imagine it would be otherwise. But I'm a bit old-fashioned in some ways, I guess. I have a need to make sure every member of my family is safe and cared for."

"I'm not a family member," she said, an adorably confused look on her face.

"You're an Argent employee, are you not?"

"Well, yeah. At least, I'm an intern."

He shrugged. "Same difference. At Argent, we are all family. Alexei, Giovanni, and I see it as our duty to protect every single person working with us. Their spouses and children as well. It's something you should think about before you consider an offer from Rush. There's a reason Argent Technologies has one of the lowest turnover rates of any company out there. We only hire the best, but we also only hire people who work well with us and have the capacity to care for their coworkers."

Azriel couldn't help himself. He raised his hand to stroke her jaw. She sucked in a breath, but didn't move away from him. "At one time or other, all three of us have been on our own. We swore first to ourselves, then to each other, that when we found a family, we'd protect them to the death. As we built Argent, we decided that was the kind of relationship we wanted among everyone who worked with us. We're all family. If someone is hurting, we help make it better. As head of the family, the three of us expect to know when there is trouble with anyone under our care."

"Sounds a little out there," she said quietly. She looked like she wanted to believe it but didn't dare.

"It's true. Ask anyone you work with. Anyone. A chemist. A physicist. A janitor, or a maid in my home. Everyone has a role to play, and we all have each other's backs."

She cleared her throat and made one more delicate swipe at the corner of her eye with her finger. "I can appreciate that, Mr. Ivanovich. Hopefully, I'll have the opportunity to belong that tightly to your family."

"Keep working as hard and as well as you have been the last couple of months, and you will, my sweet." He grinned down at her. "Now. If you won't let me take you home, I'll simply have a car take you." He tapped something on his watch. A few seconds later, a Rolls-Royce pulled up to the gate.

"Wow," she said. Azriel smiled.

"Rolls-Royce Phantom," he said. "One of the most luxurious cars in the world."

"Wow," she repeated. He chuckled as the driver got out and stepped around to open the door for her. "Sean, my driver, will take you anywhere you want to go and wait for you until he drops you safely off at your home. Anything you want, you tell him. He'll take care of it on my behalf."

She looked at him for a long moment. "You realize I just want to go home. Right?"

"I do. However, if there is anything you need on the way, I'm making sure you have it. Even if it's just a quart of Ben and Jerry's."

Once again, she giggled. God, he was in trouble. Was there anything he wouldn't do, anything he wouldn't endure just to hear that sound from her? Given that he was pretty sure she was an industrial spy, that was not a good position for him to be in.

He guided her to the car, his hand at the small of

her back. She turned abruptly and stumbled. Azriel caught her, wrapping his arms around her for the second time that night. This time, however, he had a better hold on her, and his grip was tight by necessity. She looked up into his eyes, her own wide and round. Electricity seemed to arc between them. Everything protective and possessive in Azriel rose up, trying to be unleashed. This was his woman. In that moment, he knew he had to have her. Not just for a few hours. He wanted to take his time with this one. Days at least. More likely weeks. Or months. Or *years*.

Finally, he relaxed his hold slightly. She took a shaky breath and pushed slightly at his chest once he'd given a sign he would let her loose.

"I appreciate it, Mr. Ivanovich." Her voice was shaky. She cleared her throat delicately.

"Azriel," he said as he helped her into the car.

"Family. Right. Somehow, I doubt everyone calls you Azriel."

"You'd be right," he conceded. "With you, however, I find I'd prefer to be a little less formal."

Just like that, she shut down. Giving him a tight smile, she said, "I appreciate that, Mr. Ivanovich. But it's just not appropriate."

Azriel tried not to wince and nodded. "Understood. Before you go, however," he held out his hand. When she looked at it, a lovely confused look on her face, he smiled. "Your phone, please, Miss Newsome." She hesitated, but shrugged and handed it to him. She didn't have the latest phone out there. In fact, it was an off brand she probably used with a no-contract plan. Azriel quickly figured out how to operate the thing. "I just sent myself a text. Which means you have my phone number." He pulled out his phone and showed her the screen which showed a text message to him from her number. "I expect you to use that number if you need anything. Do you understand me?"

"Not really, but whatever," she muttered.

Instead of insulting her by explaining himself, he simply smiled. "Have a good evening, Miss Newsome. If you lose my phone number, I'll be exceedingly displeased." As he shut the door, Azriel decided it was time for him to really delve into Lamb's background. If she was working with Luxemberry, wouldn't he have seen to it she had a phone with encrypted security or something? He'd surely want her to have something capable of capturing more high-resolution images if necessary. One thing was for sure, Azriel wanted to make fucking sure she was what he thought she was. If she was innocent, he was in a world of shit. The last thing he wanted to do was hurt someone who wasn't deserving. Especially not a woman. Especially not a woman who seemed as sweet and innocent as little Lamb Newsome.

* * *

Lamb tried to get Sean to drop her off at the end of the block from her house. It wasn't so much that she didn't want the man reporting back to Azriel where she lived -- he probably already knew. She didn't want her neighbors thinking she had money, because she was sure she'd have a break-in soon after, and the few things she did have, she wanted to keep. Finally, she just broke down and told him. The man hadn't been happy about that, but had agreed with the provision she allowed him to see her home.

"Mr. Ivanovich won't be pleased if I don't see you safely inside with the door locked."

"Mr. Ivanovich might be my boss, but he's not my keeper," she retorted.

Sean only grinned. "No. But he's my boss, too, and part of my job tonight is making sure you get home safely. Are you trying to get me fired?"

She sighed, frustrated because she knew he had her. "Fine. Just try not to look too much like you work for a billionaire. I'd rather not have anyone sniffing around just in case they think I've acquired a rich boyfriend."

"You know I have to report your concerns about a break in. Right?"

"Oh, please. Like Ivanovich doesn't know where I live. I seriously doubt there is an employee of his anywhere he doesn't know exactly where they are at, what they are doing, and what their plans are for the rest of the week."

"Picked up on that, did you?"

"Wasn't hard."

They walked the block to her apartment at a brisk clip. She'd secured the place soon after returning from the Keys. She unlocked the door before turning to Sean. "Thanks for the escort." She smiled. "I'd invite you in, but you really should get that car out of this neighborhood."

Sean smirked. "You're not wrong, but I promise you, no one will touch that car."

"I suppose it could only belong to one of three people, huh?"

"Well, there are several people at Argent who could afford that car, but the point is, they'd know it was someone who worked at Argent. There are very few people in this city who would chance the wrath of anyone associated with Argent."

That startled her. "Are they bullies? Doesn't sound like they're very well thought of in town."

"On the contrary. Most people in the city love

them. Argent has brought much needed employment to this city. It's thriving under its influence. But Argent Tech is a worldwide deal. As such they have added security measures. For the everyday things, they bring in some friends from out of state. They're often rough-looking, but they are all highly trained military types. They form two clubs. MCs. One from Palm Beach, Florida. The other from Somerset, Kentucky."

"MCs." She thought for a moment. "Motorcycle clubs?"

"Exactly." He smiled at her.

"Seems kind of a ghetto solution when they're so rich."

"You're overlooking the highly trained military-type thing. There's a paramilitary organization that specializes in security details both domestic and foreign. You've been here long enough you might recognize the name. Ever hear of a company called ExFil?"

Lamb thought for a moment. "Sounds familiar. Weren't they involved with something in Rockwell a month or so before Christmas?"

"Yes. They were. ExFil and Argent work closely together and often help each other out when one of the two companies, or any of the associated MCs, is in need. Not sure, but I think the owners are old military buddies. I know the clubs are called Bones and Salvation's Bane, and that there is a whisper the bosses might work even closer with a group called the Shadow Demons."

Lamb's eyes grew wide. "You mean, that's a real thing? The Shadow Demons?"

"It is."

"I've heard people talking about them. Some say they're vigilantes, others say they're the saviors of the city. All sounds very Dark Knight-esque."

Sean chuckled. "I don't know about that, but I know they guard Argent and every person working for them zealously. I also know more than one person has died when they crossed the Demons."

"Well, they sound like a mixed bag."

"They are. My advice is to keep your nose clean. Don't talk about your work at Argent unless you've been given specific permission."

That was odd. Lamb cocked her head to the side, trying to puzzle out his words. "That was in my NDA. I signed it long before I actually got here. I was allowed to make known I had an internship, but not to discuss anything I did for the company."

"Look. I like you, Miss Newsome. I've watched you interact with other team members, and you're a good influence on everyone. You make people around you smile. I just don't want to see you get hurt."

She sucked in a breath, suddenly not feeling safe. "Are you threatening me?"

"No," Sean said immediately. "Not at all, and I don't want you to take it that way. It's just that James Luxemberry works for a rival company who's tried on more than one occasion to get entry into Argent Technologies. He'd taken an interest in you even before you officially started with us."

"You have no reason to worry about Mr. Luxemberry. Certainly not about me revealing any secrets to him."

"Good. I know you were seen at the party with him. I just wanted you to know he's bad news around here."

"Bad news here, too," she muttered. "You can tell your bosses no worries here." She smiled brightly, but she was on the verge of tears again. Could this day get any worse? James had hinted at them being a team. What did he mean by that? Did she even want to know? "Thank you again. Have a good evening." With that, she shut the door and turned both deadbolts before latching the chain in place.

What a fucking night!

Chapter Four

"Is there a problem, Azriel?"

That was a loaded question if ever there was one. Azriel glanced at the man they all knew as El Diablo. He was the president of an MC called Black Reign out of Lake Worth, Florida. He was also one of the world's most successful assassins. While Azriel was more comfortable dealing with Bones and Alexei's longtime friend Cain, Azriel liked keeping El Diablo close. He and Azriel had belonged to the same organization years earlier, and both men were still trying to feel each other out. It was possible El Diablo was trying to keep as low a profile as Azriel was, but there was always the possibility the assassin had been activated to kill Azriel. If so, he'd prefer to know where the other man was.

Enlisting his help had served both to track him and to establish a rapport with him. Alexei had been hesitant, at first, but it was Azriel who knew the Brotherhood best. If El Diablo was still actively working for them, Azriel would be able to tell. Hopefully before it was too late. He debated how much to tell El Diablo, but, in the end, making sure the man had all the information he could give him about the situation was the best choice.

"How sure are you the girl's aware of what's going on?"

El Diablo shrugged. "Hard to say. I've been focused more on Luxemberry. He's the threat to your company. The girl is simply a naïve sideshow interested in a wealthy man."

A surge of anger flooded Azriel he had to tamp down. Getting emotional with El Diablo would simply be seen as a sign of weakness. "But is she an *innocent* sideshow?"

Again, the other man shrugged. "As innocent as any woman sleeping with a married man, I suppose."

"I need more information." Azriel studied the readout of Lamb's movements throughout the facility. She never ventured into an area she wasn't working in, and she never asked for information or access to projects outside her own. If it weren't for the specter of James Luxemberry and his desire to get a piece of Argent, Azriel would have admired the thoroughness of her work, and her overall work ethic. The girl threw herself into the projects she was assigned to, contributing as much as, or more than, anyone in the company.

"Always a good idea. You should be certain before you strike." No one knew that better than El Diablo. His strikes were life-and-death decisions. If he was wrong, an innocent perished.

"Something just doesn't feel right."

"I'll have my men watch her more closely. I'm also putting a man on Luxemberry's wife. The person who knows a man best is usually his wife."

"Good idea. I want to know if Miss Newsome meets or talks with Luxemberry. Record every conversation you can. If they so much as meet up in a parking lot, I want to know about it."

"That's what we're here for. Though, I think perhaps it's time to more aggressively approach Miss Newsome. Since she's hesitant about letting you get close due to your position as an owner of the company, perhaps I could step into that role?" The bastard gave Azriel a smug, superior look as if he just knew he could get the girl to fall head-over-heels in love with him by the end of the week.

"No," Azriel answered. He knew he'd shown his

hand by answering so quickly, but the word seemed to be pulled from him against his will. "If anyone's doing this, it will be me. I can convince her. If she's really spying for Luxemberry, it won't take much. All of that before could have just been her playing hard to get."

El Diablo smiled. "Of course. This is your show."

"Damned straight," Azriel muttered.

* * *

The next couple of weeks passed in frustration for Azriel. For more than one reason. James had attempted to meet Lamb on more than one occasion. The first time she had been startled and flustered until he tried to put his arm around her. She'd shut him down hard, looking as angry as any woman he'd ever seen. This time, there were no tears, only genuine anger. If Lamb thought she'd been getting her a sugar daddy, it might explain her anger at that first meeting after the New Year's party, but when it continued and she made no effort to throw him a bone, Azriel began to suspect there was more to her feelings.

Which was when he decided it was time to accidentally run into her again. He chose the city park. There was always an outdoor ice-skating rink set up around the public fountain. During fair-weather days in the winter, the place was always packed with people wanting a day outside with fun and socializing. There were hot chocolate stands, a coffee bar, places selling baked goods as well as soups and chili. It was a gathering place for the entire city, all of it free, provided by the Shadow Demons. It was a fact no one knew. They preferred to keep that bit of information quiet because, really, it was no one's business. It was a way of giving back to the community in a way everyone could enjoy. Their estate manager, Ruth McDonald, took care of the planning every year, and no one had ever figured out who was behind it. Only that it had become a treasured season in Rockwell.

Azriel found Lamb quietly sipping a cup of hot chocolate as she watched people skating around the rink. There was a soft little smile on her face, and, as he approached her, Azriel could hear her humming softly with the music.

"Fancy meeting you here," he said, grinning at Lamb as he sat next to her on the bench. She immediately stiffened in surprise, her mouth making a little "O."

"Mr. Ivanovich! I -- what are you doing here?"

He couldn't suppress his chuckle. "Same as you, I suppose. Enjoying the merriment." He pointed to her cup. "Best hot chocolate in the world."

That got her to grin. "I'll say. I've never tasted anything so decadent."

"Did you get the Milky Way hot chocolate?" Azriel leaned closer and sniffed, referring to the drink famous in the area, which was a hot chocolate with caramel sauce. A drink guaranteed to warm the coldest reveler.

"Oh, yeah." She took a sip, eyeing him over the rim of her cup, as if afraid he'd try to take it from her. "So you should get your own, 'cause, if you've had it, you know I ain't sharing."

That got a startled laugh out of him. The sound got them more attention that he'd have liked, but then he noticed James Luxemberry off in the background, watching them intently. Perfect. He was paying attention.

"You don't want to share, I suggest you hold tight to that cup."

In response, she raised an eyebrow and downed the rest in three large gulps. Giving a loud, gasp she wiped her mouth with the back of her gloved hand. "Try to take it *now*."

Even if he hadn't been observed by Luxemberry, Azriel would have laughed just as hard. The woman was priceless. "I take it you approve?"

"Who wouldn't?"

"Good point."

She stared at him a moment, then, just like that, she shut down. The light banter they'd shared for a few seconds was gone in the space of a few heartbeats. Lamb sighed, setting her cup on the ground by her feet. "What can I do for you, Mr. Ivanovich?"

"Why do you have to assume I need something from you?"

"Because I believe we decided you were my boss, and it wasn't appropriate for us to socialize."

"Hmm… Don't remember that in our only conversation. Since you didn't call or text me, I know we only had one conversation." He tried to make it both a reminder and a soft reprimand.

"Maybe the conversation was in my head, then," she said softly, looking away from him. The woman looked sad. It physically hurt Azriel to see her like this. Why did he care? She was likely betraying him. His brothers. If she was an industrial spy, they'd kill her without hesitation. Argent was theirs. The Shadow Demons wouldn't exist without Argent Tech. He, Azriel, and Giovanni had dedicated most of their adult lives to making the Shadow Demons a reality. *No one* was going to take that away from them.

"Look at me, Lamb." Even though he knew it was a bad idea, Azriel was about to do something he couldn't take back. Something that, once she found out, Lamb would never forgive him for. She stiffened, but finally sighed and turned her head. "You're a beautiful woman. You're also one of the most intelligent people I've ever met. The combination has me fiercely attracted to you."

Before she could do or say anything, Azriel leaned in to press his lips softly to hers. It was just a simple, chaste kiss, one meant only to show affection. Interest. The second his mouth touched hers, however, Azriel had to fight to stay in control. In that moment, he realized he'd never wanted a woman so badly in his life. For a man like him, someone who could have any woman he wanted, that was saying something. Maybe it was her innocence. Maybe her intelligence. Azriel thought it might be both, plus the fact that she didn't take shit she didn't want to take.

Which was another thing. As he continued to gently move his lips against hers, just getting a feel for her and enjoying the taste of her sweet lips combined with the lingering chocolate, caramel, and whipped cream, she didn't fight him. In fact, her little fingers curled in the material of his jacket before he finally ended the kiss slowly and with great care.

"You… are exquisite, Lamb. In every single way that a woman can be attractive to a man, you are for me."

She sucked in a breath, her eyes going wide. "Don't say that."

"Why?"

Lamb shook her head, closing her eyes tightly before opening them. When she looked at him this time, her gaze was hard, her facial features tight. "Because men like you use women like me until you've taken everything we have to give. Then you throw the tattered remains of our hearts in the trash to be carted off with the rest of the garbage." She probably tried to sound bitter, and she almost succeeded. Instead, Azriel heard a sadness and real hurt in her voice.

"Tell me what happened to you, Lamb. Who hurt you so badly you won't take a chance on a rich, good-looking, nice guy." He grinned, trying to lighten the mood without changing the subject. This was the information he needed. If she was looking for an in, he was handing it to her.

"Does it really matter? Tell me I'm wrong, and I'll take that chance."

He wanted to lie to her. To tell her he only wanted to get to know her better, but, though Azriel wasn't above lying, he didn't like the idea of lying to Lamb. She'd said she didn't like being deceived, and he believed her. He might betray her trust in the most horrible way, but he was going to try to be as gentle as he could. And not outright lie to her.

"You're not wrong. Doesn't mean you're right about me. Just means I need to work harder to earn your trust."

She picked up her cup and stood. "Don't waste your time, Mr. Ivanovich. I'm not interested."

Without another word, Lamb Newsome walked away from him. Azriel wanted to follow, but movement from the left caught his eye. Luxemberry. He was on a line to intercept her.

"You got eyes on Luxemberry?"

"Two of them." Giovanni's voice was strong but quiet in his ear. "She's spotted him and isn't happy."

"Have the feed cued up when I get back. I want to know everything that was said. Every facial expression on both of them."

"On it. El Diablo's got four men from Black Reign on them. Two on each of them."

"Good. They need to make sure Miss Newsome is safe. If Luxemberry feels threatened, or like she won't cooperate with him, he could try to harm her."

"My men know their job." Apparently, El Diablo was listening as well.

"Who invited you to the party?" Azriel didn't like anyone being in on the technical side of an operation. Some of the equipment they used was highly sensitive, and he didn't want anyone -- especially someone like El Diablo -- getting the idea they could have access to their equipment or computer software.

"I invited myself," he said without hesitation. "Unlike Cain or Thorn, I won't allow my men to sit in the dark waiting for someone else to hand down their orders. Our arrangement requires a certain amount of trust, but not that level. My men take their instructions from me. I make those orders based on what I want for their safety. That means I have to have all the information you do. Which means I'll be in on every single communication and meeting that involves my men."

Azriel wanted to tell the man to fuck off, but Alexei was right. They needed him and his unique expertise. "Fine, just stay off the fucking radio."

Chapter Five

When Lamb had taken this internship two months before, she imagined working long hours and late nights, with little food or rest. Now, after her little encounter with Mr. Ivanovich, she found herself being pulled off projects nearly every single day by either Azriel himself or someone running messages for Mr. Luxemberry. It was both humiliating and maddening. Azriel had always come himself, seeming not to care if anyone saw them together or not. She'd begun to get knowing looks from the other employees. No one smirked at her or in any way made her feel like they thought she was trying to gain favor by seducing the boss, but Lamb couldn't imagine any of them *not* thinking along those lines.

James, on the other hand, never approached her on company property. It wasn't unusual. He wasn't an employee of Argent Tech, as such he didn't have direct access to the campus. Instead, he'd send co-workers with messages for her to call him. Sometimes he'd call her both on her office phone and her personal cell. She had no idea how he'd gotten the number, but she'd finally had to block his number. Which he soon figured out and started using a different phone. The number she'd blocked had always shown "unknown caller," while the one he currently used had his name on the caller ID.

More than once over the following weeks, James had shown up at a restaurant she was eating at, or at her car when she was leaving work. He even showed up at the little house she'd rented when she'd first moved to Rockwell. That had been the height of embarrassment. She could tell by the disgusted look on his face he hadn't been impressed with her choice of residence. The ensuing conversation hadn't been fun. As a rule, Lamb hated confrontation, but it seemed like she was doing a lot of it lately.

She sat at a table by herself in the employee dining room in her building on the Argent campus. It was more like an upscale restaurant, but she hadn't been able to enjoy it much. If she wasn't working, one of James's flunkies was always in her space.

Speaking of the Devil, she'd just given the server her order when she spotted James coming toward her, a huge shark-like grin on his too handsome face. Where in the Keys she'd found his features pleasing, now she saw them as bait. He was obviously a predator and, for whatever reason, had put her in his sights. Lamb just suppressed a groan and resisted dropping her head into her hands.

"Lamb, my love! I'm so glad I found you here." His voice seemed to echo across the expanse of the dining room. Lamb wanted to grind her teeth in frustration. She couldn't resist clenching her fists for several seconds.

"What do you want, Mr. Luxemberry?" She used his last name purposefully, trying to keep things professional when she really wanted to slap his face. Or kick him in the balls. Either would work.

He gave her a mildly hurt look. "Now, why would I have to want something from you just to visit?"

"Because we're not friends? Because it doesn't really matter what you want, I'm not giving you anything, and I'm pretty sure you know it?"

"Now, sweetheart." He lowered his voice to a caressing murmur, leaning in close to make it look like he was keeping it private when Lamb was certain everyone around them heard his remarks. "Is that any way to talk to the man you spent nearly a week with in the Keys? Of course, if you're ready to turn our vanilla lovemaking into something a little more... aggressive, I'm into that as well."

Lamb wanted to vomit. More than one of the people in the area turned to look at them. At least a couple had disapproving looks on their faces.

"Mr. Luxemberry," she said, placing her hands on the table and standing. "I've been very clear when I told you, had I known you were married, that week would have never happened. I don't appreciate being lied to, and I certainly don't appreciate you trying to manipulate me into taking this discussion private. I'm not sure how you got in here, but this area is for employees only."

"Please sit down, sweetheart," he cajoled. "You'll only make a scene, and I'm sure you don't want to do that until you've gotten a permanent position."

The bastard was right, but if she gave in now, she knew it would be more than a small retreat. He'd jump in and take more ground than she was willing to give. Looking around her, however, she realized she didn't have much of an option. At least, not right now. She'd talk to her supervisor when she got back to work. Maybe she'd have a recommendation.

She sat, but kept her hands from the table so he couldn't reach across and touch her. "Fine," she said, raising an eyebrow. "I'm sitting."

He smiled again, obviously pleased with himself. "I'm so proud of you for making the right decision."

"Never said it was the right decision, Mr. Luxemberry. In my view, I simply had no alternative."

He nodded at her once, conceding the point without actually saying so. "I thought we might talk a little. I know you're upset I didn't explain things more clearly for you, but I assure you, I meant no disrespect." He looked expectantly at her, apparently waiting for a response. When none came, he cleared his throat, clearly not knowing what to do with her when she wouldn't rise to his bait. "I, uh, thought we might go out to dinner tonight. Discuss your objections to our arrangement. I'm sure we can find a compromise or a solution we can work toward."

"Not following." Lamb made her tone as clipped and terse as she could.

"You know. We can talk about our arrangement and make plans to make it a more permanent situation. I've been wanting to discuss it with you since the party, but you've been avoiding me."

"We have no arrangement, Mr. Luxemberry. Anything we had ended in the Keys. And if I've been avoiding you, it's because I don't want to encourage your behavior. I'm not interested in anything to do with you. Period."

"You didn't think so when you jumped into my arms at the party." Yeah. He'd jumped all over that. "In fact, I believe you were happy to continue our relationship."

"I'm not too proud to admit that I was, Mr. Luxemberry," she said softly. "But it never would have gotten as far as it did if I'd known you were married, or even had someone you were seeing seriously. I don't encroach on other women's territory."

"Just have dinner with me, Lamb. I don't want to lose you."

"That ship's sailed. I don't date married men, and I don't date men who lie to me." As she spoke, the server brought her order. She also carried a to-go box in her hand, raising her eyebrow without saying anything. Lamb nodded. She would definitely be taking her lunch to go. The server didn't stop at the table. She just continued past them and took Lamb's lunch back to the kitchen to pack. Lamb pulled out a twenty and another ten, intending for the woman to keep the extra as a generous tip for reading the situation correctly.

"Come on, Lamb. It's just dinner." Then he sat up straighter. "Or, I have a better idea. Why not come away with me. Back to the Keys. I have a private jet. We could leave after you get off work Friday."

"Are you out of your mind?" Lamb was becoming desperate. If the server didn't hurry, she was leaving without her food. "I'm not going to dinner with you. I'm definitely not going away for the weekend with you." As if she'd read her mind, the server appeared once again.

"Here you go, ma'am." She smiled warmly at Lamb, setting the food packaged in the box and a sack for ease of carrying. "I hope you have a wonderful rest of the day." The drink was in a reusable insulated Argent Tech cup with a spill-proof lid. The cup probably cost more than the meal. Shit. Lamb hoped she had enough money out. The last thing she wanted was for James to try to pay for her lunch. She glanced around looking for the check. When she didn't see it, she simply handed the thirty dollars to the woman. "Oh, no, ma'am. Your meal is already covered. The tip as well."

She glanced at James, who was frowning. "I --"

"Mr. Ivanovich. We have instructions any time you order."

"I -- what?"

James scowled. "Bastard," he muttered. Which made Lamb nearly lightheaded with relief. That was her way out. At least, for the moment.

"Please send my gratitude to Mr. Ivanovich. That was very thoughtful of him."

The server smiled brightly. "He comes across gruff sometimes, but he and the other bosses are very generous with everyone working for them."

"Thank you --" She glanced at the girl's name tag. "-- Maria. And thank you for packing this to go. I have so much to finish today." Lamb stood, turning her attention back to James. "Mr. Luxemberry, this is my workplace. Please don't approach me here again."

"If you call security, Benedict and Sebastian will make sure to divert any guest you're not able to accommodate during working hours." Maria had phrased it so as not to offend, and Lamb appreciated it. When she made that call, she'd be sure to let them know she was being harassed.

"Come on, sweetheart," James cajoled. "Don't try to keep me away from you out of spite. I think you want me as much as I want you. You're just angry that I didn't disclose everything to you."

"Please don't contact me again, Mr. Luxemberry."

"You know I can't promise that, my love."

The endearment she'd overlooked at first now made her cringe. "You called your wife that. Perhaps you shouldn't address other women that way."

"I told you, we have an arrangement. "

"And I told you I didn't care. I don't willingly sleep with married men. Ever."

He moved around the table to stand in front of her. Out of the corner of her eye, Lamb saw Maria texting on her phone. The young woman hadn't moved from her spot next to Lamb and Luxemberry.

"You seemed pretty willing in the Keys. *And* at the party." He took another step forward into her personal space. When she would have stepped back, he gripped her upper arm and pulled her closer to him. Lamb glanced around, mortified at the number of people witnessing this. She recognized a man from the weekly department meeting advancing on them. He was older with stark white hair and piercing blue eyes. If she remembered correctly, he was the department manager. Great. She'd probably be fired now. "All I'm asking for is a couple hours of your time. I think we can work something out between us. And I have a business proposition for you."

"If you'll excuse me," the older man said as he moved beside Lamb, then gently inserted himself between her and James. "It looks as if the lady isn't appreciative of your company, sir. This area is for employees only. If you're new and simply weren't aware of it, name tags are to be worn at all times. May I see your Argent I.D. card?"

James straightened himself, standing his full six-foot height. "I'm not an employee here, but I do enough business with Alexei that I'm granted full access to the facility."

The man stuck out his hand. "Grayson. Lucas Grayson. I'm head of the physics research department. I'm afraid we haven't been introduced."

James took the man's hand automatically. When he did, he winced slightly, but didn't pull back his hand. "We haven't been introduced because we are in no way equals in the corporate hierarchy."

"More likely," Lucas said, his eyes narrowing, still gripping the other man's hand, "we haven't been introduced because you're not supposed to be here. No one has free access to this facility without an escort from one of the bosses." Lucas still didn't let go of his hand. James's eyes narrowed and he shook his head.

He tried to shake Lucas free, but the other man held on fast.

"Wha' the 'ell?" James sounded like he was drunk, his words slurring.

"We don't like intruders here," Lucas said, continuing to squeeze his hand. "I'm not sure who let you in, but rest assured, they won't be in a position to do so again."

Moments later, there were three security personnel and someone from medical hurrying to James. Just in time, too, because his legs gave out and he crumpled. Thankfully, the security personnel caught him and eased him onto the floor. Almost before he hit the floor, two more men from medical entered with a stretcher and placed James on it to roll him away. They weren't at all cruel or disrespectful, and no one in the area seemed to mind. In fact, more than one of them gave a satisfied nod as they watched him being carted out.

"What happened?" Lamb didn't particularly care if James was all right or not, but she didn't like secrets. From the work she was doing here, she was beginning to suspect this place was full of them.

"Just a little tranquilizer," Lucas said, holding up a small ring with what looked like a tiny injector on the inside. "He'll be fine." The older man smiled at her kindly. "We don't like intruders. A few of us are given the means to be rid of them in the event someone like Mr. Luxemberry here manages to get into a common area."

"Could this day get any worse?" she muttered to herself.

"I do apologize, Miss Newsome," Lucas said, looking for all the world as if he truly was sorry she'd had to endure this. "Sebastian and Benedict, our heads of security, are on this. Has Mr. Luxemberry ever approached you here before?"

"Not here. But he's had messages delivered and he's called me." She felt like a tattletale.

"Both are simply unacceptable," Lucas said. "If you wanted the interaction, the messages and phone calls are one thing. But, it's obvious to me that wasn't your wish."

"Absolutely not," she said without hesitation. "I'm so sorry to cause such a ruckus. And this mess?" She referred to what had just happened. "I can't express how sorry I am."

"There's nothing for you to apologize for," Lucas said. "None of this is your fault."

She shook her head. "I do have a responsibility in this," she said quietly. "He and I spent time together several months ago before I realized he was married." Lamb couldn't help the tears that threatened to fall. One did, making an accusing track down her cheek. Angrily, she wiped it away. "When I saw him at the party a few weeks ago, I was happy to see him. I was the one to break things off, and I'm sure that's part of the problem."

"Ah, I see." The older man looked all too much like he did understand. "The fragile male ego."

She shrugged. "I don't know for sure. It seems unlikely, but I can't imagine what other reason he'd have for continuing to pursue me. If I gave in to him and let him be the one to break things off…"

"That's unlikely to happen, Miss Newsome. You're a lovely woman, and James Luxemberry is known to have a thing for young, beautiful women." Lucas shook his head. "No. If you gave in to him, he'd never call an end to it."

"Call an end to what?"

Yep. This day could get worse. Striding in with two of the biggest men Lamb had ever seen was Azriel Ivanovich. Where before when she'd seen him, he looked good but sedate in his expensive suit, this man was the powerful corporate billionaire in the flesh.

"Miss Newsome was just telling me she's afraid Mr. Luxemberry had fixated on her because she was the one to break off their interaction." Thankfully, Lucas didn't stumble over his wording. The man must have had experience phrasing things delicately. "She was pondering whether or not she should give in to him and let him be the one to end things."

"Lamb." Azriel turned to her, reaching for her. For some reason, her stupid hand found his, and she let his fingers close around it. Instantly, a shiver of awareness flooded her body. She wanted to crumple into tears and throw herself at Azriel, to let those strong arms hold her again. It had felt so good before, a heady combination of safety and acute desire. Just being near him with his attention focused on her made her stomach flutter. Had she thought she'd been attracted to James? The sensations she felt when Azriel touched her or spoke to her like he actually cared about her made anything she'd thought she felt for James feel tepid in comparison. "James Luxemberry is a swine. Don't cater to his needs. Remember our conversation before? He's *that* man. Giving in to him would be the worst mistake you've ever made."

"Can't argue with that," she said, ducking her head, trying to tug her hand free. He didn't let her. "On any account."

"Why not get your lunch and come with me? We'll find a quiet, tranquil place for you to eat and let your stomach settle."

She looked at him for a long moment. He was

putting nearly as much pressure on her as James was. Why, all of a sudden, did she have two handsome, rich men vying for her attention? Something didn't add up. Sure, she was young, intelligent, and passingly pretty, but there was more going on than met the eye, and she was smart enough to know it.

Lamb nodded. She didn't necessarily want to go with Azriel, but she didn't want to do anything more in public. While no one was standing around gawking, Lamb hated being the center of attention. The potential for ridicule was high in this situation. If she managed to score a full-time position, there would be many who thought she got there by screwing the boss.

Feeling a profound sense of defeat, Lamb went with Azriel willingly. He addressed the server. "Have her lunch made fresh and billed to me. Deliver it to my office. Add a hundred-percent tip to both you and Constance. She'll no doubt wonder why she's been asked to make the same dish twice. I don't want her thinking Lamb didn't enjoy her creations."

"At once, Mr. Ivanovich." When the woman hesitated instead of going about her duties, Azriel tilted his head quizzically. "Is there something else, Maria?"

Maria glanced at Lamb, then seemed to make up her mind about something. "Miss Newsome is very loyal to Argent, sir. I've heard the others talk about how hard she works and is never in areas she shouldn't be. She never talks about her projects over lunch and when others do, she leaves." She gave Lamb a small smile. "I just thought you should know."

That was odd. Had someone accused her of going against the NDA she'd signed? Wouldn't surprise her, the way this day had gone.

"Thank you for supporting Miss Newsome,

Maria. It's a testament to her character -- and yours --
that you felt the need to say something positive.
Especially in that regard since everyone knows how
important secrecy about our projects is to me and my
associates." Pretty words, but Lamb noticed he didn't
reassure either her or Maria that he knew she hadn't
broken the contract. "Now, Miss Newsome. Let's go
someplace more private." He dropped her hand to
place his arm around her shoulders. For some reason,
she let him. In one heroic moment, Azriel had inserted
himself publicly into her life, and she hadn't done a
thing to stop him. Instead, she went willingly as he led
her from the dining room to his office.

Chapter Six

Azriel knew things weren't going to go well if he didn't come clean soon. He had to find out if Luxemberry had delved to get information from Lamb, and if she'd wittingly or otherwise given away any hint as to what she'd seen or worked on while at Argent. He was damned close to throwing caution to the wind and just asking her, but he'd already fucked up once when he'd kissed her. If she was a traitor to Argent and he showed his hand, they would lose all the groundwork they'd laid with Luxemberry and fucking Rush Developments.

He kept possession of her hand until he shut and locked the door to his office firmly behind him. He didn't have to tell his assistant he wasn't to be disturbed. He never took women into his office, so he hoped it looked like he was angry with Lamb and intended a dressing down in private. While he had no intention of having sex with his little Lamb now, he did intend to secure her presence with him for the weekend. After that, he'd make sure she never wanted to leave him. Then he'd work out how to tell her about his role in this. With luck, she'd never have to know.

Once she was safely inside his office, he locked the door, taking a much-needed calming breath. "Have a seat." He didn't turn around just yet. Looking at her now might be his undoing.

"Why are we here?" Lamb's voice quivered a little, but he heard her clothes rustle and the couch settle as she sat on the soft leather.

"You and I need to talk." He should just lay it all out for her right here. Tell her about Luxemberry's desire to take over Argent and that he was trying to use her to do it. Instead he found himself unwilling to divulge company intrigue to someone not in the inner circle.

"I'm sorry about the scene in the dining room. I didn't know Mr. Luxemberry would be there."

He waved it away. "That's of no consequence. In fact, you conducted yourself with extreme grace and poise." He sat on the opposite end of the couch from her. "Someone is betraying us all by letting him inside the campus and smuggling messages to you from him without going through proper channels. I have to ask this, Lamb. I'd be negligent if I didn't." He took a hesitant breath, as if reluctant to bring up the subject. "Did you welcome his attention here?" Even asking that much was close to revealing his hand, but she would likely expect the question. Not asking it would be just as big of a gamble.

She shook her head almost violently. "Not at all. You know what happened the night of the New Year's Eve party. Nothing has changed my feelings. He's a married man. Off-limits no matter what he says."

Azriel nodded. "I figured as much. You're to tell me if he tries to contact you again."

"Yes, sir." Her tone was meek, her posture defeated. Azriel found her distress uncomfortable in the extreme. Thankfully, there was a soft knock at the door.

"Ah! That would be your lunch." Azriel was grateful for the interruption. It allowed Lamb to compose herself and him a moment to get himself under control. He let Maria in. She placed the food on a table in the corner of the room next to a floor-to-ceiling set of corner windows that overlooked the city. "Come, Miss Newsome," he beckoned. "Lunch is served."

She hesitated a moment, then shuffled to the table, obviously not wanting to eat. "I think I'm too upset to eat much."

"Just try." He smiled at her. "Please."

Lamb nodded and sat in the chair he'd pulled out for her. She'd ordered a lobster salad with a citrus spritz and a butter sauce.

"Looks interesting." Azriel smiled at her. "Why not try a bite? I'll get you a glass of wine. I'm sure it will go much better than water with your meal."

"I'm working, Mr. Ivanovich. I don't think it's appropriate."

He waved that away. "You've had a rough encounter. I think one glass of wine is an excellent idea. Besides. That's part of what I wanted to talk to you about."

Immediately, her gaze shot to his. Her eyes were wide and round, real fear and dread on her lovely face. "Are you… are you firing me?"

Azriel blinked several times, taken aback at her swift and immediate distress. "Absolutely not, Lamb. Absolutely not. I've been getting regular reports from your project preceptors, and they all say you're doing fantastic work and that you learn very quickly. No. If anything you'll be offered a permanent position when your internship is over, assuming you keep up your work ethic." When she slumped in the chair again, Azriel couldn't resist reaching out to cover her hand in his. "I don't offer internships to just anyone. If I didn't fully believe you'd be a good fit for this company, you wouldn't be here."

"Thank you," she said, her voice small. Azriel didn't like this side of Lamb because it made it nearly impossible for him to keep his distance.

"Look. Let's forget about that for a while. It's Friday. You've got the whole weekend to relax and forget about this mess." This was it. If he played his cards right, he could get her take on what went down with Luxemberry since the party, and get her to himself for the weekend while Giovanni and El Diablo picked apart Luxemberry's reasoning for targeting Lamb. If she hadn't supplied him with information, then why continue to hound her? If she'd promised it and then hadn't delivered, he needed to know that, too. Azriel was confident he could get it from one or the other of them. If not, maybe El Diablo could get it from Luxemberry's wife.

"Believe me. I'd love nothing more."

"Good." He smiled, nodding toward her food. "I realize you might not feel up to much, but try to eat something."

Obediently, Lamb picked up her fork and dug into the salad. As she forked one slow bite after another into her mouth, she grew more relaxed, her eyes heavy lidded as she chewed. Azriel could almost believe she'd forgotten he was in the room, she was so engrossed in the food. Either it was extremely good, or she was just as hungry.

The way she savored each bite was a fucking turn-on. Azriel had never thought the act of eating particularly erotic, but Lamb made it so. He could imagine her opening her mouth not for the lobster, but for his cock. Which just thrust images of what she must have done with Luxemberry into his head. It was an exercise in frustration he couldn't seem to stop.

When she'd finished the last bite and wiped her mouth delicately, Azriel grinned at her. "Constance always made the most delicious Lobster Spritz. Did you enjoy?"

"More than just about anything. It's my favorite from the restaurant." She gifted Azriel with a small, but genuine, smile. "I could eat it nearly every day."

"I'll have to remember that." He straightened and cleared his throat. The sight of her obvious enjoyment of her food had turned him on mightily. If he stood right now, he'd embarrass himself and remove any chance he had at wooing Lamb slowly. "So, on to the topic of conversation."

"Which is?"

For a long moment, Azriel debated on how to approach Lamb with this. He didn't want her to feel threatened, but he needed this time with her for multiple reasons. "Alex and his wife, Merrily, have invited Giovanni and myself to a weekend retreat. Since Merrily will be the only woman in attendance from Argent, I thought she might be more comfortable with a fellow female wonder in the tech field along."

"Mr. Ivanovich, I don't think it's a good idea."

"Just… hear me out, Lamb. Argent has been under fire for several months. We've woven a trap for our enemies and need to spring it. Naturally, we'd prefer not to be in the vicinity when it all goes down. While Merrily isn't involved, she will stay with Alexei, and her daughter will be sent to Kentucky with a friend of mine. Cain owns one of the largest paramilitary organizations in the world and will protect Bellarose almost better than we could. Merrily needs to be with Alexei. I could use your help to keep her company. The three of us are difficult to deal with at the best of times." He gave her a small, self-deprecating smile. "This hasn't been the best of times." He continued, "Some friends of ours own a stretch of beach in Lake Worth, Florida near Palm Beach. They've generously offered us the use of it and all the protection that goes with it for the weekend. I guarantee you'll meet many interesting characters while you're there. You'll also enjoy the sun and sea at no expense to you."

"So you want me to come with you to keep Mr. Petrov's wife company?"

He shrugged. "Essentially, yes. You'd still be my guest and therefore my responsibility. This costs you nothing, and you get to relax and have a weekend away from worry. In fact, should you come with us, I'd insist on it."

Had he worded the offer any other way, for any other reason, Lamb would have slapped him and stormed off. Might have even kicked him in the balls for her trouble. Instead, she found the prospect of spending time far away from James the best idea in the world.

"I shouldn't do this," she said, taking a deep breath. "It's a horrible idea, but I think I might." She held up a hand when he opened his mouth to speak. "But I'm not sleeping with you. I'm not your 'date.' I'll be a guest, but nothing more."

"I'd never expect more, Lamb." His shark-like smile said otherwise. Still, probably because she'd spent the last few weeks trying to be smart, she decided to throw caution to the wind. Probably because, the longer she was in his presence, the more she relaxed around Azriel. He was gentle with her, and unfailingly kind. Even when James had been doing his best to get her back into bed, he'd not treated her with as much respect as Azriel had. While Lamb was under no illusions that anything good could come of this, a wild side of her simply wouldn't be denied.

"Fine. I'll do this. I'm taking you at your word, Mr. Ivanovich. Foolish as it is."

He chuckled. The sound was warm and inviting. It made her want to smile when she knew she shouldn't. Hell, she should be running out of this office like her hair was on fire, but Goddammit, she wanted to see what happened next. She wasn't so naive to think he didn't have an ulterior motive. She just couldn't give a fuck. Worst case? He would use her, like she'd described their first encounter, and throw her away. Hadn't she asserted men in his station in life used women like her all the time? So what if he did? She knew what she was getting into, and she'd still get a vacation out of it. Not to mention an internship she already had with the most sought-after company in her field. Even if it was cut short by several months, it was still more than most women in her field ever got. She could make it worth the heartache if she had to.

"Good. Go pack. I'll pick you up in an hour."

She cringed. "How about I meet you back here?"

"Little Lamb, I know where you live. I also know your concerns. Which is why I'm seeing to it that, while we're gone, you're moved to a part of town more fitting to your employment. Argent owns an apartment building two blocks from campus where many of our employees live. When we come back, you'll have a place all set up. No more worries about my Rolls-Royce getting its hubcaps stolen." Judging by the look on his face, he was trying to make it a joke.

Lamb just shook her head. "Too soon."

"Ah. My bad." The arrogant man actually winked at her.

Chapter Seven

The retreat Azriel brought her to wasn't what she'd been expecting. They all four shared a three-bedroom bungalow oceanside. When they said "ocean side," they literally meant on the ocean. It was built on a man-made island offshore. Privacy was a hundred percent assured. There was a pier with a covered deck and a sun deck with lounge chairs, a full bar, and freshwater showers for rinsing off the salt water if one decided to swim.

Azriel had driven them to the island in the little speed boat they'd been given and tied the craft to the pier. Soon after, they'd been met by a very handsome man in a crisp, tailored suit. He had a British accent, but had Latino coloring. He wasn't as tall as Azriel or Alexei, but seemed to be more muscular. And so charming that, though Lamb's internal alarm was pinging all over the place, she found herself unable to fully distrust him. Without a doubt, she knew he was into some shady shit, but he had such charisma, Lamb found she didn't care.

"Security is as you specified," the man drawled in that accent. "With a few modifications of my own. No one can get on or off this island without me knowing. You'll find enough food and drink stocked for your entire stay, so no one will disturb you." The man turned to Lamb then, extending his hand. "Who is the lovely lady, Azriel? Please tell me she's not with you. I'll gladly take her back with me and show her the sights." His smile was wolfish but didn't reach his eyes. Though Lamb found herself automatically taking his hand, she had the feeling there was more going on with him than she realized.

"She's not for you." Azriel snagged Lamb's other

arm and pulled her close. The man had to let go of her hand or risk a tug of war.

"I see." He winked at Lamb. "Another time, then. I'm sure the lady would enjoy my… company." There was an intensely sexual vibe coming from him, but dark with a hint of violence. It was like the cultured civility he presented to them was just a shell, and the man underneath was poorly hidden. Probably because he didn't care who saw him, but it suited him to confuse people and keep them off balance.

"Just do your job." Azriel's voice was mild, but there was an underlying whip of command. The other man obviously didn't like the tone, but grinned at him anyway. There was a promise of retaliation in that showing of teeth, but if Azriel saw it, he didn't back down.

"I suppose it's what you pay me for." He turned to Lamb. "I sincerely hope you and I get officially introduced. Playing with you would be a pleasure. No matter the nature of the play."

There was no way to take that as anything but a threat. Lamb shivered and inched closer to Azriel before she realized it. The smirk on the man's face told her he'd only been half serious. The undertones were massive. Obviously he was making a point to Azriel since Azriel practically growled, putting himself between Lamb and the other man.

"Bastard," Azriel hissed.

"I believe it's time for you to leave." Alexei Petrov, though he'd been quiet up until now, asserted himself. His wife, Merrily, moved solidly to Lamb's side. Lamb had never met the woman, but her reputation preceded her. Merrily was a genius with a computer. She was the last line of testing when a security protocol rolled out. If she couldn't break it, they were given the green light to start the final coding. "We appreciate the hospitality and the lodgings, but now's not the time for this." Which implied... what? That there would be a time for him to threaten Lamb?

"On the contrary." The man waved Alexei's statement away. "I learned many things from the exchange. Some will help you in my investigation. Other things will help Azriel."

"You're overstepping." This time, it was clear Alexei was done with the conversation.

"I'm even more dangerous than you, Demon," the man said mildly. "Don't try to intimidate me, because you will fail. You paid me to do a job, and I'm doing it. This was free." He gave Lamb a slight bow of his head before turning to leave.

"Who was that?" She asked the question as she eased a little closer to Azriel, not feeling any safer as she watched him walking away from them. "What's he talking about?"

"Nothing," Azriel said as he tightened his arm around her. It wasn't until then that Lamb realized she'd relied on Azriel to protect her when she had no idea if he would. "He's working for Argent during this mess."

"But why --" She was cut off when Alexei clapped his hands together.

"Who wants burgers? It's been forever since I've grilled a burger."

"You can't cook," Merrily said mildly. "Which is why it's been forever. Literally. I'm pretty sure you've never used a grill."

Alexei pulled his wife into his arms and kissed her soundly. "I'm sure you'll help me, won't you?" He grinned at Lamb. "We've got a guest to impress. Besides, I'm hoping to make a mess so I can get you to skinny dip with me and clean me off."

Merrily's laughter was like music. Despite her earlier trepidation, Lamb found herself relaxing once again. She hadn't missed the fact that no one had called the stranger by name. She also realized they'd successfully changed the subject. She was willing to let it go because she really needed this. Just relaxing in the sun by the water. While she had no illusion there was more than an infatuation between her and Azriel -- she wasn't here as his girlfriend by her own insistence -- she now thought he might just protect her to the best of his ability while she was with him. She'd seen that when the stranger had given her that veiled threat.

"I'm not skinny dipping with you, Alex." Merrily ruined the admonishment by giggling, which meant Lamb should probably enter the water around the pier with caution if she hadn't seen the other couple for a while.

"Maybe you should," Azriel said, looking serious. When Alexei turned and raised an eyebrow, Azriel shrugged. "I just mean that if you two did, I might be able to coax my date to skinny dip with me."

There was a silence around them. Alexei and Merrily hid grins and ducked their heads. Lamb just gasped, her mouth open.

"You… you *brought* a… a *date*?"

Two emotions overwhelmed Lamb at the thought. Confusion and anger. First, the bastard had lied to her. He'd said he'd invited her to come with them because Merrily would be more comfortable with a woman around. Which implied she'd be the only woman without Lamb. But if Azriel had brought a date with him, wasn't that another woman? If not, was it a man? Was he gay? If he was gay, why had he kissed Lamb? And what was she doing here in the first fucking place?

Without thinking, she launched herself at him, throwing a punch that he neatly caught and following it up with several open-handed slaps with her other hand. Azriel erupted into laughter, not really needing to do much to defend himself because, as far as she could tell, none of her blows connected.

After a few moments, Azriel wrapped her up in his strong arms, pulling her close against his body. Gradually, her struggles ceased, and she registered his body shaking with laughter. Then she realized one more, very important thing. She'd felt more than anger or confusion. There'd also been hurt. And a seething jealousy she had no hope of controlling. That was when she'd realized her cheeks were wet with tears, and her throat was raw from screaming at him.

"Looks like you've got a fierce little kitten there, Azriel," Alexei said.

"She's not a kitten. She's a lamb. My little Lamb."

"Not your anything," Lamb muttered from his chest. His arms were securely around her, one hand stroking up and down her back. She even felt his lips in her hair and shivered in reaction. God, he was so potent!

"I think you might just be," he said softly. "We'll see."

"You let that girl go," Merrily said, gently tugging at Lamb. "And if you bait her like that one more time, Azriel Ivanovich, I will change your legal name to Pussywillow Snodgrass."

Lamb couldn't help her sharp bark of laughter. Once she started, she couldn't stop it. Her laughter triggered everyone else's until they were all hanging off each other as they shared their merriment. Perhaps Azriel had been right. This was something she needed.

The only problem was, she thought she might need him too. In her short life, she could never remember anyone making her feel the way Azriel did. She'd moved to him to protect her when that man had threatened her. She'd been blinded by a sudden, sharp jealousy and pain when she'd thought he'd brought another person with him as his actual date. He was the one man she could never have. Yet she recognized in herself the yearning need she had for him. Even if it was just for the weekend. She had no doubt he'd take her up on an offer of sex. No man kissed a woman the way he did and didn't want to fuck her. The question was, could she do it, then let him go?

* * *

He had her. Azriel *knew* he had her. The moment she relaxed in his arms and started giggling, he knew she was his. Which made this whole fucking situation impossible. There was no way to keep his true motivations from her once this was over. He'd have to tell her he was pumping her for information, and that getting her secluded with him and his brother in the Shadow Demons was the quickest way to do it, and that would be the end of any relationship they had. She'd see him as no better than Luxemberry, and he wouldn't blame her.

El Diablo had wanted to just take Luxemberry and question him with a delicate touch, but Alexei wanted to make sure they got the very top. None of them believed Luxemberry had the brains to attempt something like this on his own. There had to be someone pulling his strings. As far as he knew, Luxemberry had been seen in medical, then escorted off the property. He'd threatened to sue, but Alexei had pointed out he was the one trespassing, and he was sure he could find a reason to have him arrested and spend at least one night in jail. Giovanni had a handle on the security breach. No matter what they'd told anyone, Luxemberry and Lamb included, Giovanni had been aware of the security breach the moment it had happened. Those men were now unnecessary and had been flagged for no entry and fired. They'd only been hired in the first place because Giovani had known Luxemberry was trying to gain entry to Argent. They'd wanted to see what would happen, and if the two men could give them anyone beyond Luxemberry.

Despite all the obstacles he had to overcome with her, right now, she was his. He'd treat her as such and maybe, just maybe, he could convince her he was worth a second chance later.

"Go inside," he said, pushing her away and turning her toward the bungalow they all shared. "Your luggage is in the room you picked out. Change into swimwear and come back outside."

"You're not my boss this weekend. You do realize that, right?"

"Honey, I'm always the boss."

"You're also bossy. One I can deal with. The other? Not so much."

Merrily giggled. "I can relate. I've got one the exact same way." She looked up at Alexei with so much love Azriel groaned.

"You two need to get a room."

Alexei scooped his wife up in his arms. "Now, that's the most intelligent thing you've said all day, Azriel." He stalked off with Merrily in his arms with her clinging to him as she nibbled at his ear, continuing to giggle as she did.

Lamb glanced back at him, a speculative look on her face. "You planned this all along. Didn't you."

He shrugged. "Does it matter? You're a beautiful woman. What man wouldn't use any means necessary to be alone with you if he could get you in a receptive mood? Hell, just being in your company gives me a thrill."

"You're full of shit, but I think I might be game. First, though, you know I have to ask. Do you have a woman somewhere I'm going to run into at a party?"

Azriel strode the two steps separating them and reached out to cup her face. "Absolutely not, my little Lamb. There is no woman anywhere who has any kind of claim on me. I'm not married, nor have I ever been. I've had my share of women for pleasure, but never for long and never for anything other than sex. As a result, I've never had sex without a condom. No reason to give a woman a chance at getting her claws into me when she's not who or what I want."

"I've never had sex without a condom either." She sounded small and shy, but probably knew this had to be done. Azriel hated seeing her uncomfortable but knew it would be worse before it was over.

"Not even Luxemberry? He seems like the type who'd use the possibility of you carrying his child to control you." He was fishing. He wouldn't actually call it subtle either. But it was a place to start.

"He tried to, but I always insisted." She frowned slightly as if just realizing something that she didn't like. "Those last couple of days especially. He really pressured me to let him go without a condom. It had been an issue from the first time, but he actually tried to force the issue once. One of the last times we had sex. I was honestly afraid I couldn't stop him."

Azriel frowned. Not only did he not like the thought of that bastard assaulting her like that, but he was just one more small piece of the puzzle. He wanted to fuck her bare... why? The only explanation was so he could possibly get her pregnant. At the very least, he'd have used that as an excuse to see her more and, quite possibly, to get her to let him fuck her again without a condom because the deed was already done. Which would make sense if he'd kept in touch with her. But he hadn't. Not until he'd seen her at the party. Which meant he probably had a backup plan. Since he was now actively chasing Lamb again, his backup must have fallen through.

"While I can understand why any man would want to secure you for himself any way he could, he and I will have words over that the next time we meet."

She shook her head. "There's no need for that. It's done. Over. I'll never willingly sleep with that swine again." Her delicate features scrunched slightly in distaste.

"Just so we're clear," Azriel pressed. "When we have sex, we use a condom."

"Yes. I'm sure you'd have more reason than me to insist on protection, but I have no desire to get pregnant."

Azriel couldn't help but push her. Just a little. "Oh, really? I'm a billionaire. Part owner of a trillion-dollar tech company. If I got you pregnant, you'd come away with a sizable chunk of money, no matter if you kept the baby or not. All it would take would be a good lawyer and a paternity test."

She stepped back, looking for all the world as if he'd slapped her. Azriel winced, bracing to take the onslaught he'd just brought down on his own head.

"Do you honestly think I'd use a baby as a payday? Besides, since you obviously didn't listen to my story, I was the one to insist on protection. Not him. By your way of thinking, shouldn't I have been the one to try to not use protection?"

"Easy there, little Lamb. I was simply telling you a man in my position doesn't take a woman without protection unless he intends on keeping her. James Luxemberry intended to keep you."

"But he's married? Did he think he could keep me as some kind of plaything?"

"Good question," he hedged. The man wanted her in his pocket. Likely wanted her dependent on him so he could get the information he wanted. Assuming they didn't already have an arrangement. Azriel was beginning to believe his gut telling him Lamb was entirely innocent. "One for another day. Right now, I want you out here in a swimsuit that shows plenty of skin. If we're going to play tonight, I want you feeling the burn before we start." He gave her his best wicked grin. "Which means teasing you the rest of the afternoon. By the time the sun sets, I want you so ready for me that you're the one making a move."

She sighed. Her smile was slow in coming but when it did, she seemed to light up the world. "I guess that's only fair since I'm the one who said I wasn't sleeping with you."

"Was that you? I thought it might have been my other date."

Lamb giggled. "You're such a cad. Fine. I'll go change. But I expect you to be shirtless when I get back. I want to see what I'll be getting later."

Chapter Eight

Azriel had been right. Lamb was practically jumping out of her skin by the end of the day. He hadn't done anything overt, but the sexual innuendo and heated looks had been enough to heat Lamb's blood to near boiling. Add the gentle touches and the brush of his lips over her cheek and mouth occasionally, and Lamb was, indeed, on fire for him. The bastard knew it, too.

Merrily had giggled with her off to the side, as if they were sharing a joke they didn't want the men to know about. In reality, the two women were making friends. Lamb loved Merrily's wicked sense of humor and her keen mind. She was one of the few women outside of her college clique she'd ever been able to converse with about code and computer geeky stuff. Though Lamb was more of a mechanical engineer than a computer engineer, she still loved the language. Occasionally, she poked her head inside the world of a computer nerd, but she was nowhere near the level that Merrily was. Which seemed to be perfect, because Merrily told her about all kinds of tech she was dreaming up.

"With your help, I bet we can give Giovanni a run for his money in the cave." Apparently, "the cave" was a workshop the men played in beneath their house. Merrily jokingly referred to it as the Bat Cave and had assured Lamb she wasn't exaggerating. It was in the back of Lamb's mind that Merrily probably shouldn't be telling her this, but she'd had more than a couple Captain and Cokes and was past censuring the other woman. As far as she knew, the facility Merrily referred to wasn't part of Argent's campus and, therefore, a private workshop for the three Argent executives.

"I don't know about that. I'm still learning stuff every single day. But you've got some very interesting ideas. I'd love to explore them." The fact was, some of what Merrily had shown her and described Lamb found eerily similar to a few of the projects she was working on. Was this some kind of test? If so, Lamb wasn't biting. She'd hedged her responses, claiming to be too drunk to see straight let alone think tech speak. Lamb found the thought that Merrily's friendship might not be genuine disturbed her nearly as much as the thought of Azriel's interest being feigned. Lamb liked both people. Azriel in ways she probably shouldn't.

Which brought her to the current situation. Azriel stood, holding out his hand to her. "It's time, little Lamb." That velvety soft voice he normally used like a third hand to caress her was gruff. A husky whisper. His erection was prominent behind his swim trunks, but it didn't seem to bother him.

All the play of the day rushed through Lamb's buzzed head. The muscles bulging beneath Azriel's skin. The various scars over his smooth, naked chest. Heated looks passing between them all day made Lamb want to throw herself into his arms and fuck him six ways to Sunday. God, the man was sexy in every possible way! What got to her the most, however, was the singular way he focused on her. It didn't matter where she was or what she was doing, Azriel always had her in sight. Like he was afraid she'd somehow escape their island paradise and leave him before he could sample her. There was no doubt what he'd had on his mind the entire day. He stayed hard and she stayed wet, the attraction mutual.

He led to her room, taking care to shut and lock

the door. Lamb was nervous but so turned on she was almost beyond caring that Alex and Merrily were on the other side of the bungalow in their own room.

"Won't the others hear us?"

Azriel shrugged. "Possibly. Do you really care? It's not like they're not going to be fucking, too."

That made her giggle. "I guess not."

"Neither are going to judge you, Lamb. You're a grown woman invited here by me. Under some duress, I might add." He grinned. "You made quite an impression on both Alex and Merrily. I think they like you better than me."

"I doubt that. But I really like Merrily. Maybe she and I can get together for a girls' night out sometime."

"You wouldn't like working with her?"

"I think she's a little beyond my skill level. Maybe one day I'll get there."

Azriel smiled at her, a predatory grin if ever she saw one. "You'll get there. Right now, I want you naked so I can get you there."

"That's not exactly what I meant." She laughed, genuinely happy. Then Azriel took her in his arms and kissed her. And she didn't care what she meant.

All her life, Lamb had wondered why people loved to kiss. Or have sex. She'd never really understood it. No one she knew had ever confirmed the overwhelming orgasms she'd read about in books. Part of her had disbelieved such a thing ever happened at all. She'd had some pleasant times with a couple of men -- James included -- but no man had ever turned her insides to mush the way Azriel Ivanovich did with only a single kiss.

He grunted, his body stiffening the second their lips made contact. Lamb shivered, and she could have sworn she felt Azriel do the same. It was only a pressing of their lips together for a few moments. Then he deepened the kiss, sweeping his tongue over the seam of her lips once before delving between them for a long lick.

Lamb whimpered when Azriel pulled back. He gazed down at her for a long, long moment. She leaned into his palm as he caressed her cheek, never looking away from him. The angles and planes of his face were starkly beautiful to her. Classically handsome, but a few thin, white scars that looked like they'd been surgically diminished gave him a slightly roguish appearance. As did the dark stubble on his cheeks. As perfect as James had seemed to her, Azriel was equally *im*perfect, but he had more substance. Like the surface was only part of what she was getting. There was a deeper side to Azriel she'd only scratched the surface of. She wanted more. Of everything.

Looking up into his eyes as he studied her made Lamb all the more hungry for him. His fingers dug into her back as he pulled her ever closer, holding her tighter. "You're so fucking beautiful," he whispered. "And more innocent than I normally like, but I'll be damned if I'm letting you escape me, little Lamb."

She was sure she should be offended that he just assumed he knew her experience level, but when he took her mouth again, she let it go. If he thought she didn't know what she was doing, she'd just have to get him to teach her.

Vaguely, Lamb knew he'd pulled the string at her back, releasing her top. It fluttered to the floor, but all Lamb could process was that her breasts were now mashed against Azriel's chest. She moaned and rubbed herself over him, unable to stop. Sweat from their time in the sun made their bodies glide together sensuously.

"Azriel," she gasped.

His arm tightened around her back even as he slid down her body to take one nipple into his mouth. Lamb tunneled her fingers through his hair, gripping and loosening her hold almost spasmodically. The sensations overwhelming her weren't foreign, but she hadn't been prepared for the intensity. When he pulled strongly, then nipped the tip, there was no way she could contain her cries.

When Azriel tried to pull away from her, she whimpered and held him tighter. "No!"

He chuckled darkly. "Oh, my little Lamb. This is just the beginning. Before we leave here, you're going to grow addicted to me."

He freed himself, continuing down her body. Tugging at the little string that held the bottom of her bathing suit around her hips, he kissed the skin over her hip bones. First one, then the other. The material pooled at her feet with her top. Before she could register what he was about to do, Azriel leaned in and swiped her cunt with his tongue.

The jolt was wicked and sharp. Lamb gasped just before her knees buckled. Luckily, Azriel was very strong. He didn't let her fall. She was lightheaded and weak as a newborn kitten, hyperventilating even as she gasped for air. Azriel picked her up and laid her on the bed before stripping off his shorts. Then he followed her, settling himself between her legs, his arms around her thighs to hold them open.

"You taste sweet, my little Lamb. I think I might be down here for a long, long time." His smile was wicked, but his voice sounded strained. Sweat dripped from his chin to her leg as he lowered his head and latched his mouth onto her clit, never breaking eye contact with her.

The jolt of pleasure was so sharp, Lamb bucked

her hips. Thrashing beneath the onslaught, Lamb cried out. Never had anything been so... overwhelming. The passion he created just with the flick of his tongue and the movement of his lips over her clit was beyond anything she'd ever experienced. Was this the passion and intensity she'd been looking for? Craving? When she felt Azriel probe her opening with two fingers, she suspected this might just be her answer. Sweat slickened her skin, making her legs slip against his forearms as he tried to hold her in place for him. The sensations were too much, and she fought him, trying to twist from his grasp as she cried out.

"T-too m-much! Azriel! Oh, God!"

He growled and smacked her inner thigh. The sting only added to the sensations already overwhelming her. An orgasm was eminent. And Lamb was certain it would be a doozy. Several times, he pumped his fingers into her, filling her cunt with the thick, blunt digits and spreading her open for him.

"Don't you dare come, Lamb," he growled. "Not until I'm snugly inside you. Gonna fuck you 'til we both come."

"C-can't hold o-off! Can't!"

Immediately, he withdrew in one swift motion. "You will, little Lamb. You'll do exactly what I tell you and hold in your orgasm. Your pleasure is all mine."

As he spoke, Azriel reached up to the nightstand and pulled out a condom box. He sat up, licking her juice off his fingers before breaking the seal on the box and pulling out a little foil packet. He tore it open and rolled it down his thick, impressive shaft, giving himself a few pumps as he surveyed her body. Lamb felt the inspection like a caress. Like he'd actually touched her. Her nipples hardened even more, aching for his mouth on them once again. Without him covering her, blanketing her with his larger frame, Lamb actually felt bereft. She wanted his touch and possession like she wanted to breathe.

"Please, Azriel," she sobbed. "Oh, God, please fuck me!"

He grunted, his eyes narrow as he lowered himself to her, his cock still in his hand. "You're dripping wet for me, aren't you, my lovely little Lamb?"

"Yes," she breathed. "All for you."

"Show me." The demand in his voice was as much a turn-on as his big, muscular body blanketing hers. Lamb managed to get her hand between them, dragging her fingers through her pussy. When she pulled back, she wiggled her fingers in front of his face. Sure enough, they were wet, practically dripping with her desire. "Suck them, baby," he told her. "Taste yourself and what I do to you."

Lamb didn't hesitate but licked her fingers, then sucked them into her mouth, humming as she did so. On some level, she realized she was following his orders easily, without question. This wasn't who she thought she was. She'd always had her wits about her during sex. Had always made sure she kept herself out of trouble. She remembered watching Azriel put on that condom, but in that moment, she realized that, even if he hadn't, she'd still beg him to fuck her. She was that far gone.

"That's my girl," he praised her, taking her wrist in his hand and sucking her fingers into his mouth as he lay fully on top of her. His cock poked at her entrance, the head tucked against her pussy just waiting to thrust home. "Are you ready for me?"

"Azriel!" Lamb knew she was nearly screeching now, but really, the man was making her suffer needlessly. She clawed at him, scoring his shoulders with her nails until, finally, with a mighty heave, Azriel surged into her.

"Fuck!" he shouted at the same time she screamed.

Lamb's world imploded. The only thing she was able to process was Azriel looking fiercely into her eyes and his cock wedged so tightly inside her. He made her stretch and burn with his size and length. He hit something deep inside her that caused her both pleasure and pain. For several seconds, Lamb lost the ability to breath. When he started to move slowly inside her, she sucked in a breath before a long, loud scream escaped her. The orgasm that followed blindsided her. There was no way to prepare for the intensity or duration. Her body seemed to contract over and over, never letting her get her bearings.

Finally, Lamb just let go. She went limp in Azriel's arms, her own wrapping around his neck to hold on loosely. Her body finally calmed, small contractions gripping her every few seconds but not building again. It was then she realized Azriel had stopped moving. And that her eyes were closed. The roaring in her ears finally subsided, and she heard Azriel call her name. His hand stroked her damp hair away from her face gently, but it shook slightly.

"Talk to me, Lamb. I need to know you're good."

"I --" Lamb squeezed her eyes shut and shook her head a little to clear it. When she opened them, Azriel was staring into them intently. She nodded her head. "I'm good." Her throat was raw from her screams. God, how loud had she gotten?

"You're sure? I don't want to hurt you, baby."

"I've never felt anything like that." The confession slipped from her lips before she could censor herself. It was too much information for him to have and she knew it. He could use her body against her if she let him. And she knew she'd let him. Willingly. If he kept making her feel this level of pleasure, Lamb knew she'd become a slave in his arms without a fight.

* * *

The drive to fuck rode Azriel hard. It was nearly a compulsion, as if his base nature had taken over. A demon with his chosen mate. Sex was pleasant, a necessary pastime to relieve tension that sometimes coiled itself inside his body. This was altogether different. Everything about Lamb called to him on a purely primitive level. She was necessary. The woman he'd been looking for all his life. And it had taken that one, cataclysmic orgasm from her for Azriel to understand just how much he needed her.

When she told him she'd never felt anything like it, he believed her. It was there in her eyes. In her lovely face. She'd come harder than he imagined any woman could. Hell, she'd nearly squeezed his dick off! He regretted two things about this encounter with Lamb. First, he hadn't come clean with her. He needed information from her and was using their connection as a way to get it. He was doing the very same thing James had done, only it was worse. He did it after she'd told him how much it had hurt when James had done it. She would see it as the greatest betrayal, and Azriel wouldn't blame her. Second, he'd promised to always use a condom when he fucked her. Azriel told her the truth when he'd said he'd never taken a woman without protection. He hadn't. Had never wanted to. Now he wanted nothing more than to mark Lamb by filling her up with his come, making her pregnant so he'd always have a hold on her. Not for information or anything else. Just because he wanted her. The smart, funny, sexy woman he thought was betraying his company.

He had to finish this. Had to find out what the fuck was going on with James Luxemberry and fucking Rush Developments. He might still believe Luxemberry was trying to pump Lamb for information, but he no longer believed Lamb was willingly involved. Or involved at all, really. She was too smart to leak information she shouldn't accidentally, and she'd never reveal it on purpose.

When she nodded that she was, indeed, OK, Azriel stroked her hair some more and smiled at her. "Good, baby. Good."

"I need more."

"With pleasure."

Azriel began to move. Slowly at first, then with more vigor. He lay fully on top of her, letting his chest mash pleasantly against her breasts. Her hard little nipples stabbed into his chest as he kissed her, his hips thrusting slowly. He circled his pelvis, hitting inside her at a different angle and was rewarded with a little gasp from her. Taking full advantage, Azriel thrust his tongue inside her, mimicking what his cock was doing to her pussy.

Lamb gave as good as she got, locking her ankles around his waist and digging her heels into his ass. She urged him forward. Faster. Harder. Her nails scored down his back in a slow, deep scratch that made his body shiver and his cock twitch.

"Love the feel of you around me, Lamb. All that glorious heat tempting me to let go and just come inside you." He watched her eyes widen and her breathing quicken, which just made him move faster. He was becoming close to desperate to come now. He needed it, craved it. The tension in him built with every single second. "Need to fuck you. Make you mine. Make you never want to leave me."

"Don't say things you don't mean, Azriel." She spoke softly, her eyes glistening now. Tears?

"Honey, I never do. I've never said that to anyone else. Man or woman. But I'm telling you now, I'm not letting you go. When this vacation is over, you're coming home with me. We'll figure out a way to work things out, but we'll do it together."

"You can't say that! Don't --"

"Don't what? Don't want you? Don't want you for my own? I have no idea why other men let you slip through their fingers, but I'm too smart for that. You're a shining beacon in a murky cave, Lamb. I see that, and I'm keeping you."

Without another word, afraid he'd simply confess everything to her on the spot, Azriel began to move inside her faster. He surged forward, moving her up the bed with every stroke until she had to brace her hands on the headboard. The ride was teeth clattering, their bodies slapping together at a furious pace.

Finally, when Azriel felt her orgasm start to squeeze the life out of his dick, he let himself go. It took several strokes, but when his orgasm overtook him, when his cock swelled inside of her ready to burst, Azriel held himself as deep as he could, shouting to the rafters as he came in spurt after spurt of scalding come. Nothing in his life had ever come close. *Nothing*. The explosion was painful in its intensity. The sensitive head of his cock was too tender to move as he pulsed and ached and throbbed inside her.

Finally, when he could breathe again. Azriel's body relaxed. He lay limp and weak as he'd ever been on top of Lamb. She clung to him, her little body still quivering in his arms.

He raised his head, trailing kisses over her cheek to her mouth. She sighed as he kissed her tenderly, tasting the sweat of her skin where it beaded on her upper lip.

"You OK?" Now his voice was as hoarse as hers had been. He was sure to take a ribbing from Alex tomorrow. Assuming they left the bed at all.

"Yes." Her affirmation was drowsy, her eyelids heavy, but there was a contented smile on her face that was completely unguarded.

"Don't move."

Azriel rolled out of the bed, getting to his feet. He had to be careful as he strode to the bathroom so he didn't fall on his ass. His legs were rubbery after that intense orgasm. For the first time ever, a woman had made him weak in the knees, and he couldn't be happier about it.

He disposed of the condom and cleaned himself before returning with a wet cloth and cleaning her as well. After tossing the rag in the general direction of the bathroom, Azriel pulled a dozing Lamb into his arms, pulled the covers over them, and slept like the dead.

Chapter Nine

Lamb awoke just as dawn was lightening the sky. It was still early, the light vague and shadowy in the room. She glanced at the clock. Five in the morning. Then she remembered where she was.

She glanced behind her. Azriel lay with an arm draped loosely over her body, not pinning her in place or anything, just in a casual possession that made her want to smile with happiness. Unfortunately, she knew this was the very height of stupidity on her part. How could she possibly have done this a second time? Sure, he'd said he wasn't married and didn't have a relationship with anyone, but how much did she believe? And was that even the point? No matter what kind of bullshit she'd fed herself the night before, sex with Azriel could only end in heartache for her.

And the stuff he'd fed her during sex? Did she really believe he was going to stay with her after this weekend? She wanted to, but Lamb knew better. No. This was bad judgment run amok if ever she saw it.

Carefully, doing her best not to wake Azriel, Lamb slipped from under his arm and out of bed. She was naked so hurrying out wasn't an option. She had to at least find her bag and the change of clothes she kept there. She'd get the rest of her stuff later. Or not. The only thing she was worried about right this second, was getting out of this bungalow and back to the mainland. From there, she'd have to rent a car or something to get back to Rockwell. An unscheduled flight would not only cost her an arm and a leg, but would probably be impossible to find. She could do this, though. Leave this paradise. And Azriel.

She tugged on clean underwear and snagged a clean change of clothes from her open suitcase. She'd just started to tug on her pants when she heard Azriel stirring in the bed.

"Lamb?" He sounded sleepy and confused. "Lamb? You OK?"

"I'm fine," she said, trying to sound cheerful. "I just thought it might be better if I go on home." It took every ounce of effort she had to keep the tears at bay. Thinking about leaving and actually telling Azriel she was leaving was harder than she suspected it would be. Leaving James had been a little wistful, but it hadn't filled her with such sadness. Like she was leaving part of herself behind. She'd known she hadn't loved James, but she'd thought she'd had pretty strong feelings for him. Now, she realized what she'd felt for him had been nothing. Not when compared to what Azriel had brought to life inside her in such a short period of time. He was completely off-limits. Yet here they were.

"What? Why would you think that?"

She thought about lying. Telling him she had forgotten a meeting or something, but she could never lie worth a damn. She could deflect and dodge, but she couldn't seem to actually lie. Maybe that was why she hated being lied to so much.

"I guess the harsh light of day made me realize what a horribly bad idea this was."

"It wasn't a bad idea, Lamb." Still lying in the bed, the sheet over his body and one leg bent and out from under the cover, he reached out a hand for her. "Please don't leave me."

Had he phrased it any other way, had he demanded she stay with him, she might have been able to hold the course she knew she needed to be on. But he'd said, "Please don't leave me." Like she was important to him. Like he was the one who would be hurt if she didn't stay.

"I don't think it's a good idea," she managed to whisper, looking down at her feet. She wasn't dressed, but she at least had a T-shirt covering her. "I -- I don't belong here."

"I know," he said, scrubbing the hand he'd been reaching for her with over his tired face. "You don't belong here, but it was the safest place. It's not so bad, though." He looked around and winced. "Little small. Not nearly what you deserve."

"That's not what I meant, Azriel."

He sat up, swinging his legs over to sit on the side of the bed. "I know what you mean, Lamb, and you couldn't be more wrong. More than any person I know, other than Merrily and her daughter, Bellarose, you belong in my world. Hell, the three of us, my brothers, we don't deserve the good fortunes we have, but we hold on to them ruthlessly. Alex found the woman who means everything to him in Merrily. If he hadn't had all the wealth he does, she wouldn't have all the things he can give her." Once again, he held out his hand to her. "I want to be that for you, Lamb."

She sighed. "I don't want all that. I just..." She swallowed. "I just want something... I don't know. Something *real*. Nothing about this situation or you is real for me, Azriel."

He dropped his hand, scrubbing the other one over his face. "It's real, baby. I swear to you, what I feel for you is so fucking real it hurts. Just give me a chance to prove it to you. Just one chance. It's all I'm asking. It's all I'm *begging*..."

Azriel looked at her with such pain and longing in his eyes, on his face, Lamb found herself taking a step toward him before she even realized it. Somehow, she managed to stop herself from taking another.

"You're my doom," she whispered. "Nothing can come of this but heartache for me. I might enjoy myself, might fall completely in love with you. I know I'll enjoy every second, and that's the whole problem. It will make the ending that much more painful." She clutched one fist to her chest. "It already hurts, Azriel." She was mortified when she realized tears were tracking slowly from her eyes down her cheeks.

"I need you, Lamb," he admitted, looking at her with a kind of dark possession. He hadn't changed his tone or his expression, but there was something there that hadn't been before. Lamb knew in that moment he wasn't letting her go. She might run. Might even make it back to Rockwell, but Azriel would be there. Waiting on her when she arrived. Then she recognized the relief blossoming inside her. She didn't want to leave him. It was so different than when she'd left James in the Keys. She'd thought about their time together fondly on her drive home. If she left Azriel, it was quite possible she wouldn't make it home. Hell, she probably wouldn't make it past the pier. The next thing she knew, she'd find herself on a beeline right back into Azriel's arms.

"I made a fool out of myself once. With James. It was a little place much like this in the Florida Keys. He made me think he felt something for me, though he never outright said anything to the effect. He didn't give me a way to contact him or promise we'd always be together or any bullshit line. Just told me how he loved being with me. That I was intelligent and hardworking. That he hoped we could become very good friends. Even said he hoped that, when my time at Argent was done, I would consider working for the company he used to run. Rush Developments. When I left the Key and him behind, I had no regrets."

She swallowed, blinking back another tear, determined not to let any more fall. Especially not because of James Luxemberry. "When I saw him again at the party, I was happy. I thought maybe we'd have a chance to work out a relationship between us. No matter the age difference, I really thought there was a shot. Older men like younger women. Right? But not five seconds after I inserted myself back into his life, he introduced me to his wife. The betrayal, more than anything, hurt me. I didn't care about James. Only had an infatuation with him. He had money, power, and even though those things didn't matter to me, the way he wore them did. His charisma drew me to him, much like you do."

She took a breath. "Finding out I was sleeping with a married man was only part of the reason I felt betrayed. He made me believe I was special. Being singled out by a man like that was thrilling, I'll admit. Finding out he was just using me for sex made the whole week feel slimy and dirty. I promised myself I'd never feel that way again. So, if sex is all you're after, just tell me now. I can deal with it and accept it. But I can't let you make me feel like I mean something to you only to find out I'm a means to an end and disposable afterward. It made me angry with James. With you, it would shatter me."

There. She'd said it. It probably made her look weak and definitely made him aware how susceptible she was to him, but she had to lay it all out. In her heart, she didn't believe Azriel was the type of man to intentionally hurt an innocent, especially not a woman. He might be brutal to his enemies, but not to people who had never done anything to him or his.

"I understand, little Lamb. Now, please. Don't make me beg a second time. I'm not sure my fragile pride could take it."

There it was. His humor. The one thing that could make up her mind and ease the tension between them in only a few simple words. How could any woman resist him? She knew the answer to that without even thinking. They couldn't. At least, she couldn't.

With a sigh, Lamb walked back to him, taking the hand he offered the third time. Azriel moved her hand around his neck as he wrapped his arms around her middle and buried his face in her belly. For long moments, they didn't move. Lamb rested her cheek on the top of his head while he clung to her just as tightly as she did to him. This had been her chance. Her one chance to make a clean break and deal with her emotional fallout. It would have been hard. She'd have cried herself into an exhausted stupor, but it would have been over in a few weeks. Maybe. Now, she knew she was throwing herself into whatever Azriel had planned for her. She could never get this close again. Not and keep her heart somewhat intact.

After what had to be a full minute, Azriel moved. He pulled off her shirt and slid her panties down her thighs. Once she was as naked as she was, he pulled her to straddle him on the bed. Tangling his fingers in her hair, he pulled her to him gently to kiss her. The taste of his kiss never ceased to thrill her. It was a combination of wild man and sinful sex. She didn't fool herself into thinking there was love in there. She wasn't entirely sure the man was capable of it. Given the string of broken hearts all over the country -- according to the tabloids -- she doubted it.

There was also possession. The more she kissed him, the more she tasted it. For some reason he'd fixated on her for the time being. How long remained to be seen, but Lamb knew there was no point fighting it. Men like Azriel always got what they wanted.

* * *

The next three weeks were the busiest, fastest, and most exciting of Lamb's life. Not only was she brought in on several more projects, but Azriel was rapidly becoming an obsession. He came to her tiny office every afternoon and insisted she leave with him. Then he took her to dinner. Sometimes he took her out on the town. Sometimes they stayed in. Didn't matter at which of their places they stayed. Sex was always involved. Heavily. A few times, Lamb cooked for him. He always loved it when she made dessert. She loved it when he made dessert. Out of her.

Life as she knew it was the best she'd ever known. The only thing that marred her happiness was James Luxemberry. He still tried to contact her. Never when Azriel was around, so not often. But he was determined to accomplish something. Lamb just didn't know what.

Today was the first day Azriel hadn't picked her up at her office. He'd stopped by earlier in the afternoon to tell her he had a meeting that would last late, but he'd call her afterward. She found she was actually relieved at the same time she was disappointed. She was beginning to feel more for Azriel than she should, which was dangerous for her heart. No matter how he reassured her, there was still a little niggling of doubt. Something that tickled at the back of her mind saying there was more going on that she knew.

With Azriel not with her, she was free to run some errands, the most pressing of which was going to the grocery store. When she cooked for Azriel, she only let him buy what she needed for the meal, though he'd sometimes slipped things into the cart he'd noticed she was out of. Or, rather, had the delivery boy slip it in. This time, she was free to go in and do her own shopping. Strange that she found she'd missed it when she used to hate it. Probably was the fact that Azriel hadn't let her spend a penny of her own money since they'd started seeing each other. She didn't have to be so careful with every choice.

She was loading her groceries when a sleek little Jaguar rolled up to park directly behind her in the parking lot. Even if she could get inside her car before he hopped out of his, she was blocked in.

"Lamb!" He called to her as he hurried around the front of the little sports car. "Lamb!" When he reached her, he gave her that megawatt smile of his, opening his arms like he fully expected her to step into them. Lamb pulled her shopping cart solidly in between them.

"What do you want?"

"Come now, my love. Is that any way to treat an old friend?"

"When did we become friends? We fucked. We parted ways. No one had expectations we'd continue. Besides, that ship sailed when I found out you were married. I can't be your friend without your wife getting hurt, and she's innocent in that business."

He waved her argument away. "I already told you she and I have an open marriage."

"Well, my relationship isn't so 'open.' So, I need you to leave."

"Relationship? With Azriel Ivanovich?" James grinned at her, his smile full of pity. "Sweet girl, don't you know he eats young little things like you for breakfast? I'm not sure what he's doing or what he's told you, but, rest assured, he has a reason for it, and it isn't love."

"I never said I was in love with him, or that he was in love with me. We have merely enjoyed each other's company."

"Like there's no sex involved. I realize I'm not the greatest lover in the world, but surely he hasn't completely blinded you with sex."

It was quite possible he had. Lamb found herself more and more relaxed with Azriel every day, letting her guard down when she never had before. Not that she was going to admit it to James.

"I'm well aware I'm not the kind of woman men like him settle down with. Or men like you. But I am, after all, human. I have needs. So does he. He scratches my back. I scratch his. Only he's not married or involved with another woman."

"That you know of," James countered. "You can't tell me you've spent every single minute with him, because I won't believe it. Does he act secretive? Insist he has places to go without you?"

"We're not married. He can go wherever he wants. So can I. Sometimes we go together, other times we don't. I don't see your point."

"I just hope you realize you can't trust him." He tried to look like he had her well-being at heart, but Lamb knew better.

"Any more than I can trust you?"

For long moments both of them just stared at each other. Lamb saw a myriad of emotions cross his face. Aggravation. Frustration. Anger.

"You're really not going to believe me, are you? I have to say, Lamb, I thought you were more intelligent than this. I thought you'd see through even the great Azriel Ivanovich. I can tell you're starstruck, though. If you're looking to score his money, you won't."

"Why does everyone insist I must be out for the money? Didn't land one fish, I must have moved on to a bigger fish. Why can't you just accept the fact that maybe I just want to be with someone I can relate to. Not in lifestyle, but intellect. I'm not saying I'm as smart as a man like him or you. But I can hold my own, and I know my field of study."

"I'm fully aware you do, my love. That's one of the reasons I'm here. I want to offer you a job with Rush Developments."

"You know I'm contractually obligated to offer Argent first refusal."

"We can buy out your contract."

"And be locked in to Rush for the rest of my career? I don't think Azriel would make me stay anywhere I didn't want to be, but if he tried to and I left like that, he could blackball me anywhere else I wanted to go."

He grinned like he'd finally proven a point. When Lamb just stood there, he pointed at her. "When did he become Azriel instead of Mr. Ivanovich?"

"When I started having sex with him? I'm sorry you don't approve, but I didn't ask your permission!"

"Which brings me to the second reason for my visit." He tried to move the shopping cart away, but Lamb held it fast. Finally he just sighed. "I want you to come home with me, my love. I can't get you out of my head. You got to me body and soul. Whatever Azriel Ivanovich is giving you, I swear I'll do anything in my power to do for you, too. Sexual or material. I don't care. If you need something, I'll figure out a way to provide it for you."

Lamb couldn't believe this. "Why? Why are you doing this? And nothing changes the fact that you're still married! Or that you lied to me! What the hell,

James?"

"I just don't want you to make a mistake with a man like Azriel. He's… not right for you."

"Oh, and I suppose you are."

"I've never claimed to be, but I'll be better for you than he will."

"Not from where I'm sitting, James. Does he have secrets? Yes. I'm fully aware, and I make a point not to discuss work with him because I don't want him to have to lie to me because I'm being nosey. As to the implication that we're together for the long haul? I won't deny that I really like him. I might even feel more for him than even a deep friendship. I have no idea if I love him or if he loves me, but that's for us to figure out. If he's really stringing me along, he'll eventually tell me to get lost. So, yes. I know what I've gotten myself into. I also know that I'm not throwing it away because you say I should. You've already proven you'll lie if it suits your needs. While I have no doubt Azriel is capable of lying if it suits him, I've not caught him in one. Until that time, I'm going to continue to believe in him because of what I feel for him."

Lamb closed her eyes and took several calming breaths. The more she let escape, the more ammunition James had and the more she realized just exactly how much Azriel meant to her. When she had herself better under control, she opened her eyes. Reaching into her pocket, she pulled out her phone and hit the one-touch dial for Azriel. With the phone on speaker, she heard the ringing line. James heard it, too. His eyes narrowed.

"If he's in a meeting, like you say, he won't answer."

"Maybe not. But I can leave a voice message and he *will* get back to me."

Just when Lamb thought the phone would go to voicemail, it was answered. There were some men talking in the background in what sounded like a heated discussion, but she couldn't make out the words. Then the noises faded, and she heard the faint closing of a door.

"Sorry about that, little Lamb." Azriel's voice was comforting to her. Lamb's knees nearly buckled she was so relieved. "Is everything all right?"

"I -- yes. No! I mean..." Lamb started trembling. James was unnerving her more than he should, but the look in his eyes now promised retaliation. If she told Azriel, she had no idea what he would do. She didn't want to really cause James trouble, but she also wanted to know what Azriel's reaction was. Would he be angry at James? At her? Would he ask her what she wanted him to do about it? Would he give a damn? "I'm at the grocery. James has me blocked in with his car and is between me and the driver's side of my car. I have a shopping cart between us. I don't exactly feel threatened --"

"I'm on the way. Sean should be there in less than three minutes. Do not close this connection. Am I on speaker?"

It was James who spoke. "You are, Azriel. I'm in the process of making Miss Newsome an offer she can't refuse."

"Keep talking, James. Sean will be there before I will so, by all means, keep talking."

"Are you threatening me? Because your girl here isn't the only one with a phone."

"I never threaten, James."

Tires squealed in the distance, and Lamb saw a car speeding up the back of the parking lot in their direction. It turned down their aisle and came to a screeching halt. Sean stepped from the vehicle, a gun in his hand aimed at James. Not wanting to get caught in the crossfire, and not wanting to give James anything to hide behind, she stepped backward away from the shopping cart and toward the Rolls-Royce where Sean stood.

"Put the car between you and Mr. Luxemberry, Miss Newsome." Sean's voice was quiet and calm. "Mr. Ivanovich will be here in another three minutes."

"How did you get here so quickly?"

"He's got your car tracked, my love," James said, his arms up and away from his body. Obviously he wasn't giving up on her. "I told you, he's using you for something. There's no need to be loyal to him when it's obvious he's got more up his sleeve than simply showing you a good time."

"Be that as it may, I'm not going anywhere with you. Not now. Not ever."

"Be very careful what you decide in the heat of the moment, Lamb." There was something in James's expression that sent a chill through Lamb straight to her bones. "I'm offering you a chance at a top-level position at one of the leading technological companies in the world. If you stay at Argent, your talents will be underutilized, and you'll be used for your mind and not given the proper recognition."

"Not interested," she said without hesitation.

"Why do you trust him so readily?" Now James looked furious. Sounded it, too. "He's using you!"

"And what's your motivation? I'm not qualified for a top-level position. What's your motivation for putting me there?"

Just as James opened his mouth to answer, another car came screaming around the bend just out of sight. Soon after, though, the car could be seen along the same path Sean had taken. James swore under his breath and hurried around to the driver's side of his car.

"I'll be seeing you again, Lamb. Next time, have the right answer." Then he slid inside, slammed the door, and sped off.

Azriel's sleek little Aston Martin screeched to a halt just behind the Rolls. Azriel stormed out of the car, his own gun in hand. He moved straight to Lamb, but his eyes were on the retreating form of Luxemberry's car.

"Did he hurt you, Lamb?"

"No," she said softly. Lamb didn't hesitate to go into his arms when he reached for her. He kissed the top of her head, his gun still at his side in his free hand.

"Sean, get someone to take Miss Newsome's car back to her apartment."

"I'll see to it, sir."

"I'm perfectly fine, Azriel. I have groceries in the trunk."

"I'll see to those as well, sir," Sean answered before Azriel could give him more instructions. Lamb didn't offer her key and Sean didn't ask. Which meant he had a way into her apartment. It wasn't really surprising since Argent owned the building, but it did lend credence to what James had said.

"Are you keeping tabs on me, Azriel?" she asked in a small voice. "How did you know where I was?"

"Honey, you know I'm keeping tabs on you. I've not been secret about my interest in you, and we've been all over the city together." He didn't hesitate at all in answering her question. "I put a tracker on your car and your phone. That way, if something like this happened, or if one of my enemies got to you, I'd know where you were."

"Oh. I never thought of that."

"Of course you didn't, baby. That's what I'm for. You're coming home with me tonight. No arguments."

She didn't want to argue. Same as she didn't want to believe anything James had said. But he'd planted the seed of doubt, and her imagination was very fertile.

The ride back home was quiet. Azriel held her hand the entire way, only moving when he had to shift gears. When they reached his house, he escorted her inside. She knew the place well, having been there several times, and he'd given her free rein to explore. Mrs. McDonald met them at the entrance to the pool area with a smile.

"Mr. Ivanovich, the pool is yours. You and Miss Newsome won't be disturbed. So good to see you again, dear," she addressed Lamb. "I look forward to you being here more often." The older lady patted her cheek in a motherly kind of way before taking her leave.

"I think we need a soak and to relax a bit." Azriel held the door open for her before taking her hand and leading her to the hot tub. It was half in, half out of the room, with the outside part truly being outside among plants and a furnished patio. Along the back side of the area was a bar. Lamb longed for a glass of wine, but didn't say anything.

Azriel pulled her into his arms, holding her tightly as he rested his chin on her head. "How close did I come to losing you today? Is James about to win you over?"

She stiffened, then pulled back to look up at him. "Azriel, James is a swine. He offered me a 'top-level position' at Rush. I'm not qualified nor am I interested in anything like that. Also, I'm not interested in being his mistress or whatever other arrangement he has in mind for me on a personal level. If you lose me, it won't be to that sorry bastard."

"I'd think a top-level position would be tempting, even if you weren't qualified."

"I also signed a contract with Argent. You guys are holding up your end admirably. I'm learning so much, and everyone has gone out of their way to make me feel like one of the family. I don't go back on my word, no matter how much I don't want to. With Argent, the thought hasn't crossed my mind."

Azriel caressed her cheek gently with the backs of his fingers. "Did he tell you why he was doing all that? What he wanted from you?"

She shook her head, then frowned. "I think he might have been going to say something, but you were screaming through the parking lot and he decided to get out. But, no. He didn't say why."

He smiled down at her. "Get undressed and into the hot tub."

She nodded and did as he asked. When Azriel sank behind her into the hot, bubbly water, Lamb sighed and leaned back against him. She groaned when he used his fingers and thumbs to press into the tense muscles at her neck and upper back. And when she felt his hard, thick erection pressing tightly into her back and pulsing with every moan she made, she looked back over her shoulder at Azriel and smiled.

"You want me."

"Always, my little Lamb."

"I want you, too."

His smile was both gentle and carnal. "All you have to do is ask, baby. I'll give you as much as you can handle."

"I can handle quite a bit," she answered, her grin

growing larger.

"I had a feeling you might."

She showed him that she could, indeed, handle what he needed to give her.

Chapter Ten

Though she tried not to dwell on James's words, they kept her awake at night. Especially when she was away from Azriel. That first night when he'd picked her up after the confrontation with James, she'd convinced herself James was wrong. But the next morning, Azriel had seemed a little distant. Nothing spectacular or overt, just that little bit impersonal. He'd told her he had meetings all day and wouldn't be home until well into the night, but he'd call her when he got home. He hadn't. Naturally, she'd been hurt and even afraid for him. When she'd texted to ask if everything was OK, he'd sent back a single word. "Yes." She'd gone to bed hugging her pillow and struggling not to cry. Sleep hadn't come easy.

That had been the beginning of the week. It was Thursday. Azriel had arranged for her to take off on Friday, and he'd said he would take her anywhere in the world she wanted to go for the weekend. If they were a little late getting back the next week, well. He was part owner of the company and managed all personnel issues. Her job would be safe. He'd been so warm and inviting when he'd told her about that gift to her, she'd let her worries drift away, dismissing them as insecurity in her relationship with him.

They were supposed to leave when she got off work. Azriel had arranged his private jet to be ready this afternoon. But, in her excitement, Lamb had let slip to one of her friends in the department about her plans for the weekend, and her boss had sent her home with a smile and an extracted promise from her that she have the most wonderful time and to bring back plenty of photos. She was four hours earlier than she should have been, but she wasn't certain she could have made it through those extra hours if she'd had to work. She was so excited she was practically bouncing.

As she drove as fast as she dared straight to Azriel's home, she couldn't contain the smile on her face. She turned the satellite radio to the eighties station and sang at the top of her lungs to Blondie, Cindi Lauper, Def Leppard, and INXS. It had been a long time since she'd been this excited. It truly felt like the world was smiling at her.

Inside the house, Mrs. McDowell met her with a hug. "It's so wonderful to see you, child! I wasn't expecting you until later, but you're always welcome anytime.

"I really didn't mean to intrude. I was just so excited --"

"No need to explain, child," Mrs. McDowell chuckled. "He misses you as much as you miss him when he's not with you."

That startled Lamb. "He does?"

"Oh, absolutely. Azriel is quiet and doesn't wear his feelings where anyone can see them, but I've practically raised those boys. Believe me when I tell you, that man misses you when he's not with you."

Lamb couldn't help the huge smile she knew split her face. "You have no idea how happy that makes me."

"I have an idea." Mrs. McDowell just shook her head. "You go on now. He's in his office. Second floor, east wing. End of the hall on the right."

She didn't need to be told twice.

As she raced up the stairs in a most unladylike fashion, the staff waved and smiled at her. Lamb returned the friendly gestures feeling, for the first time, like she might actually get to be a part of all this. Not the big house or the servants waiting on her every need, or any of the wealth it implied. The family. This house, no matter how big it was or how expensive the decor or how the servants were everywhere, felt like one big family. They treated each other that way too. Every single person serving in that house was loyal to each other. That included Alexei, Azriel, and Giovanni. Everyone was loyal to them, but the men were also loyal to their household. Lamb had been around Merrily and Bellarose enough to know those two were held in as high regard as the three men.

The thick carpet along the hall muffled her steps as she hurried along. She'd slowed by the time she reached Azriel's office. She'd had no intention of entering without knocking, but the door was cracked just that little bit and she overheard a conversation between Azriel and what sounded like Alexei on speaker.

"She's coming by this afternoon. I've arranged for her to be off work the rest of the week. We'll be going to a destination of her choice."

"Does she suspect anything? That we're investigating her?" That sent dread and a deep pain through Lamb's body. She actually bent double and would have cried out had she not been paralyzed with shock.

"She's highly intelligent. There's always the possibility." That was Azriel. "I don't think so, though. If she does, she's the coolest customer I've ever come across. El Diablo? What have you found out so far?"

"Whoever's bankrolling Luxemberry is very good at covering their tracks. I have a theory, but it's not something I'm comfortable discussing over the phone." The mention of James's name was another fist to her gut. What was all this about? El Diablo had a slight British accent, and she recognized the voice from the pier beside the bungalow. There was a slight edge to the silky-smooth tone, but it might have been the connection. Where she'd once found James's accent sexy, with this man, it made her shiver in fear. Not desire. Probably because she'd felt so threatened by him before. He sounded pious. Like he thought he might be just a little bit better than either man in on the conversation. "Even Giovanni and Merrily are having trouble finding the information you need. If I'm right, though, I'll have it for you before the vote. You'll either be able to lock it down before the scheduled day, or do it just before the vote after each member makes their positions known."

"Which might work out better because we'll know if any of the other board members are doubting our direction for our own company." That was Alexei again.

"The man seems to have control of at least three of the board. That leaves five still loyal with you to break any tie in our favor, Alex." Azriel again. "Those three have managed to get the rest of them to hold a vote of confidence in us so there are bound to be more than one he's gotten to."

"I'm not worried about that," Azriel sounded irritated but not worried. "We can control any dissent among the voting."

"I realize that," Alexei replied. He sounded like he was trying to soothe Azriel's temper. "But it's not just the bankroll or even the mastermind we need to find. We need to know if any information was passed on to Luxemberry without us knowing. The deposits to him were quite sizable. You don't pay a man in that amount to simply stage a hostile takeover. Hell, I doubt whomever he's answering to expects something like that to be successful. Most of the board is too loyal to us, and they make no bones about it. Luxemberry is expected to gain information about Argent's projects. Something of more importance than a failed coup within our own house."

"If she's given him information, she's the best I've ever come across," Azriel said immediately. "I can't find any chinks in her armor, and she's never been caught saying or doing anything inappropriate. I set up the meet the same day we found out Luxemberry had met and struck up a relationship with her. Sure, there was some time before when she could have spoken to him, but there's been no evidence whatsoever of it. Afterward, well, she had no chance. Not without us knowing about it. All the bugs and trackers we had on her? No way."

"The fight with Luxemberry could have been staged," Alexei said. "Wouldn't be a first time a spy had used those tactics."

There was no doubt in Lamb's mind they were talking about her. Azriel had lied to her. He was using her to get to James. Using her because he thought she was some kind of industrial spy who had been feeding James or someone else information about what she was working on at Argent. *And Azriel had orchestrated their first meeting.*

It all made sense now. She'd been brought in on some of the most sensitive projects in her field. Things she shouldn't be working on at her level. Things no other had ever been allowed near -- she'd been told that by more than one project manager. All of it had been to see if they could catch her leaking information. Which begged the question whether or not those projects were even real. Were they simply giving her something to do that looked impressive because they were expecting her to go blabbing to someone like

James? For what? Money? She'd never risk jail for money, and she'd never sully her integrity for it either. She damn sure would never risk her relationship with Azriel for money.

Tears rolling down her cheeks, her heart in tatters, Lamb quickly headed back down the hall. With any luck she wouldn't meet anyone on the way out. It was just after lunch, and the staff usually took an hour to themselves.

She made it to her car without incident. When she turned around and headed away from the estate, Lamb couldn't help but believe she'd just left part of her heart in that deserted hallway. Did Azriel really think so little of her? Had anything in the last few weeks been real? He'd said he needed her, and he hadn't been lying. He *had* needed her. To confide in him what she'd told James. Had he even once considered she hadn't betrayed Argent? Or him? He'd tempted her with his wealth and power, even when she'd told him that wasn't important to her. He'd never truly believed her. It had all been a farce. She'd gotten caught in the middle of a turf war, and the collateral damage was her heart. And certainly her reputation. She'd never be able to get a job in her field after this.

Halfway to her apartment, she'd had all she could take. She pulled over to the side of the road and just screamed. It was a tortured, anguished sound that had her throat raw and her chest aching. Azriel had done exactly what she'd known he would. He'd used her, ripped out her heart, her hopes and dreams, then thrown her away like yesterday's garbage.

This was it. She couldn't take anymore. There was no way she could show her face on campus again. Not after this. He was right to call them a family. There wasn't much in the company, outside of specific project details, that everyone who worked there didn't know. If Azriel was playing her like this, letting her in on different projects, she knew every single person involved knew what was going on. They were likely laughing at her naïveté, thinking it was all an act. Just like Azriel did. Leaving town was the only option. There was no way she'd ever find a job to complete with the one she was leaving, but maybe there was someplace Argent wouldn't blackball her from, though it wasn't likely. Leaving so abruptly would only confirm her guilt in Azriel's eyes. No matter. She couldn't face him. Not after this. Not since she'd gone and fallen in love with the fucking bastard.

* * *

"The fight with Luxemberry could have been staged." Azriel knew Alex was just thinking through every possible event, but he had a visceral reaction to the thought. "Wouldn't be a first time a spy has used those tactics."

"No," Azriel said sharply. "But it would be the first time a spy's ever gotten around our defenses."

"I don't think so." Surprisingly, it was El Diablo who came to Lamb's defense, nearly on top of Azriel's denial. "That girl is pure as driven snow on Christmas Eve." Then he chuckled. "Or was, until Azriel got to her. Can't say I'm sorry we bugged the bungalow, but the little thing has a set of lungs on her. Made for some rather loud listening."

"Watch your mouth!"

"Ahh," El Diablo purred. "Little testy, are we? Alexei, I do think your Demon brother has a thing for our little Lamb."

"She's no one's but mine, El Diablo," Azriel growled. "I'm doing the responsible thing by including her in our investigation, but that woman is innocent. And you will keep your fucking hands to yourself."

El Diablo chuckled. Underneath that, he could hear Alexei sigh. "Fine. Never thought she was really in on it anyway. Never made sense. Not after the interview you had with her. She's too open and honest about everything to be a spy. She needs to be protected, not interrogated."

"She's supposed to be here in four hours. I need to be ready for her."

"So, we're in agreement? El Diablo gets us the information we need to move on the board at the vote. We keep a tail on James, and we keep security on Lamb in case James doesn't stay away from her." Alexei was always the voice of reason. At least he was now that he had his woman secure. Merrily had had Alexei tied up in knots. Still did, but Alex had locked her down by marrying her at the first opportunity and adopting her daughter, Bellarose, at nearly the same time. Even if Merrily decided he wasn't worth the trouble, Rose adored him.

"Yes. Now, if you'll excuse me. I need to pack."

"Bring that girl home with you, Azriel." Alex said softly. "You need her, and she needs someone to keep the big bad wolves away."

"That's the plan, brother." And it was. Azriel knew he'd do everything in his considerable power to lock Lamb to him. Forever.

Chapter Eleven

"She was supposed to be here an hour ago," Azriel muttered as he dialed Lamb's number for what had to be the hundredth time. Just like all the other times, she didn't answer. "Where the fuck is she?"

"Giovanni and Merrily are on the trail of someone El Diablo put them on, but I can pull one of them off to find your woman if need be. She doesn't seem like the kind of woman to stand you up."

There was just the smallest bit of humor in Alexei's voice that Azriel didn't like. He glared at his brother, his only acknowledgement of the barb.

A moment later, Mrs. McDowell entered his office, a confused smile on her face. "I thought you were leaving with Miss Newsome? Is everything all right?"

"Lamb isn't here, Grace. Have you seen her today?"

"Of course. She came by earlier. Just before lunch. I thought you'd be on your way with her by now." She clasped her hands in front of her, a grin spreading her lips. "You take care of that girl. She's a treasure. Just like my lovely Merrily."

"That was four hours ago. Did she leave? If someone here's kept her away from me there'll be hell to pay!"

"Relax, Azriel," Alexei said. "No one would try to keep that girl away from you. They like living too much." He took out his phone, his thumbs flying over it for a moment. "There. If she was in the house, Giovanni can see what happened to her."

Less than five minutes later, a ping sounded on Azriel's phone. He snatched it up, looking at it intently. "She stood outside my office door for a short while before leaving in a hurry." His brow furrowed, then realization dawned on him. He looked up at Alexei. "She overheard my conversation with you and El Diablo."

Alex shrugged. "So? Just coming clean with her before she can bring it up should smooth things over. Besides, you didn't do or say anything you didn't mean. You love that girl, and we all know it. Does she?"

"She might have been figuring it out. Unfortunately, the one thing she can't get over is being lied to. She told me that from the very beginning. What I've done to her is no different than what Luxemberry did to her. And she still doesn't know he was trying to get information from her. At least, she didn't until today." Alexei scrubbed a hand over his face. This was bad. This was real bad. "Fuck!"

There was silence while Azriel stared at Alexei, looking for something. A way to pull this out. Something to save his relationship with Lamb he wasn't seeing.

Finally, Mrs. McDowell broke the silence. "First thing you need to do is find her. Then you apologize. Then you spend the rest of your life making it up to her, dear boy." She shook her head sadly. "I can't believe one of my boys did this." Her gaze snapped to Azriel, and she shook her finger at him. "If you were still ten, I'd turn you over my knee."

"I know, Ruth," Azriel said gently. "Perhaps, if I can get her back here, you can ease her worries about me?"

"That, my boy, is up to you. I can tell her of your merits all day, but, in the end, you're the only one who can win her heart."

Azriel crossed to the older woman and kissed her

head as he passed. "I have to find her."

"See that you do. That girl belongs here. Why in the world you set her up in an apartment when you should have brought her home with you is beyond me," Ruth said, a fierce scowl on her face.

Azriel hurried from the mansion to his car. A ping from his cell let him know that Giovanni was ever vigilant on his behalf. He'd found Lamb. She was at the little apartment she'd rented before he had her move into an Argent building. And it looked like she was about to have company. James Luxemberry had just pulled into her neighborhood and was headed to her apartment. Giovanni didn't think she'd invited him over, but El Diablo thought things were rapidly closing in on Luxemberry. Giovanni said El Diablo had pulled a few invisible strings and discovered Luxemberry was being backed by the Brotherhood. Just in a roundabout way so they couldn't be found.

The revelation set up three problems. First, if Luxemberry was in bed with anyone in the Brotherhood, if he couldn't produce what they wanted, he was a dead man. Second, if what he needed to produce involved Lamb giving him information, then she was in great danger. And third? El Diablo was still active with the Brotherhood, which meant he might not be as firmly on their side as they all wanted to believe.

All of it meant Azriel needed to get to Lamb as quickly as possible.

* * *

It took Lamb precious little time to pack her things at the Argent apartments. Even less time to get anything remaining at the apartment she rented when she first came to Rockwell. It had been hard to stop crying long enough to move from place to place without drawing attention, but she'd managed. Once inside, though… Away from everyone else, Lamb had let her tears flow. There was simply no way to stop them. Azriel had broken her heart. Shattered it into tiny fragments. Staying in Rockwell wasn't even an option for her, leaving her only one choice.

She was finishing packing up the few personal items from her living area when there was a polite knock at the door. Lamb froze. No one knew she was here. At least, she hoped Azriel didn't. One thing she absolutely could not do right now was face him. Not like this.

The knock came again, harder this time. "Lamb! I know you're in there! Open the door so we can talk!" That was James. What was he doing here?

Instead of answering, Lamb continued the last of her packing. She was so fucking out of here! Azriel thought she was selling secrets to James. James was trying to seduce her into doing just that. Even Merrily was in on it! Lamb had thought she'd found a friend there. Hell. She'd thought she'd found a home with Azriel. Even though she'd known it wasn't sound judgment, she'd let herself be taken in by his charisma and expert lovemaking. His pretty words. All the time he'd been playing her. She'd thought James's betrayal had been bad. It was nothing compared to what Azriel had done to her.

She'd just picked up the box of personal items when the door opened. James walked in like he owned the place, smirking.

"Going somewhere?"

"Yes." Like she was telling him where she was going.

"I hate to say I told you so, but I did tell you Azriel would show his true colors."

"No one said this was about Azriel."

"You didn't have to tell me. I can tell by the look on your face. He hurt you."

"Everyone in this fucking town hurt me, James. Now, if you'll excuse me, I'm late."

"For what?"

"For a meeting with It's None of Your Fucking Business." She kept her voice neutral, trying not to sound the way she felt. Hurt. Angry. Disgusted with herself. If he thought nothing mattered, maybe he'd just go.

His smirk stayed in place. "OK." He gave a little chuckle. "I get it. But I can offer you a way to get back at him. Hurt him the way he hurt you."

It was Lamb's turn to laugh. "What? By telling you everything I know about Argent Tech and what they're working on? Yeah. I know that's what you want from me. Not sure if it started back in the Keys and don't much care. All I know is I'm leaving. And you're not getting shit from me, asshole."

That seemed to startle him. Good. Bastard. "Lamb, you're not thinking clearly. Besides, I know you want to get even with him. You loved him. Didn't you." It wasn't a question. Did she? She thought she might. Not that it was any of James's business.

"Irrelevant since I'm leaving. Excuse me, please." She tried to go around James out the door, but he sidestepped, blocking her path.

"We need to talk. Forget all the pretty words and the sex. We can keep it business."

"I've got nothing to discuss with you. Even if I did want revenge against Azriel, I still signed many NDAs preventing me from saying anything. Nothing is worth my integrity. Not money. Not Azriel. It may not make a difference to anyone but me in the future, but I don't break promises. Or lie."

"Is that your final say, my love? Be sure because this is the last time I make the offer. I promise you, the financial reward will be enough to soothe your wounded pride."

"Spoken like someone with no moral compass," she muttered. "Let me pass, James. I'm leaving."

Instead of moving, he stepped forward. Before she realized what was happening, James backhanded her. Hard. Lamb went spinning to the floor, the box she'd been holding skidding across the hard surface to crash into the wall, objects flying everywhere.

There were several beats of silence broken only by her whimper as she held her stinging cheek. Tears tracked down her face from the shock of the blow, and pain seemed to explode through her head.

"Now, Lamb. Let's start this again." James shut the door and locked it. Then he walked to her and helped her gently to her feet. He eased her down to the couch and knelt in front of her. "I want you to tell me everything you know about Argent. I want to know what projects you worked on, and what they were intended to do. When I'm satisfied you've given me everything, you can leave. I'll even compensate you in untraceable cash. You can leave, and no one will know you ever had a part in the transfer of power within the tech giant."

She stared at him, still in shock. Lamb might have had to work and scrape for every single penny she'd ever had, but she'd had a good life to this point. No one had ever struck her. She'd never once been in a fight. Never struck anyone in anger or otherwise. The fact that it was happening now was nearly as much a shock as the actual blow. This was a man she'd been intimate with. No matter his reasoning, he'd still shared her body. Now he was willing to hurt her simply to get information?

Power.

Money.

Greed.

She'd been right all along. These were people she had no hope of ever understanding. She didn't understand them or their lives. Didn't much care to.

"No," she said softly. "I won't."

James stood, his face thunderous with rage. "Be very, very careful, my love. Now isn't the time for this. Just tell me what I want to know, and this will all be over. A bad dream."

Lamb clenched her fists at her sides, sticking her chin up definitely as she looked at him square in the eye. "My answer is still no."

She saw the hit coming this time. A strong backhand, then, when she snapped her head back to him, a closed-handed punch to the other side of her face. The combined blows hurt more than anything Lamb had ever experienced. Had she not been so stubborn, she might have spilled the information and worried about her pride and honor later. But she had a stubborn streak in her that just she just couldn't control.

There was a sharp, metallic taste in her mouth, and she spat, not caring if she hit James or not. Blood. She raised her hand to her mouth and winced as she discovered the cut on her lip. She looked back up at James. There was a look of satisfaction there. Like he'd just been waiting to hit her and found himself gratified by the action.

"Go fuck yourself, James. Better yet, take Azriel with you and you can both fuck each other."

His satisfied look turned to one of anger and…

something else. Frustration? Fear? Before she could puzzle it out, James reached behind him and came back with a gun, pointing it straight at her face. He pulled the hammer back, his finger curling around the trigger.

"Last chance, Lamb."

She stared at the gun. There was no doubt in her mind that James was going to kill her if she didn't give him what he wanted. The rational part of her mind argued that she had everything to lose and nothing to gain by not talking to him. Hell, she could probably even give him bits and pieces, and he'd never know she wasn't giving him the whole thing. What would it matter in the long run anyway? Azriel and his team were smart enough to know what information she could give them and counter anything James thought he was doing. Once she was done, she could just leave. Azriel might not care anything for her, but she stood by her assessment that he wasn't a bad person. Also, even though he'd betrayed her, Lamb still thought he did care for her. It might have been unintentional or unwelcome on his part, but she was sure he had feelings for her. Given that, he wouldn't hurt her or keep her from getting a job somewhere else. If she gave James what he wanted, she would lose nothing and quite possibly save her own life.

But that little stubborn part of her was telling her she was delusional if she thought James would let her live after she talked. If he was going to kill her anyway, why should she submit to what he wanted?

Her stubborn side won.

"Then I guess you've got no choice but to shoot me." She spat again. "'Cause I ain't tellin' you shit, motherfucker."

* * *

The moment Azriel pulled onto Lamb's street, he spotted James's Jaguar. It was already minus a couple of center caps with a kid sitting off in the distance eyeing it, obviously waiting to see if he could get the other two. Azriel pulled his car in behind the Jag. As he got out, he motioned to the kid. He thought it was a boy, but, as the kid got closer, he could see it was a girl of about ten.

He pulled out his money clip with its thick bundle of one-hundred-dollar bills. He waited until the kid's attention was focused squarely on him before peeling off two crisp bills and handing them to the girl.

"This is yours if you guard my car from center-cap thieves." The kid grinned, taking the bills and stuffing them in her pocket. Before she could turn away, however, he caught her arm gently. "If you prevent anything else from walking off my car, I'll give you the rest." He held up the money clip for good measure, letting her see the wad of cash. The girl's eyes widened, and she reached for it, but Azriel pulled it back. "Huh-uh," he chided. "What's your name?"

The kid dropped her hand in disappointment, looking very disgruntled. "Flick," she said, her looking turning into a glare as if she expected him to make fun of her name.

"Well, Flick. You get the rest when I come back outside and my car is still sitting here and intact. You can take anything you want off the Jag."

Flick's expression transformed into one of mischievous delight. "Awesome!"

Azriel chuckled as he set the alarm on his car, then jogged to Lamb's apartment. He'd raised his hand to knock when he heard Lamb's voice.

"Then I guess you've got no choice but to shoot me. 'Cause I ain't tellin' you shit, motherfucker."

Everything in Azriel went into autopilot. Not wasting time to see if the door was locked, he gave a hard, solid kick. The flimsy thing actually splintered, coming apart from one of the hinges. None of that registered. In the tiny living room, Lamb sat, a defiant look on her face as she faced James Luxemberry and the gun he had trained on her.

With a bellow of rage, Azriel took a running step, lowered his shoulder and plowed into James, taking the other man to the floor. As he did, the gun went off, the sound deafening in the enclosed space. Lamb screamed...

And Azriel unleashed hell on his enemy.

* * *

When the gun went off, Lamb couldn't hold back her cry. It took several seconds to realize she hadn't been hit, that she wasn't hurt anywhere other than where James had struck her. She saw the gun lying about a foot from James's hand as Azriel proceeded to pound the guy. Somehow, she had the presence of mind to grab the weapon and take it out of play for either man. Azriel obviously didn't need it, and she didn't want James to have it.

She thought that, once Azriel realized he had the man subdued, he'd back off. Maybe roll him over and tie his hands behind his back or something. Didn't they do that in the movies? Then he'd call the police and they'd take James off to jail or something. Right?

Only, Azriel didn't stop. He kept hitting James. Over and over. Blood was everywhere, both from James's face and Azriel's fists. Lamb called to him twice, but Azriel didn't seem to hear her. He just kept beating the other man. There was no doubt in her mind that Azriel would kill James. Even then, she suspected it would be a long time before he stopped whatever madness had overtaken him.

"Hey! Hey, mister!" Flick, one of the kids from the neighborhood, stood in the doorway. Her eyes widened momentarily, then she seemed to dismiss the violence. "Hey, mister!" She yelled louder this time. Surprisingly, Azriel looked over his shoulder at her. He was covered in blood spatter, looking for all the world like some demon from hell. The kid didn't bat an eyelash. "They's some of the kids tryin' to take shit off your car. I told 'em to get shit off the Jag first, but they think yours is better."

Azriel stood, not even looking at James. "Thanks."

Flick looked from Azriel to James and back. Then she narrowed her eyes. Lamb could practically see the wheels turning in the girl's mind. "This what you do to guys who fuck with your car?" Lamb winced at Flick's language. She'd been trying to get her to stop swearing so much, but it didn't seem to take no matter what she did.

"Yeah."

"You don't talk much, do you, mister?"

"No."

Flick looked over at Lamb, waving happily like nothing had happened. "Hi, Lamb!" Without waiting to see if Lamb returned her wave, the girl dashed off. Lamb could hear her yelling as she ran. "You better not! You should see what he does to people who fuck with his car! There's blood everywhere!"

In any other situation, Lamb realized she might have laughed. Now, the adrenaline rush was leaving her, and she realized just how close she'd come to dying only moments before. She was still sitting on the couch and doubted her legs would hold her if she tried to stand, but all she wanted was to be in Azriel's arms.

The second the little whimper left her, Azriel reached for her, pulling her to her feet before she even realized she was leaning against him. His embrace was warm, his arms strong and tight around her. That was when she realized how good it felt. How... right. This was where she was supposed to be. With this man.

"Are you hurt, Lamb?"

"N-no. I d-don't think s-so."

He ran his hands over her, but didn't attempt to push her away. Probably a good thing since Lamb's arms were locked around his neck. "I don't feel any blood," he murmured at her ear. His arms tightened around her again. "I need to look you over, but I --" Did his voice break? He cleared his throat. Must have gotten a tickle or something. "I need to hold you right now."

She needed him to hold her. Needed to be with him. How could she need him this much when he wasn't what she thought he was? He'd played her for a fool. Had lied to her. He'd made love to her, made her think he wanted more with her, when all the while it had been a ruse to get close to her and find out if she'd been selling secrets.

Before the tears could really start, Lamb pushed back, needing out of his arms. "Let me go," she said softly. Immediately Azriel loosened his grip on her.

"Did I hurt you? Are you OK?"

"I'm fine. Just let me go." She knew there were a few tears falling from her eyes and hastily wiped them with the back of her hand. "I'm fine," she said with more force. She looked around the room. James's battered body was still beside the couch where Azriel had left him. He was breathing, but it was obvious he needed immediate medical attention. Normally, she'd be the first one calling for help. Now, she just wanted out of that confined place where Azriel seemed larger than life. Her avenging angel. Only he wasn't an angel. He was a Demon. A Shadow Demon. The Demons were the protectors. Argent was in the center of their circle of protection. She had to remember that.

"If you'll excuse me."

"Baby, you're upset. The adrenaline is making you shake, and you might be injured and just too much in shock to realize it."

"Upset?" This was the fight she needed to pull her out of her shock. "You think I'm upset? Why would you think that, Azriel?" Her voice was still shaky, and a stray tear still managed to escape, but she was refocusing her attention to the problem that mattered most.

"I know you overheard part of my conversation with Alex and El Diablo. I want to explain."

"Not really much to explain. It is what it is."

"But it's not like you think." He actually looked like he was desperate for her to listen to him. Azriel moved closer, gripping her shoulder gently. She shrugged him off.

"Oh really? So you didn't arrange to meet me that night at the New Year's Eve party? You didn't suspect I was feeding James trade secrets or something? You didn't get close to me, make love to me, all with the purpose of getting me to confide in you everything I'd told James, or maybe get me to tell you about his company? Because that's what I think it sounded like."

He swallowed, opening his mouth only to close it and shake his head. "Well, I guess that's exactly what happened, but --"

"That's all the information I need, Mr. Ivanovich. I don't need anything that comes after the conjunction."

She moved toward the door, but he caught her arm. "Lamb, just listen to me."

"No!" she screamed at him. "You had your chance! You knew what James did to me! I confided all that to you, yet you did exactly the same thing! You both schooled me like the amateur I am!" To her utter mortification, the tears kept coming. She was sobbing now, having to take great gulps of air just to feel like she wasn't smothering. "Well, I'm done! Thank you for the lovely time and the wonderful vacation. While I appreciate the internship and appreciate all I've learned with the incredibly talented and intelligent people at Argent, I regretfully resign my position. Any possessions I have can be donated to the appropriate charity. You should have my direct deposit information for my final check."

"Lamb --"

"Good day, Mr. Ivanovich."

As she spun around to leave, both Alex and Giovanni Romano, the third man in their Shadow Demons organization, entered, blocking the door. Fortunately, both men moved out of her way on reflex, letting her escape when she'd been sure Azriel would have chased her.

Before they could change their minds, she sprinted from the little apartment to her car. It took some maneuvering to get out of the drive since both James and Azriel had blocked it. Once on the road, she peeled out and took off. She had no idea where she was going, but she wasn't going to stay here.

With every mile she put between her and Azriel, the more her chest tightened. The more tears fell. The more she struggled to keep her grief and desolation at bay.

Chapter Twelve

Why did crying give one such a horrendous headache? Lamb had done nothing but cry every waking minute since she'd left Azriel two days ago. She'd thought about texting him a tepid "thank you" for saving her life and all, but knew that one thing would lead to another and she absolutely could not go through this again.

A soft knock at the door of the motel she'd booked for the weekend startled her from her thoughts.

"Lamb? Are you there? It's Merrily." More polite knocking.

Lamb debated on not opening the door, just pretending to not be there. After all, Merrily had played a part in the deception. Whatever she said would just be more lies. Wouldn't it?

"Lamb?"

With a sigh, Lamb opened the door. The two women looked at each other. Merrily had a worried expression on her face, and she clutched her phone tightly.

"Can I come in?" Merrily looked so hopeful Lamb couldn't deny her request. Why couldn't she be strong? If she was going to survive this, she had to toughen up.

Taking a step back to allow the other woman entry, Lamb lowered her gaze. Dammit! She'd just gotten her tears under control. The headache had eased off. Was she expected to do this all again?

"I'm sorry to bother you, Lamb. I know you're upset, but you need all the information before you leave Azriel."

Straight to the point. Lamb respected that. Didn't

mean she liked it.

"He lied to me, Merrily. You were part of it while pretending to be my friend. Of course I'm upset."

Merrily winced. "I know," she said softly. "But you have to understand, none of us truly thought you were part of it. Alex and Azriel would have been negligent if they hadn't at least looked at you."

"I can accept that," Lamb conceded. "But he didn't have to sleep with me."

"Which is the reason I came to see you." She raised her phone. "Can I send you something?" When Lamb shrugged, Merrily poked some buttons on her phone with her thumbs, the movements fast and precise. When her phone beeped, Lamb looked at what she'd been given. It was an audio file. "Because the guys are paranoid, and because El Diablo was listening to the conversation, they recorded it. Just like they do every conversation with someone outside of Argent listening. Azriel doesn't know I have it, but he'll get over it. You only heard part of the conversation. They saw you leave on the security feed, so they know what you heard."

God, she wanted to believe. She wanted there to be a reasonable explanation for all of it, but how could there be? He'd still lied to her.

"I'll listen, Merrily. But the fact remains he still lied. I can even understand his reasons. I have to live with his decisions, too."

"I understand. Just..." Merrily trailed off. To Lamb's surprise, she caught the glint of tears in the other woman's eyes before one spilled down her cheek. "I'm so sorry, Lamb. You're a good and honorable person. You didn't deserve to be investigated at all. You never did, and they all know it."

Lamb nodded, her own eyes filling with the

familiar tears she'd been shedding for two days. How many more tears could one woman have? "I'll listen to it."

Merrily moved closer to Lamb, as if she intended to hug her but then thought better of it. "I really hope I see you again, Lamb."

It was all Lamb could take. She hurried to the other woman and hugged her tightly. "You're a good person, Merrily. I think we both got caught in the crossfire. You work for the men, and they had you doing a job."

"Shadow Demons," Merrily said softly. "I work with the Shadow Demons."

"Wait. I knew they were closely associated with the Shadow Demons. Sean said as much. Are you saying the men who own Argent Tech are actually part of the Shadow Demons?"

"Not part of, Lamb. Alex, Azriel, and Giovanni *are* the Shadow Demons."

Lamb wasn't sure what to think. It kind of made sense. Just… was it just one more lie to go with the rest? Or a secret from Azriel she hadn't yet earned?

"I'm part of them now. You could be, too. If you can find it in your heart to forgive the boys. Especially Azriel." Merrily pulled back enough to look Lamb in the eyes. "He loves you, you know. He'd never admit it, but I think he fell in love during your interview before you ever started working for Argent. He watched it all from a monitor, but you affected him."

"He -- he does?" That was surprising.

Merrily nodded vigorously. "He does. He was pretty hard up before, but with you gone, he's miserable. He just doesn't know what to do to get you back."

With a sigh, Lamb looked at her phone. "I'll

listen. But that's all I'm promising."

"If you do that, I think you'll understand."

As Merrily left, Lamb stared at her phone. She pulled up the audio file Merrily had sent her. Looking at the screen for long moments, Lamb finally decided it was worth a shot. She loved Azriel. Wasn't love worth just one listen?

* * *

How could two fucking days seem like two years? Christ! Had it only been two days since Lamb had left him? In that time, Azriel had thrown himself into work in the lab. Giovanni was trying to perfect that fucking portal, and Azriel had put himself out there to help test it. High voltage cables ran in all directions from the circular metal frame to different areas of the lab. Azriel was tempted to have Giovanni program it to dump him in the middle of that fucking hotel room Lamb had rented for the weekend. She'd probably kick him out -- once she got over the shock of him appearing amid the chaos of the event horizon -- but he'd at least get to see her. Smell the sweet scent of her skin and hair. If he startled her enough, maybe she'd let him hold her. Just for a moment. Like she had in her apartment after he'd nearly beaten James to death. That is, assuming he survived the experience. Giovanni's inventions were not always safe. Alex had gone through it once but hadn't recommended it to Azriel.

That was a memory best left alone. The one time he'd attempted to sleep, he'd woken up in a cold sweat, reaching for Lamb as she lay dying in a pool of blood. She hadn't even let him really look her over before she'd left him. Not that he blamed her. He'd fucked up and wouldn't even try to deny it.

Giovanni had left to bring down supper, leaving

Azriel free to tinker with the settings on the portal. If he could just see Lamb! Oh, he knew where she was. He'd always know. Keeping tabs on her was second nature now. Only, where before he hadn't worried she'd give him the slip, now he worried constantly about it. Other than some of the Brotherhood deciding she needed to be taken out for some reason only known to them, his biggest fear was of Lamb managing to get away from him and disappearing off the grid. He doubted she'd do it. After all, slipping grid wasn't easy, and she'd have to care enough about him to put that much effort into it, but the fear was still there. He doubted Lamb wanted to put anything more of herself into anything to do with him.

He heard the door to the underground of the Shadow Demons opening but filed it away. He didn't think Giovanni had been gone that long, but it was possible his mind had drifted off to thoughts of Lamb and lost track of time.

"Azriel?"

He stood up straighter, whipping around so fast he nearly got tangled in all the electrical cables around his feet. "Lamb! What are you doing here? Are you hurt?"

She raised a hand and took a step back when he moved toward her. "I'm fine. Just stop for a minute."

He did as she asked, laying down the wrench he'd been using and wiping his hands on his jeans. "I -- " He had to stop. Swallowed. Then tried again. "I've missed you, Lamb."

"I've missed you too," she said softly. "Merrily gave me the recording of the whole conversation I heard. Is it true?"

Azriel chanced a single step toward her. "That I intend to marry you?" She nodded. "Absolutely." He dug into his back pocket and brought out the ring he'd had made. "I had this made before that conversation ever took place. I just could never find the right time to give it to you."

He held out the most extraordinary ring Lamb had ever imagined. The center stone was a dark red, surrounded by pink stones. Two clear diamonds were set on each side along the band of rose gold. "Rubies?"

"No, my little Lamb. They're all diamonds."

She gasped and looked up at him, a look of horror on her face as she hastily tried to give it back to him. Shaking her head emphatically, she said, "I can't take this! That's a fortune in stones! What if I drop it? Or lose it!?"

He would have chuckled if he hadn't been so heartsick. "Then I'll buy you another, bigger one. One not so easy to lose."

"Azriel this is… it's lovely, but it's just… too much!"

"It's not nearly enough, Lamb. Not for you. You're worth everything to me."

She looked at the ring for some time, just studying it. Then she slipped it on her finger. "Looks like you had it sized to fit me."

"I did. Since I had it sized, I can't take it back." He threw that bit in just to guilt her a little. He'd use anything he could to keep her.

"Well, I suppose if you can't return it, I should try to get used to it."

"I'd appreciate it."

Lamb looked up at him. Then, somehow, she was in his arms, clinging to him as tightly as he was clinging to her. He felt her slight body trembling against him. Hell, he was probably shaking just as badly.

"Just to be clear," he said in her hair as he continued to squeeze her to him. "You're marrying me."

She let out a little giggle that sounded suspiciously like a sob. "Yes, Azriel. I'll marry you."

"Thank God! I'd've hated having to grovel, especially when El Diablo is still lurking around somewhere, but I'd have done it."

Finally, they both eased up. Azriel stared down into her lovely face. "Has there ever been a woman so lovely?"

She blushed becomingly. "Maybe you just need glasses."

"Or maybe you just need to learn to take my compliments. I have a feeling I'll never tire of giving them to you." He brushed a tear from her cheek with the pad of his thumb. "What made you change your mind?"

"The audio file. And I realized that I loved you. Knowing that you loved me back and hadn't wanted to lie to me helped. I'm still not happy with you."

"I swear, I'll never lie to you again. No matter what."

"I'll make sure you never forget because I'll be bringing this up often. So often you'll get sick of hearing it and will probably regret marrying me because of it."

"Baby, that will never happen. Do it. Bring it up every fucking day. Three times on Sunday. I'll forever be contrite and will never lie to you again."

"See that you don't," she said sternly. "I can forgive you once. Two times shows a pattern I won't tolerate."

"I understand."

"It also includes anything you're doing with the

Shadow Demons. Merrily told me she's part of that group. I want in as well."

"Done. Anything else?"

"Yes. Take me upstairs and make love to me." She reached up to brush a kiss along his lips. "I've missed you so much!"

* * *

Thankfully, there was an elevator from the basement lab that went straight to the topmost floor of the massive compound Azriel called a house. From what she knew, Azriel, Alexei, and Giovanni each had a top floor on a different wing of the house to himself. As such, each had an elevator leading from the foyer of his suite to the lab. This expedited travel, and Lamb was exceedingly glad at the moment.

The moment they were inside his suite, Azriel started tugging at her clothing, trying to get them off.

She giggled. "I got my own clothes. You get yours off."

"No," he bit out. "If I get you naked before me, it's less likely you'll make it off this floor before I can catch you."

Laughter bubbled up inside her where there had been only sorrow. Instantly, she felt lighter. Yes. She'd definitely made the right decision.

She let him finish undressing her before picking her up and laying her carefully in the center of his big bed. He had to crawl up on the thing fully clothed to do it. Even then, he didn't let her go. Instead, he moved over her, lying between her spread thighs before taking her mouth with his.

Lamb opened willingly, lapping at his tongue when he thrust it deeply. There was no holding back her sigh of content. This was where she wanted to be. She knew she'd have to address everything else, but it could wait. Not long, but it could wait until they'd each taken what they needed. And given it back to each other.

Azriel blazed a trail down Lamb's body from her neck to her breast, to her hip, and finally settled in on her pussy. He sucked each lip once before circling her clit with his tongue. Groaning loudly in almost a defeated tone, he covered her with his mouth, sucking and licking as he growled and snarled. His body trembled nearly as much as hers did. The arms wrapped so tightly around her thighs shook almost violently with every moment that passed. The material of his clothing added to the sensations he created. Whisper-soft movements followed by scratchy abrasions from his T-shirt and jeans both tantalized and maddened her.

Finally, finally, Azriel sat up, her thighs still draped over his. "Need inside you, Lamb." His voice was guttural, his eyes wild with need. Sweat dampened his upper lip and brow. She knew his shirt was probably damp with it as well. He whipped the material over his head and went for the buttons on his jeans. "Not using a condom, Lamb. This is a permanent thing. You're not leaving me. I'm not leaving you."

She supposed that was as close to asking permission as she was likely to get with Azriel in this state. Truthfully, she wasn't much better off. In answer, she reached for him, pulling him down on top of her. Then, she reached between them to guide his thick shaft inside her cunt. As he slid in slowly, he dropped his forehead to hers. Lamb whimpered, tightening her legs around him.

"Going to fuck you, Lamb. Going to fuck you until I come inside you. When you're pregnant with my child, you'll never in hell be rid of me."

The grin tugging at her lips was tempered only by the intense need she had for exactly that. It was the heat of the moment, but Lamb yearned for a permanent tie to this man with all her heart.

"You know I'm not letting you do this for the money. Right?"

To her surprise, he grinned. "Little Lamb, you're not the kind of woman to do that. Your heart is pure. Me, on the other hand… I'm going to shamelessly use any advantage I have to keep you with me. If that means I have to keep you pregnant for the next twenty years, I'm more than capable of it. Anything I have to do to keep you with me. I'm that ruthless."

With a sigh, she stretched, arching her back and tilting her pelvis, moving on him and putting as much friction on her clit as she could and still tease him. "Well, in that case, I suppose you'd better get started. I might walk out the door otherwise."

Azriel growled and nipped her neck sharply before sucking hard on the spot. Lamb knew she'd have a love bite for all to see and contemplated wearing something strapless and her hair up the next time they went out together. He'd placed his mark. She'd wear it proudly. Then Azriel started to move in earnest within her, and she forgot about everything other than the pleasure blossoming inside her.

Arms tightening around her, his breath coming in pants, Azriel surged deep, trying to concentrate on Lamb. He needed her to have a much pleasure as he could give her. She wore his ring, but he wouldn't rest easy until he was legally bound to her and she had no way out of the marriage. He wasn't lying. A baby would go a long way toward that end, and he was just desperate enough to make it happen.

Unbidden, the thought of a little girl with Lamb's

shining hair and big doe eyes looking up at him and smiling flashed through his mind. The vision was sharp and crisp as if he were actually seeing it. He cried out sharply, the need to plant his seed in his woman nearly overwhelming.

"God, Lamb!" His cries were echoed by Lamb's. Her nails scored down his back until she gripped his ass and dug them in hard like little spurs. It wouldn't surprise him if she'd broken the skin. But it meant she was as far gone as he was. Which was his permission to come.

"Come for me, baby," he bit out. "Come on my dick so fucking hard!"

She did. Her cunt pulsed and pulled at him, taking the seed he was so ready to give. Lamb screamed shrilly, her head going back on the pillow and her back arching. Her muscles clamped down on him so tightly, he could hardly move. When he shot his load, it went deep inside her. She jerked with each jet of semen as if the bursts were strong enough to jar her.

Azriel gasped for breath as he lay there, Lamb pinned beneath him. She made sounds that almost sounded like a little purring kitten, obviously well-pleasured. There were things they needed to discuss, but he wasn't ready. Not yet. He wanted her sated and sleepy before they had that talk. Then maybe he'd have a chance of keeping her. Sure, she'd taken his ring, had agreed to marry him, but Azriel wasn't a man to take chances with what he wanted.

"More," he growled, pushing himself off her only to flip her over to her knees. She let out a startled cry, then did it again when he swatted her ass.

"Ow! What was that for?" She looked over her shoulder at him. Her expression was angry, but there was a definite interest shining in her eyes.

"For trying to leave me. You're never to do that again." He swatted the other cheek.

"Azriel! Stop it!"

"Not until you promise," he said, swatting her again. One cheek. Then the other. Her ass was a nice shade of pink, but he wanted it to be a deeper red. Wanted to look at those luscious globes as he fucked her and know he was the one who'd made them that particular color.

"Oh, God!" Lamb cried out as he kept spanking her, arching her back and leaning into his hand with each swat. "Oh, fuck!"

Azriel grinned as she swore. Yeah, she was enjoying the moment as much as he was. So he continued, and every now and then, he brushed his fingers through her pussy lips. She was wet with his seed and her own moisture, and it was nearly as big a turn-on as her reddening ass. On impulse, he swatted her pussy, making sure to get her clit when he did. Lamb let out another scream, this time lowering her head to the bed and raising her ass as high as she could get it.

"Goddamn," Azriel muttered. The sight was more glorious than anything he could remember in recent memory. He'd seen subs at the Playground -- a BDSM club owned by Salvation's Bane in Palm Beach -- present themselves thusly but never thought to have one do so for him. Mainly because he never cared to take a sub. Now, he could well see the appeal. The sight she made was droolworthy, practically straining for his hand and willfully showing him her drenched and well-used pussy. Well-used by him. Which made him hard as fuck. For her.

Azriel delivered several more slaps to her pussy before moving back behind her and mounting her in one swift stroke. Lamb cried out again, this time stretching her arms out in front of her and pushing back as much as she could.

He fucked her with all his might, gripping her hips and pulling her back as he thrust forward. When that wasn't enough, he pulled her arms back, gripping her at the elbows and pulling her back to him hard. Lamb kept her upper body low, giving him the best angle to pull her roughly against him. Both of them grunted and whimpered and moaned in the silence of the room, the sound of their bodies slapping against each other the perfect cadence.

Muscles strained. Bodies sweated. And Azriel and Lamb convulsed together as they both came in a hot, wet rush. Azriel pulled her up to wrap his arms tightly around her body as he shot his seed inside her. One arm was tight across her breasts, but the other drifted down her body to where they were joined and cupped her pussy, his fingers around his dick where he was nestled snug. Her pussy milked him, her body shuddering in his arms as her climax crested, then ebbed.

For long moments they stayed like that. Azriel held Lamb upright when she might have collapsed. His dick was empty, but still it was hard enough to stay put. Azriel intended on keeping it there as long as he could.

"You good?" His voice was hoarse from his yells. The way it should be after sex this fantastic. "I wasn't too rough? I don't want you hurt, Lamb."

She chuckled softly. "No, Azriel. You didn't hurt me. That was the best sex of my life!"

That put his shoulders back and his chest out just a little. "Good. Because I intend to be the only man you get sex from for the rest of your life."

She stiffened, then turned her head, resting it on his shoulder as she looked up at him. "Are you sure? I'm in love with you, but I don't want you to do this because of what we just did."

He sighed. "I hope you know me well enough by now to know that no one makes me do anything I don't want. Yes. You're marrying me. Why?" He kissed her softly before answering his own question. "Because I love you, Lamb. I want a child with you because any boy you have will be one more strong male to protect his mother, and any girl you have will be one more female to wrap me around her little finger. I want you, Lamb. In my life. In my bed. In my heart. My own little Lamb."

Lamb smiled, the happiness showing brightly in her eyes. "I love you, too. And I want all those things as well. But only with you, Azriel."

"Good." He said, gently extracting himself before urging her back on the bed. He snagged a tissue from the nightstand and wiped her gently before tossing the thing in the wastebasket. "But we have one more thing to discuss before I fuck you again."

She giggled. "Oh? What's that?"

He grinned. "About those spankings I just gave you…"

Yeah. Azriel knew they were going to have a blessed life. Together.

Marteeka Karland

Erotic romance author by night, emergency room tech/clerk by day, Marteeka Karland works really hard to drive everyone in her life completely and totally nuts. She has been creating stories from her warped imagination since she was in the third grade. Her love of writing blossomed throughout her teenage years until it developed into the totally unorthodox and irreverent style her English teachers tried so hard to rid her of.

Marteeka at Changeling: changelingpress.com/marteeka-karland-a-39

Changeling Press E-Books

More Sci-Fi, Fantasy, Paranormal, and BDSM adventures available in e-book format for immediate download at ChangelingPress.com -- Werewolves, Vampires, Dragons, Shapeshifters and more -- Erotic Tales from the edge of your imagination.

What are E-Books?

E-books, or electronic books, are books designed to be read in digital format -- on your desktop or laptop computer, notebook, tablet, Smart Phone, or any electronic e-book reader.

Where can I get Changeling Press E-Books?

Changeling Press e-books are available at ChangelingPress.com, Amazon, Apple Books, Barnes & Noble, and Kobo/Walmart.

Changeling Press, LLC

ChangelingPress.com

Printed in Great Britain
by Amazon